Elaine Ellis

A SUMMER'S
Child

A heart-warming story of families coming together,
and sharing their hopes and their regrets

Elaine Ellis

A SUMMER'S
Child

A heart-warming story of families coming together,
and sharing their hopes and their regrets

ROMAUNCE
Cirencester

Romaunce Books

1A The Wool Market Dyer Street Cirencester Gloucestershire GL7 2PR
An imprint of Memoirs Publishing www.mereobooks.com

A SUMMER'S CHILD: 978-1-86151-833-0

Published in Great Britain by Romaunce Books,
an imprint of Memoirs Publishing Ltd.

The address for Memoirs Publishing Group Limited can be found at
www.memoirspublishing.com

Cover design and artwork - Ray Lipscombe

The Memoirs Publishing Group Ltd Reg. No. 7834348

The Memoirs Publishing Group supports both The Forest Stewardship Council®
(FSC®) and the PEFC® leading international forest-certification organisations. Our
books carrying both the FSC label and the PEFC® and are printed on FSC®-certified
paper. FSC® is the only forest-certification scheme supported by the leading
environmental organisations including Greenpeace. Our paper procurement policy
can be found at www.memoirspublishing.com/environment

Typeset in 11/17pt Century Schoolbook
by Wiltshire Associates Publisher Services Ltd. Printed and bound in Great Britain
by Printondemand-Worldwide, Peterborough PE2 6XD

CHARACTER LIST

～～～

Lara Allen	Linguist for the Foreign Office
Tori Allen	Lara's sister and a hairdresser/beautician
Adam Sinclair	Tori's fiancé
Debbie Allen	Lara's mother and hairdressing salon owner
Pete Allen	Lara's father and postman
Jill Simpson	Joint owner of Jilly's Restaurant with Rob
Rob Simpson	Husband of Jill
Megan Simpson	Jill and Rob's daughter

CHAPTER 1

~~~

It wasn't Lara's fault she was now stuck in customs at Bournemouth Airport, waiting to fly off to her sister's hen night, on The Algarve. The rest of the hens were waiting by the boarding gate for her. The public-address system had said 'Lara Allen on flight FR5953 to Faro, please go immediately to airport security.' As she walked with her sister, Tori, to the offices she tried to remember what she had put in her suitcase.

So, she was now taking out all the items from her case, under the gaze of a woman from *Bad Girls* and a man on the Most Wanted list of perverts. His eyes seemed to light up every time she took out an item of underwear or swimwear.

"Ah ha." Pervert spoke. He reached over and grabbed a carrier bag from Tesco and said in a pervy way, "Open it." Tori didn't like this man; she thought he was rude. Manners didn't cost anything.

"P..l..ease!" Tori said with emphasis on the P and L. Lara glanced round at her sister with an uneasy look. This really wasn't the time for Tori to play silly buggers. But to Lara's surprise, pervy man suddenly smiled.

"Please could you open the bag, Miss?" Tori thought her prompt to him for politeness was the reason, Lara knew better. She realised immediately that he knew what was in the bag and just wanted to embarrass her to a greater extent.

Lara opened the bag and out dropped a pack of AA batteries, and then a very pink, silicone-covered man's penis with fingers attached.

"Ooh, a Rampant Rabbit. I've been meaning to get one of those myself, are they any good?" The woman from *Bad Girls* was either winding Lara up, or was genuinely interested. Lara was mortified. What a start to her holiday. Tori was laughing so hard she had to hold on to the desk in front of her.

"Ok, I think you can put it all back now. We like to do these random spot checks, sorry for the inconvenience." Pervy man looked up at the clock. "You better hurry though or you'll miss your flight. Have a good holiday." He walked off through the door, leaving the woman from *Bad Girls* and Tori repacking everything into the suitcase. Lara was too bemused to do anything.

When they were finally on their way to the boarding gate, having been called twice, Tori had to make a solemn promise that it was just a spot check and nothing untoward was found. Tori couldn't keep promises, no matter how hard she tried.

"After a couple of shots I just can't keep a secret, you

know that Lala. But I'll try." Lara couldn't expect anything more; after all it wasn't her sister who had signed the Official Secrets Act. Working for the Foreign and Commonwealth Office as a linguist, Lara was used to secrets. Why oh why had she brought the pesky thing in the first place. But she knew the reason why. She hadn't had sex with a man for nearly five months, and she didn't think that weekend would be any different. That's why she had brought her own amusement. The irony was that it had been for everyone else's amusement so far!

The sisters managed to get back to Tori's party as they were queuing at the boarding gate. The hen party consisted of Hayley, the salon colourist; Kate, the junior stylist; Josh, men's stylist and his American boyfriend Chuck – Charles when Josh was cross with him, which was frequently.

"Oh Babe, thought we were going to have to fly off to hostile lands without our clucking hen!" Josh was panicking. "What did security want with you Lara?"

Lara looked at Tori for support.

"They were just checking that the suitcase they had found without a label corresponded with the luggage label they had found on the conveyor belt. Luckily it did and they have secured the label back on Lara's suitcase." Wow, thought Lara, Tori did surprise her on occasion. Perhaps she should get her a job in the government with her, she could be very useful with a quick response like that; and it was convincing too.

"That's alright then. I thought perhaps they had found something illegal in your case and you were going to have to pull the diplomatic immunity ploy." Josh had watched too many spy movies. Lara may work for the government, but she certainly didn't get diplomatic immunity. "Ooh good, we're moving. Ladies, let's go party. Whoop whoop." Josh led the way on board the flight to the Algarve. With a lot of 'whoops' and a few 'Ola's' they were on board and safely belted in.

Lara sat by the window, with Tori in the middle and Hayley on the outside. The boys and Kate were in the same row, but on the other side of the aisle. Lara looked over at her sister and saw the excitement in her eyes. Tori had always loved Portuguese holidays as a child. To be fair, so did Lara, but that was before...

Lara tried to hear what Hayley was saying to her, but her mind was in the summer of 1995, when she was last in the Algarve.

"Lara, cooee. Tori, can you get your sister to pass the boiled sweets so we can give them to the boys please? Josh doesn't want his ears playing up on take-off." Lara seemed to be staring straight ahead. Tori took the sweets from Lara's lap and passed them to Hayley. She then turned back to look at her sister and knew something wasn't right. It couldn't be anything to do with flying, her job meant she was in the air more often than on the ground.

"Lala? Are you ok?" Hearing her sister's nickname for her (r's were very difficult to pronounce as a child) jolted her back to the present.

"Of course. Just excited for you." She hugged her sister awkwardly in their seatbelts, and looked out of the window as the plane started to taxi. Lara realised that she would ruin the hen party for her sister if she continued with her thoughts. It was a long time ago, it was too late to do

4

anything about it. She'd just have to put it to the back of her mind, where it had been, unabated, for the last 15 years.

"Vilamoura here we come." Josh was so excited. He couldn't believe his luck when Tori asked him and Chuck to go on the hen weekend. It was originally going to be to Brighton, but when they scrutinised the web, the airfare was the same price as the rail tickets from Bournemouth to Brighton and with a change at Southampton, and absurdly it was also quicker to get to Portugal. The weather also swung in its favour, late September could be quite changeable in England, and so it was decided.

Debbie, Tori and Lara's mum had to stay to 'mind the shop' as Tori had taken most of the staff with her. Debbie had made Tori a partner after she had qualified as a hairdresser and beautician. The small salon had doubled in size with Tori doubling the turnover with her nail bar, sunbeds and her new fish spa, where the fish nibbled the hard skin off the feet.

Tori had chosen Hayley, Kate and Josh, as they had been at the salon the longest.

Hayley had been at the Bournemouth and Poole College of hair and beauty with Tori, and Kate had joined as the salon junior while still at school, following her big sister Hayley into hairdressing. Josh had applied for a job on the first day Debbie had allowed Tori to hold an interview on her own. Josh and Tori had left the interview room (kitchen) in hysterical laughter after only five minutes, with the job and new best friends forever. Debbie had banned her from interviewing future staff.

Josh and Chuck had helped Tori with her wedding dress and all the trimmings. Chuck now saw himself as a wedding planner, much to his parent's dismay. He had a degree in accountancy, working for an American bank in Bournemouth; a much more suitable career for an 'All American Boy'. His parents were in denial. Having met Josh they were sure it was just a phase Charles would grow out of. Josh and Chuck found it amusing. His parents loved him so Charles knew eventually they would realise it wasn't just a phase and hopefully support his choice.

Lara and Tori were the only ones who had been to the area before. When they were little they used to stay in Albufeira with their parents, but this time Tori wanted to go where the nightlife was legendary. The advantage of being a hairdresser and beautician was that you heard about everyone's holidays, good and bad. Vilamoura and Vale Do Lobo came out high on the 'places to party' list.

The flight time was just over two hours, and what with the refreshments, duty free, fake cigarettes and top-up cards for phones being peddled over the tannoy system, it didn't leave very much time for anxiety or apprehension. In the few quiet moments when nails were being painted, and iPods were being shared, Lara had time to look out of the window and contemplate 'what if'.

CHAPTER 2

2000

~

As Lara got off the plane at Faro she was hit by the oven effect. It was boiling after the cool air-conditioned plane. It was only early June but already the temperature was hotter than she had felt in a very long time. She loved it already. She followed the families and couples through passport control. Normally she'd feel lonely, but everyone was in holiday mode and was friendly and happy. She waited for her suitcase and took it off the carousel and made her way to the bus stop she had been told to go to. It was an Algarve hopper, stopping at most resorts along the Algarve. Luckily the one Lara wanted was only the second stop and would take about twenty minutes. She had chosen an area called Vale Do Lobo where there were lots of restaurants along a beach in an affluent part of the country. The point being that she would find employment more easily where people spent money.

A short distance along the coast was a town called Quarteira where she hoped to find cheaper accommodation. She knew there was a youth hostel there so she would head for it that evening, after she had hopefully found a job.

At nineteen years old, she should have been very nervous about going out to a foreign country on her own, but her great advantage was her ability to communicate through language.

She had just finished her A levels in French, German and Spanish. Having already attained GCSE A*'s in all those languages plus Russian. To her delight she had been provisionally accepted to three major universities, to study modern languages. She was lucky; she just had that sort of brain. To her, learning languages was fun. Her parents were so proud of her, but were not particularly well off. They were by no means poor, but they had her little sister still at school and her mother's hair salon was more of a hobby than a money-spinner. Her dad made an honest wage as a postman. They were all comfortable, but Lara knew that she would be a drain on their incomes if she continued in education. That was when she decided to take a working year out. She would save every penny, and with a student loan, she hoped her parents would not have to worry about her financially. Waiting on tables was her first choice – talking to the public, she would be able to use the languages she was already fluent in as visitors to the Algarve were from all over Europe, with the added bonus of learning another language, Portuguese.

The Hopper driver shouted out the resort names as they drove to the stops. Lara got out at Vale Do Lobo. It was lovely. It had palm trees everywhere. There were a few bars and restaurants around a fancy hotel. The beaches went on for miles.

Lara went into the hotel and walked up to the reception.

"Hello. I wonder if you can help me? Do you speak English?" The girl on reception looked at Lara with her small suitcase and a backpack, immediately realising she would not want a room at that hotel.

"I vill try," she said politely, with a smile forced onto her face. Lara recognised the accent. She asked her question in fluent German.

"Could I possibly leave my suitcase with you while I walk down the beach in search of a job?" The girl's face seemed to catch up with her smile. She was very flattered that Lara had talked to her in her native tongue.

"We're not supposed to, but I can put it in the cupboard where residents leave theirs when they have to vacate their rooms and have a while to wait for their flights. It will be safe in there." Lara thanked her and made sure she kept the ticket safe, to retrieve her case later. If Renate (her name was on her ID badge) wasn't on when she got back she had to bluff to the new receptionist that she had been a guest. Lara was beginning to realise that the power of language was fundamental to a genial stay in a foreign country.

So, with the heat of the day at it's most vehement, she walked off in the direction of the beach. She decided on beach restaurants as she hadn't any training, so didn't want to try the smarter inland ones. Her main advantage of choosing June was that it was early season and most of the restaurants hadn't started to take on summer staff.

After a few rejections, she was thinking about a career change, when she came across a group of shacks on the beach. They consisted of two restaurants and two bars. To her it looked like a scene from an Australian soap. Surfboards decorated the bars. The area obviously was a favourite with the younger holidaymakers, and those who liked fish. They looked informal and relaxed. As she passed the first restaurant called 'Jilly's', she could hear a heated argument. Trying not to listen, but not having much choice, she recognised the language, again German. The father of the family was trying to tell the English waiter that he had not ordered any bread or olives, and therefore did not see why they were on his bill. Unfortunately only a few words were in English, not enough for the waiter to make out what the customer was saying.

Lara went over to the woman behind the bar and asked if she could speak to the manager.

"You want my husband over there, Rob. He's a little tied up at the moment though." The woman laughed. "Can I help you? My names Jill, by the way." She put out her hand and Lara shook it.

"Hi. I'm Lara Megan Allen, and I'm looking for a job." The voices were getting louder. Rob had realised what the German gentleman was annoyed about and was trying to explain that a cover had to be charged, as tips were optional, and that was what the bread and olives were, the cover. Lara felt obliged to help these two men. It was obvious that the family were getting embarrassed and so were the other customers. She put her rucksack on the counter, smiled at Jill and then went over to the German gentleman and in her most pleasant German she explained.

"Sir, we are very sorry that we have to make this charge, but some people do not leave tips, this makes it impossible for staff members to make ends meet as they rely on tips to boost their wages. As our countries are affluent at the moment, we do our best to help those less fortunate, like Portugal. Look at it as a thank you for letting us enjoy their beautiful country." The German gentleman embraced Lara and then Rob who was completely stupefied. The gentleman got out his wallet and placed the money with a very generous tip, on top of the cover, on the plate, and left with his family, smiling.

"I'm not entirely sure what you said to him, but thank you." Lara smiled at Rob.

"My pleasure. I'm Lara. Is this a good time to ask for a job?" Rob looked over at Jill and they both smiled.

"I think you will come in very handy, we have a lot of German visitors." He escorted her over to Jill. Hiring was her department.

"I have a few more languages that might come in handy, and hopefully within a few weeks I may even have Portuguese sewn up." Jill thought she was manna from heaven. She was always having problems with the kitchen staff as most of them spoke very little English.

"When can you start?" asked an eager Jill. Lara laughed.

"Now would be good. I've just got to find somewhere to live." Jill whispered something to Rob and he nodded.

"OK Lara. If you can help us until the lunchtime rush is over, Jill can take you to one of our holiday apartments in the next town, Quarteira, yours for a modest rent." Lara couldn't believe it, a job and a place to live all at once. "Don't get too excited though, it's only a studio." She shook Rob's hand again, as if closing the deal.

"I'll take it. I don't need more than a bed and a kitchen,

oh, and a bath. Is it always this hot?" Lara was feeling the heat; she was again holding her backpack.

"It get's much hotter, but you become acclimatised quite quickly." Rob helped her off with her backpack and Lara immediately went into the kitchen with Jill to see what had to be done.

After lunch Jill left Rob to clear up ready for dinner and took Lara to Quarteira, via the hotel to pick up her case. Jill found Lara so easy to talk to. She told Lara that she and Rob had been in the Algarve for five years. Rob had sold his late father's pub back in England to a chain of family pubs for double what it was worth. They were able to buy a small villa in Almancil, the nearest town, and a restaurant on the beach, Rob called it 'Jilly's' as a surprise for her. They also had invested in some holiday apartments in Quarteira a few miles along the coast; that was where they were headed.

"Don't you miss England though?" Lara couldn't imagine living away from her family for so long. One year would feel like an eternity.

"My parents live in Brighton and come over quite often, so I don't miss them so much. Unfortunately, Rob's Mother lives in Surrey, alone now. We have tried to persuade her to live here with us but she has a close circle of friends and prefers to come and go. As for us, we had nothing to stay in England for." Lara noticed a hint of sadness in Jill's voice.

Lara turned and saw a tear in Jill's eye. She thought perhaps she should change the subject.

"Well, you couldn't have chosen a better place to live. I know I'm going to love it here." She looked over at Jill again. Jill smiled. She remembered her first few days there and knew how Lara was feeling. It was a wonderful place, with lovely, friendly people.

They passed a school with flags of different nations flying outside.

"Is that a language school?" Lara wondered if she could get a part-time job there too. The extra work would come in useful.

"No, that's the European High School for English children here. Preschool from three year olds to eighteen year olds in the sixth form. It's very successful actually, as the classes are small. Some of the teachers are our friends. We actually had their Christmas party at the restaurant last year." Jill was smiling again. Lara wanted to ask so many questions, but decided to take her lead from Jill.

Jill felt comfortable in Lara's company. She hadn't had a girlfriend to talk to for ages. Language wasn't her forte so the girls at work were unable to have a gossip with her. The rest of her English friends all worked during the day, and she worked in the evenings. Lara could be her confidante.

"I expect you are wondering why we moved here in the first place." She looked round at Lara who nodded. "Well, we left England in 1990. I was only nineteen and Rob was twenty-four. We had been married for a year when his father died leaving us with enough money to settle his mum comfortably and start a new life here. At seventeen I'd had the shock of my life when a routine smear test showed pre-cancerous cells. After treatment they decided I needed a hysterectomy." She took a deep breath. Lara was moved that Jill had only just met her but was confiding in her already.

"Oh my goodness, you were so young. Does Rob know?"

What a stupid question, but she was in shock.

"He was with me all through my treatment. He had been my first boyfriend, and I cannot believe he stayed with me after all that, but instead of running away, he proposed!" Jill and Rob were such wonderful people. Lara wanted her to go on.

"So you can't have children?" Again, another stupid question. Lara could have kicked herself at her lack of tact. But Jill didn't seem to mind.

"No, but we decided to adopt as soon as possible. Unfortunately in England we came up against a brick wall. Although we had age on our side, because I had been diagnosed with cancer, even with the all-clear, we were told it would be almost impossible. So we decided to leave England and make the most of the sun and golf in the Algarve." She sighed and looked resigned. Lara wondered if Jill was happy. Rob was such a fantastic bloke; did that make up for it? Being in such a lovely country with brilliant weather, did that help? Lara thought it probably helped, but not nearly enough. She would be a good friend to Jill while she was there. She was already honoured that Jill had opened up and explained everything to her. Hopefully from now on she'd not put her foot in it.

They had arrived at the apartment block. From her studio she could only glimpse the sea around the building in front. But it was cheap, clean and above all, hers.

She and Jill found the bus timetables, and realised that the last bus went before she finished her evening shift. Jill had the answer. They went to Rob's friend who owned a garage, he was his golfing buddy, and he had a rather ancient, but perfectly serviceable scooter that Jill bought for the restaurant and loaned to Lara for her time with them.

"It will come in handy when chef runs out of scallops. He can come over to Quarteira fish market and get them fresh himself." They both laughed picturing Jorge, the chef, balancing on the scooter. He liked to eat as much as he liked to cook!

So, life was going her way; a fun job, with lovely people, in a wonderful place. She immediately became invaluable to Jill and Rob. They gave her jobs that needed her language skills, after a couple of weeks she had mastered enough Portuguese to help with ordering, menu translations and advertising. Jill did worry about her though, all work and no play.

"She should be out enjoying herself on her days off, not helping me at the Cash-and-Carry." Jill was unpacking her shopping at home. She and Lara had finished unloading the restaurant's purchases and before Jill went home she told Lara to go and enjoy the rest of her day off. "She just shrugged and walked off onto the beach. I know she's trying to save all her money, but she will be ill if she doesn't chill out occasionally."

Rob went over and put his arm around her. She was mothering Lara, and there was only four years between them.

"Oh Jilly, you don't realise, Lara is happy when she's working. She enjoys being useful and loves all the company. Which is just as well as the school holidays will be on us very soon and none of us will have time to chill." Rob was right, once the holidays started the Algarve would be swamped by holidaymakers. It was quite a short season so they had to make the most of it.

In Lara's second month there, Rob was right. The restaurant had queues lunchtime and evening. Lara was in her element. She loved the diversity of the people. Everywhere she turned languages were flowing. She had been in the kitchen for a while, helping with a member of staff who was crying. Jill couldn't work out what was wrong with her and sent Lara in to sort it out. Having ascertained the problem between sniffs, Lara had made chef apologise to her, for calling her a "*louco idiota*". Totally uncalled for, as it was not her entire fault for leaving her foot too near his, so chef, with his large stomach, didn't see it and trod on it. That meant she was not only crying because of his hurtful words, but also for the pain she was suffering.

When she finally calmed things down in the kitchen she made her way into the restaurant to find it bustling.

"Lara, we only have one table free, for two people. The table for six is reserved and they should be here any minute. Apart from that we are full." Jill sounded so pleased. For a week-day it was a good sign of things to come that season. Rob was opening a bottle of wine at a table, but kept an eye on the door.

"Lara." He signalled to Lara and pointed to the door. She turned to see a group of lads walking in. She went over to the book to check the name the table had been reserved in. Munro – funny, she knew a Munro at school, Mark. She turned back to the group and almost simultaneously they recognised each other.

"Oh my goodness. Lara Allen as I live and breathe. We heard you'd come to Portugal, but this is too much of a coincidence." Mark Munro went up to Lara and kissed her on both cheeks.

"Mark, what a great surprise." She led them to their table and handed out menus, catching up on the gossip as she went. They had lost contact for a few years as he went to the boys' grammar and Lara to the girls', but had met again for school dances, and occasionally out in town. The others in the party she knew from middle school. Most of the evening the lads teased her mercilessly. She was actually enjoying it, in a funny way. Jill and Rob thought Mark a very nice chap. Lara said he was just an old friend, but she saw the wink Rob gave Jill and laughed with them.

When it was time to leave, Mark signalled for the bill. Rob took it over to them.

"I hope you have enjoyed the evening gentlemen." He placed the bill with Mark and left. Having split the bill between the six of them they got up to leave. Mark looked around for Lara. He went over to the bar.

"Excuse me. Can you tell me when Lara finishes tonight?" he asked Jill. She looked at her watch.

"When everyone has left, normally. But it has quietened down now, so I'll see if she wants to finish early." Ever the matchmaker, Jill went into the kitchen.

Lara was helping with the pots and pans. Nearly everyone was on coffee so they would not be needed again that night. The sooner they were put away the sooner they could close for the night. She often helped in the kitchen when it was getting late. That was why the kitchen staff loved her.

"Lara, your boyfriend wants to take you out." Jill was more excited than Lara.

"He's not my boyfriend, and I'm tired. Anyway, I don't have money to spend on nights out," Jill tutted.

17

"All work and no play makes Lara a dull girl. You've been here for a month and not had a night out. Go and enjoy one night at least. Looking at the gentleman at the bar, I don't think it will cost you anything anyway. He doesn't look the type to make a lady pay for herself." Jill had made a valid point. Well a couple actually. Lara waved to the kitchen crew and wished them all a good night. She followed Jill out to the bar.

"Lara, there you are. I was wondering if you'd like to come to Vilamoura with me. I'm only here a few days, and I'd loved to spend some time with you. This will be my last holiday for a few years as I start university this autumn. Please say yes." He looked like a small schoolboy. How could she break his heart?

"Ok, yes. But I can't be too late. I have work tomorrow lunchtime." Jill checked the rota and Lara had a day off the next day. She was about to tell her when Lara turned and gave her a knowing look and a slow wink.

"See you tomorrow, Jill. Goodnight." Jill realised that Lara might need an out clause so she wouldn't ruin it for her.

"Have a wonderful evening you two, and don't be late tomorrow." Lara knew Jill had realised her ploy. They were best friends now. She waved to Rob who was getting the card machine for the last table.

"Don't do anything I wouldn't do!" He grinned at them both. Lara poked out her tongue and hooked Mark's arm and left. Rob thought how alike Jill and Lara were, funny really, he'd just noticed that.

"They seem like a nice couple, your boss and his wife." Mark was a little too chauvinistic for Lara.

"Actually, she is more my boss than Rob. He looks after the restaurant, but Jill takes care of the staff and accounts. Far more difficult than just taking the money, wouldn't you agree?" Lara was starting to slur her words, slightly. They had been at a nightclub for a few hours where they had joined Mark's friends. She was trying not to let the side down, and at home she could compete with the best of them. The problem was, that was her first night out in over a month, and she was tired and not used to so much alcohol, especially in the heat. Mark decided it was time to take her home. They got a taxi, and he told the driver to take them to Quarteira. Within seconds of getting into the back seat, Lara was unconscious. Mark hadn't got the full address from her. Quarteira was only minutes away from Vilamoura, so the driver needed an address. Mark shook Lara, who moaned but didn't communicate in any other way. Only one thing left for Mark. He gave the taxi driver his address in Vale Do Lobo. He paid the driver and managed to get Lara out of the taxi. The driver drove away laughing.

"Thanks mate." Mark thought he could have at least help carry her to the door. Luckily it was a bungalow, no stairs to carry her up. There were three bedrooms. His he shared with his mate Tom. He could sleep on the settee for one night, Mark thought. He took Lara to his room and locked the door. The last thing he needed was for Tom to get into the bed with Lara. He managed to get most of her clothes off, but kept her dignity by leaving her underwear on. He rolled her onto the bed and grabbed a pillow for the bath in the en suite. He'd seen them do it in films and thought he'd give it a go. He stripped down to his boxers and climbed into the bath. Before he could even try to get comfortable he heard Lara groan. He ran back out to the bedroom.

"Lara, are you ok?" She opened an eye.

"No, I feel sick." Mark looked round for a container, the litterbin was made of wicker, not quite up to the job.

"Hang on Lara." He couldn't see anything usable. Suddenly a blinding flash went passed him into the bathroom. Then came the inevitable up-chuck noise. Well, he could put that night down to one of the most unromantic in a while. He stayed perched on the end of the bed until it had been quiet for a few minutes.

"Lara, are you ok?" He heard a gargling noise and went to check she wasn't chocking on her own vomit. Opening the door he could see her bent over the basin, with the mouthwash.

"That's better. Where am I, by the way?" She looked round and saw Mark standing in the doorway in his Pluto boxers. She laughed and pointed at them.

"My Mum bought them for my birthday. I didn't realise they'd be seen." He looked embarrassed. She went over to him and cuddled him.

"Don't worry I won't tell anyone. Your secret is safe with me." She threw herself onto the bed. "Come and have a cuddle." Mark didn't want to take advantage of her, but she looked so good. He had fancied her for a very long time. But for the chance meeting with her mum, at his parents' chemists where he was helping out, he wouldn't even have known she was in Portugal. They'd already decided on the Algarve for the golf with his friends. Lara was an added bonus.

He lay down beside her. She snuggled up to him. He turned and kissed her, passionately. She felt her whole body relax into his arms.

"Lara, may I make love to you?" Mark knew Lara was drunk and didn't want to take advantage of her. But if she agreed…

"Yes please." Lara surrendered into the arms of Mark.

When she woke up the next morning she looked around and realised she was in Mark's bed, in his rented villa in Vale Do Lobo. How she got there she didn't know. In fact, she couldn't remember much after they left the casino early on in the evening, the nightclub was a blur. She managed to get out of bed without disturbing Mark. She found her clothes and put them on, quietly. She felt terrible. Her head was thumping and she was desperate for the loo. Would it wake Mark? She'd have to chance it or wet herself. She didn't flush, that would be too risky. She carefully unlocked the door and tiptoed out into the hallway holding her shoes. Problem was, she had never been in that villa before and didn't know where the front door was. All the doors looked alike and she didn't want to end up in a bedroom. She moved slowly to the end of the hallway and saw the kitchen. Back door, she thought, must be one in the kitchen to take out the rubbish. Eureka, a door. She opened it very quietly and left the building. She put on her shoes and walked up the driveway. As she got to the main road she knew exactly where she was. In a short distance she was at the beach and a few minutes along the beach was 'Jilly's' and her scooter. She wasn't sure if she was over the limit still, but she had to get home and shower. Thank goodness she wasn't at work that day, she needed paracetamol and sleep. Luckily it was still early and the restaurant was closed. She couldn't face anyone until she'd showered.

She managed to get back to her flat and made straight for the bathroom. It was then she realised sex had taken place. She vaguely remembered it, but wasn't sure. She hoped he was sensible and had used protection. Lara hadn't had a boyfriend for over six months, so when her last course of contraception had run out she hadn't bothered getting any more; she thought it was better for her body to have a rest when she had no need of the Pill.

Her mobile rang a few times that morning, and it beeped a few more. She looked at the text messages and they all said the same. He wanted to keep in touch when he got back to England and he had enjoyed the evening and wondered why she had rushed off without saying goodbye. He expected she needed to get to work. He hoped she was ok and thanked her for an amazing night.

She felt awful. He was such a good guy. But she was embarrassed by what had happened. It wasn't his fault, but that didn't make it better. She felt like a slut. She got back into the shower and scrubbed and scrubbed herself until she was sore. Tears were streaming down her face. For the first time since arriving in Portugal, she wanted to go home to her mum.

By the next day she was feeling more herself. Things seemed more tolerable. Mark had sent a text from the airport to say goodbye, and again thanked her for a wonderful evening. Her headache had gone completely. She had had hours of sleep to make her feel rejuvenated, and she was ready for the weekend rush, bring it on.

The summer was a busy one. Good for takings, and tips alike. Lara had made good money. Learning her lesson, she hadn't gone out partying again. She didn't miss it; she was always too tired to worry by the end of her shifts. She had made herself indispensable to Jill and Rob. Not only because she could take on a shift at very short notice, but also, by then, she was fluent in Portuguese ("not too different from Spanish," she had told them, "but don't let the Portuguese hear me say that!") and that helped with the ordering, winter menus and advertising for the locals. Rob also wanted her to stay because she was so good for Jill. They had become very close, and it stopped Jill going down, psychologically. Lara made her laugh.

So, by the end of the season when most of the summer staff had gone, Jill and Rob agreed to keep Lara as long as she wanted to stay.

Lara was over the moon. She was worried about what to do next. She was thinking perhaps she would have to go back to England and find a job over Christmas in a department store like last year, so depressing. That really didn't appeal to her after working so long outdoors. She felt healthier than she had in a long time, and was noticing that her nails, hair and skin were all benefitting from the sunshine.

One morning in October, Jill had arranged to pick up Lara on the way to the Cash-and-Carry in Albufeira. Lara was waiting outside her apartment block, and saw Jill's car approach. As she went to open the car door she felt a little lightheaded. She hadn't had any breakfast, as she was feeling a little nauseous that morning. She knew what it was, and it was her own fault. Instead of going straight to bed after her shift, she went to her fridge and ate some prawn cocktail she had taken home a day or two before. It was past it's sell by date and she had promised to eat it that day, or throw it away. Jill wouldn't let her take it until she had promised. But for some reason Lara fancied it that night, and thought it tasted fine. She'd keep it to herself so Jill wouldn't get cross.

"Good morning." Lara said cheerfully as she got into the car. It didn't convince Jill who had noticed Lara looking very pale on the pavement as she pulled up.

"Is it? You don't look very good. Are you ok?" Jill was worried. "If you don't feel like coming, I'll understand." Jill assumed it could be the time of the month.

"No I'm fine, really. Have you remembered to put candles on the list? We were running low last night." Lara always used the 'change the subject' ploy. It nearly always worked.

"Oh no. Well done. Grab my clipboard; it's on the back seat there. Can you add it and anything else you think I've forgotten?" Jill had more confidence in Lara's memory than her own. Subject changed; her ploy had worked. Lara stretched over and got the clipboard. Then she wished she hadn't. The nausea had returned. Luckily Jill had her eyes on the road so Lara just kept still for a while until it passed. Bloody prawns, she thought. She never ate before bedtime. Why did she fancy prawns of all things? Oh Lara, she told herself, stop thinking of prawns. Another wave of nausea came over her. She had to think of something else. She looked at the list and saw more items of food. Not the best idea. Right, she thought, think of swimming with Fernando in the sea when they got back from the Cash-and-Carry. He was the winter waiter they kept on as he attracted the ladies. Lara knew she was safe as he was wonderfully gay. He also had a partner who was the maître d' at the hotel where Lara had left her suitcase on the first day. His name was Nelson and they were a lovely couple, fantastic company for a single girl. They had fun on their days off together. Before she knew it, she and Jill were parking at the Cash-and-Carry. Jill got out and found a coin for the trolley. Lara carried the list. She felt better in the fresh air. She took a few deep breaths and followed Jill into the warehouse.

Things went well and they were finished within the hour. A record, but at that time of year they needed less. Lara helped empty the trolley into the boot and back seats while Jill checked everything off. It was no good getting back to the restaurant and trying, as too many hands helped to put things away. That done, Jill went off to put the trolley back and retrieve her euro. She got back to the car and wondered where Lara was. She wasn't in the passenger seat. She looked around and there was no sign of her. She went round the car to see if Lara was hiding. She was a joker sometimes.

"Lara, are you alright. What's happened?" Jill rushed over to Lara who was on the ground by the passenger door.

"I'm fine. I stumbled, I think." Jill helped her up and noticed that the colour had completely drained from her face.

"You are anything but fine, young lady. Let's get you home." Jill helped her up and put her in the car. Jill got into the driver's seat and started the engine. "What do you think it can be? Are you due on?" Jill wondered if it was just a heavy period.

"No, I ate some dodgy prawns last night and felt sick this

morning, so I haven't had any breakfast." Lara thought the truth was the best option. She felt so ill that she couldn't think of a lie.

"Dodgy prawns may make you sick, but fainting is another matter. I'm not convinced it's just food poisoning. I'm going to take you to see Paddy. He'll take a good look at you and then I'll be happy." Dr Paddy O'Donnell was a golfing buddy of Rob's. He was a frequent visitor to the restaurant and more often the bar. He had a consulting room in the Medical Centre in Vale Do Lobo, where Jill headed. Jill got there in record speed, hoping the frozen stuff would be ok for a little longer. She left Lara in the car and ran into the Medical Centre. Hilda was on reception as usual. She was Paddy's long-suffering wife.

"Jill, how lovely to see you." Hilda looked at Jill's face. "Is something wrong dear?"

"Lara has just passed out in a carpark. Is Paddy about?" Jill tried to get her breath. Her heart was racing. She was worried about her friend. Hilda took charge and got Jill to sit down. She buzzed through to Paddy and told him to get out there. She then went out to the car to help Lara into the surgery. Paddy was talking to Jill as Lara came in with Hilda.

"Right young lady, let's get you into my room where I can take a look at you. Hilda, can you get Jill a coffee?" Hilda went over to the machine and poured Jill a strong cup of coffee. Lara was escorted into Paddy's consulting room.

"Jill said you thought you may have food poisoning. Have you been sick, or had diarrhoea?" He was prodding her stomach as she lay on his couch.

"No, I've felt like I'm about to throw-up but haven't yet."

Paddy caught hold of Lara's arm and helped her sit up. He put the blood pressure sleeve on her arm and started pumping it up. He then pulled her lower eye-lid down and tutted.

"Well, if it was food poisoning from last night I can assure you that it would have made its way out of your body by now. I'm almost sure that what is wrong with you will not be making its way out of your body for a good few months yet." He laughed at his own joke. Lara looked bemused, until it suddenly dawned on her.

"You mean I'm pregnant?" Paddy clapped his hands.

"Got it in one. By the feel of it, I'd say you were around twelve weeks already. You are lucky; most people would have got your symptoms weeks ago. Didn't you notice your periods had stopped?" Paddy was talking with his back to Lara, looking for some tablets in his cupboard.

"Not really, I've never been that regular. I've been so busy recently that it hadn't occurred to me." She was in shock. Paddy handed her some tablets.

"Right, these are iron tablets, you are a little anaemic; and by the way, congratulations." Lara got off the couch very carefully. She couldn't believe it. Pregnant. She knew it was Mark's. She hadn't had intercourse for a good six months before and not since. Should she tell him? What is Jill going to say? What are her parents going to say? Paddy opened the door and walked out to Jill and Hilda.

"Well, how is my favourite restaurateur?" Jill stood up and looked for Lara behind Paddy. "It's ok. She's fine." He smiled at Lara.

"Thank you Dr O'Donnell. Bye Hilda." Lara made for the door. She turned to Jill. "I'll wait in the car." Jill said goodbye to Hilda and Paddy and hurried out to the car.

"What are those for?" She noticed the tablets Lara was holding.

"I'm slightly anaemic. It goes with the territory when you're pregnant." Lara decided not to beat around the bush. Jill's mouth was wide open. "Not an attractive look there, Jill." Jill closed her mouth. "And before you ask, it's Mark's. One night of debauchery." She burst into tears. "I'm so sorry Jill. I've let you down. I've let myself down, and I've let my parents down." Jill held her until she stopped crying. Suddenly Lara pulled herself together. "Come on, let's get to the restaurant before the frozen stuff thaws." They looked at each other and smiled.

As they drove Jill asked her if she was going to tell Mark. Lara wasn't sure. Mark had told her how thrilled he was to have been accepted into the university where his parents had met and studied.

"I know I should, but he's just started his three-year biomedicine course. His parents own a chemist shop. They are both pharmacists, but his father is going blind. His poor mum is coping with the bulk of the dispensing and trying to help his dad feel useful. Obviously it's too dangerous for him to dispense any more. Mark decided to help them both and when he finishes his course he will take over the running of the chemist so they can take it easy. He's an amazing son. I can't let him ruin his plans for one night of stupidity." Jill understood, but thought Mark ought to make that choice. She kept her opinion to herself. It was all too raw for now.

"What about your parents, should you phone them?" Jill wondered if Lara's mother would help Lara make those important decisions. She sounded like a lovely person.

"Mum and Dad are extremely proud of me. I'm the first person in the family to get into university. I couldn't do that to them. There's my little sister to consider too. What kind of example would I be setting her? Oh Jill, what a mess." She started crying again as they pulled up outside the restaurant. Jill stopped the car.

"Help me put these things away and take you home and we can have a nice talk. Things will look a little better after we get some food inside you and a nice cup of tea." Lara looked at Jill and smiled. She was more like a mother to her than a friend.

"Thank you, Jill."

"For what?" Jill was puzzled.

"For not judging and being there for me. You are a true friend." She kissed Jill on the cheek and got out of the car. Jill felt fulfilled for the first time in a long while.

Lara knew she had a big decision to make. She knew in the back of her mind she had already made it. Termination was out of the question. Lara wasn't particularly religious, (she hadn't been to church since she was a Girl Guide) but she believed a baby was a gift from God. She also felt after all the kindness and friendship that Jill and Rob had shown her that it would have been a slap in the face to them and others who longed for, but couldn't have a baby. She needed to talk to Jill and Rob together. Rob was laying up the tables while Jill was helping put the groceries away. The restaurant was due to open in twenty minutes. It was now or never.

"Rob, can you and Jill meet me on the decking for a chat.

It's important." Rob knew something was up the minute the girls got back from shopping. He didn't want to pry so hadn't asked.

"Now?" Rob saw Lara nod as she walked out onto the terrace. He put his head into the kitchen and called Jill. "Jilly love, can you come out here a moment?" Jill came to the door.

"I've not finished putting all the things away yet. What's the problem?" Rob looked out onto the terrace where Lara was sitting at an outside table. Jill's eyes followed his. "Lara wants to talk to us. Do you think she wants to go home?" Jill took Rob by the hand and they went out to talk to Lara.

"This is going to be difficult for me to say, so neither of you talk until I've finished, deal?" Lara was looking very serious. It made Rob want to laugh, but he took his lead from Jill who agreed with Lara and sat down.

"Rob, to keep you abreast of all the news, I'm pregnant. Twelve weeks to be exact. It wasn't planned, but sometimes the best things in life are surprises." She was smiling. Jill couldn't believe the transformation from the quivering wreck she had just brought back from the doctors.

"I have made a decision which I need to run past you both. It really isn't the right time for me to have a baby. I will not terminate this pregnancy; the little life inside me is too precious. With your help, I'd like to give birth to it and then give it to you both to adopt. I'm not sure of the legal ins and outs, but I'm sure with a little help from Dr O'Donnell no one else need even know it isn't yours, Jill." Lara looked at Jill who had tears streaming down her eyes, then at Rob who was also welling up. They both hugged each other, and then got up and hugged Lara. "I take it that's a yes then?" Lara was welling up too. Rob took control.

"Are you absolutely sure, Lara? It will be a very difficult thing to do. But I think I speak for Jilly that if at any time you want to change your mind, I know we will be devastated, but we will understand." After so many disappointments, finally getting a baby to complete their family was more than they ever hoped for.

"I won't change my mind. I will hopefully enjoy the opportunity of having a baby when the time is right, but this baby is already yours. My gift to you both for being the best friends I have ever had." She was nineteen and knew she was giving Jill and Rob a wonderful gift, but she was sad. Had things been different, had her parent's expectations been lower, or Mark's family loyalty been non-existent, there would have been no problem, but that is what made them the good people they were. She knew she was doing the right thing. She could visit the baby whenever she wanted. She decided to stay until the baby was weaned so as to give it the best start in life. They were all crying again, but this time with happiness.

Soon after the revelations Jill and Rob insisted that Lara move into their villa so they could keep an eye on her and stop her working too hard. The baby wasn't due until mid-April, which still gave Lara time to earn more money, and also get over the birth before her university course started late in September. Rob had insisted she work less, and had set up a trust fund for her university fees. It was the least they could do, but Lara took some persuading. She didn't like the thought of selling her baby. Rob and Jill knocked that idea right out of her mind. Rob pointed out that, one, she would have been working a lot more hours had she not been pregnant with their baby, and two, if she was giving them a wonderful gift through friendship, they could reciprocate. When put like that she accepted, but only what she needed to top up her own savings. They all agreed.

It was soon Christmas and Lara was slightly showing. She decided to go home for the festivities, otherwise she would not see her family until well into the following year after she had given birth. The good thing about England was the fact she could wear baggy jumpers. Her excuse was being used to warmer weather. She had a lovely Christmas with all her relatives. Her sister, Tori, was especially pleased to see her, and re-styled Lara's hair. She'd been allowed to work as a junior in her mum's salon on Saturdays and had decided to go to the hair and beauty college when she left school. Her mum was equally proud of her second daughter. She had a wonderful talent and a way with clients that no training could teach. She was a natural. Lara stayed until just after the New Year Celebrations, and then told her parents that she was needed before the golfing season rush started. They were pleased that she was so highly thought of and was making money towards the costs of university by working so hard.

Time flew by. She was pleased that the pregnancy was mainly in the winter months – as she got bigger the heat would have been intolerable. Rob and Jill had managed to get legal advice on the quiet, and if they registered the birth at the British consulate in Spain they could get the baby a British Passport, making it a legal British citizen. Rob had easily persuaded Paddy to make house calls so Lara didn't have to make her pregnancy official. With the inducement of alcoholic beverages, Paddy was there frequently. Although it had been a few years since he delivered a baby, it was something you remembered, like riding a bike, apparently, so he was on call for the big day.

To quote Robert Burns, "The best laid plans of mice and men go often awry." Of course most baby's births cannot be planned however hard you try. So, on a beautiful day in April, Lara was taking in the washing to help Jill and Rob while they were at the restaurant, when her waters broke. She phoned the restaurant first and then Paddy's number. It went straight through to voicemail. She phoned his home number and managed to get Hilda.

"He's on the golf course dear. Mobiles are frowned upon so his is probably on silent. I'll see if I can get someone to fetch him. Don't you worry, you'll have plenty of time this being your first." How many times had she heard that! Unfortunately her baby hadn't read *The Idiot's Guide To Giving Birth*. Almost immediately her contractions were coming fast and painfully. She lay on the bed at first, but that made her back hurt. She found lying over Jill's gym ball helped, which was where Rob and Jill found her.

"Oh, you poor child." Jill knelt by her side and rubbed her back for her. Rob paced up and down looking out of the window for Paddy's car. Eventually a golf buggy whizzed up the driveway. Out stumbled a rather drunk doctor.

"I don't believe it." Rob went out to hurry Paddy along. "I thought you were on the golf course."

"Nineteenth hole actually. It wasn't my fault, I won so it was my round." Paddy looked pleased.

"But it's your round when you lose too. You really are an

idiot sometimes. The sun isn't over the yard-arm for a while yet." Rob couldn't really get cross with him because he was such a nice bloke.

"It is somewhere." Paddy laughed. "Get the coffee on, there's a good chap." Good idea thought Rob, black and lots of it.

The baby girl was born within the hour. It had been quite traumatic for Lara, being so quick, but even she had to say it was well worth it just seeing the joy in Rob and Jill's faces as they held their little daughter. Paddy checked Lara over and the baby and gave them both a clean bill of health.

"Shall we toast the baby's health? No? Well, I'll go now then. Good luck to you all. I'll be back tomorrow just to check all is well. Good bye." Lara managed a feeble "thank you" and Rob saw him to the door.

"This isn't going on record anywhere is it?' He hoped Paddy wasn't too drunk and decide to write notes.

"No, don't worry. This is completely off the record. That little baby girl couldn't have better parents in you two. Who am I to ruin Lara's gift to you. Just keep an eye on her for any depression. She's strong, but what she is doing takes a great deal of courage and in one so young who knows how things will work out for her." He left feeling very humble. Rob felt the same as he closed the door, but didn't have time to think about it. He had a family now, and had to make sure they were all taken care of.

Lara had already decided to breastfeed the little girl for as long as she could. It was the best for the baby. At least she could give her the best start by giving her the goodness and colostrum from the first few days, but during the fifth day she was very tearful. Jill had noticed she was getting depressed. Lara had to make a decision. The baby purposely hadn't been named. Lara decided she wanted to leave before the name was chosen. She felt she was bonding with the baby and that was wrong. Before she became too attached she had to go.

Jill and Rob told her that the second she wanted to visit, or if she wanted photos and progress reports, just ring them and they'd send them, in the immediate future though Lara wanted no contact, to help her get over it quicker. She said her goodbyes, and left the new happy family to a wonderful life. She cried all the way home, but hid the secret from everyone.

She felt guilty each time she thought of her little girl, but her conscience was appeased by thinking of the wonderful deed she had done for Jill and Rob.

Living in Bournemouth she was able to get a summer job in a local language school, teaching English to the numerous students from all over the world. It kept her very busy and gradually it got easier. Late September she started her new life at university in Oxford studying modern languages. Within three years having left university with a First, she was head hunted by the Foreign Office, later known as the Foreign and Commonwealth Office, as their top translator, translating at important European conferences, and became an important cog in the diplomatic wheel.

Jill and Rob named the little girl Megan, after Lara's middle name. They knew what an enormous sacrifice Lara had made, and they knew her heart was broken. She had fallen in love with that little girl. They waited for her to contact them, but she never did. They knew it was her defence mechanism.

CHAPTER 3

PRESENT DAY

~~~

"Cabin crew, seats for landing." The captain's voice jolted Lara back to the present. She hadn't undone her seatbelt, or put down her table, so no one had disturbed her. The plane landed with a bump, followed by another. They were safely down. A fanfare came over the cabin intercom system as the plane had reached its destination on time. Her group's excitement finally filtered through to Lara and she left the plane joining in their effervescence.

The hotel had sent a coach to pick up the hen party, plus a few other groups. They only had to wait for their luggage to be loaded and they were off. Lara noticed the airport was bigger than she remembered, and on the road to Vilamoura, villas had sprung up everywhere. The area still looked idyllic, just on a much grander scale.

Once they had arrived at the hotel they were allocated

their rooms, Tori and Lara in one, Josh and Chuck in another and Hayley had to share with her little sister Kate. Within twenty minutes the boys were hammering on the door to Lara and Tori's room. Tori let them in.

"Come on you two. Let's go check out the port. There may be some handsome sailors waiting to be picked up." Josh was winding Chuck up.

"You find it difficult to pick up your feet, how are you going to pick up a sailor?" They playfully spanked each other, laughing at each other's attempts.

"Boys, we will come with you, but I'm going to have to disappoint you." Lara stopped them in their tracks. They looked worried. "The Vilamoura port does not have sailors. The boats moored there are luxury motor yachts, playboy toys." Josh burst out laughing again.

"I love playing with boys' toys." Lara gave up. She realised that if she had wanted an intelligent conversation she should have stayed in the stuffy Foreign Office. She joined in the laughter and they went in search of the final members of their brood of merry hens.

Thursday night was awesome. They had hit the casino and then at least three nightclubs. Lara had gone to bed first, but couldn't sleep soundly until her sister was safely tucked up a few hours later. In fact, an hour before breakfast started being served.

By eleven o'clock they were all nursing hangovers by the hotel pool. Josh was sitting over with a group of girls chatting away, while Chuck snored on a sun lounger. Josh minced back over to his flock of hens, leaving the group of girls in hysterics. He was such a drama queen, but everyone loved him.

"Those girls are on a hen weekend too, from Dublin. The one with purple hair is the bride-to-be. They coloured it while she was asleep, we wouldn't do that to you Tor. We love you." Hayley and Kate laughed. They had tried to colour Tori's hair before they left, but Debbie took over realising what they were about to do to her daughter. "They had a fantastic night last night at a place called Vale Do Lobo. It isn't far."

"Isn't that near to where you used to live, on your gap year Lara?" Tori seemed to remember the name, but wasn't sure.

"Yes, but everything has changed since I was last here. There's been so much development that it is all unrecognisable now." Lara looked lost in thought, so Josh carried on.

"Anyway! Apparently, It's Karaoke Night in the main restaurant called Monty's. It's a bar and has a dance floor with a DJ and live bands. Then they said by midnight the Gecko Club next door is open for dancing. This is the exciting bit though, they were saying that the England football team were over getting used to training in the heat for an important match, somewhere." Josh liked watching the players, but hadn't a clue about football. "The whole area is full of the fittest players from the Premier League." Chuck woke up.

"Count me in." Chuck had almost fallen off the lounger. The idea of all those fit footballers was something he couldn't sleep through.

"I think you'd make a wonderful footballer's wife, Chuck." Tori couldn't resist teasing Josh. Josh loved being centre of attention and pouted his lips, thrust his body round and minced back to his new girlfriends. Hayley and Kate were in hysterics. Tori called him back and apologised, trying to keep a straight face. They all agreed that it would be a fantastic night and they'd go and try it out that evening. Lara was torn. It was way too close to home. She was going to say her hangover was too bad and she'd give it a miss, but she didn't want to let her sister down. So, not being a party pooper, she decided to go with them.

They ate at Vilamoura, in a wonderful Thai restaurant, with water cascading down the outside windows. Lara had joined in the fun at last. Why waste such a fantastic holiday, with her sister, on old memories. She decided it was time to make some new ones in those familiar places. So far it was easy. Josh and Chuck were hilarious. She hadn't laughed so much in ages.

In London she couldn't remember the last time she went out and enjoyed herself. Due to the very unsociable hours and unpredictability of her job, her personal life was non-existent. Her job took her to places like Geneva, Paris, Brussels and Dublin at short notice, which sounded impressive, but weighed against a social life for a woman of thirty-five years, having broken dates so often, she had decided it was easier to curl up on the settee with a good book; it was lonely.

Her sister loved coming up to London. She'd do Lara's hair and nails and they'd go out on the town. Unfortunately this wasn't very often, as Lara was called away at a moment's notice, mostly hush-hush, so she couldn't even tell Tori when or where. Tori understood and would stay flat sitting with her friends so she didn't mind.

After they had finished the meal, Lara took control. She had remembered to get the taxi number from the hotel receptionist and so she ordered a seven-seater taxi to take them to Vale Do Lobo.

As they pulled into the taxi rank at Vale Do Lobo they could hear the karaoke in full swing.

"Elvis is in the building." Chuck recognised 'Love Me Tender' being sung by someone who had drunk far too much, but was obviously enjoying himself. Josh was beginning to think it was a big mistake. He loved music, but Elvis used to sing with an acoustic guitar and it was all about his voice. Somewhere during its karaoke remix that fact had got lost.

They went over to the restaurant where a few people outside on the decking were finishing off their meals, and walked into the bar. The girls found a table and the boys had been sent to order the drinks from the bar. After a few minutes Tori wondered where the boys were. She stood up to see if they had been served yet.

"I can't see the boys. They're not at the bar." Just as Lara was getting up to check, the introduction started and great roars came from the audience. The boys broke into their song on the stage, 'It's Raining Men'! The whole place enjoyed the two lads camping up their performance. The girls were laughing so much. When they had finished the entire bar gave them a rapturous applause.

"Well, what do you think?" Josh came running over to the table, completely out of breath but totally exhilarated.

"Wonderful darling, but where are the drinks?" Tori was joking. "No, really, you two have made the evening. Who is going to be able to top that?" Chuck and Josh hugged.

"Hello, my name is Nikki and I'll be your waitress for the evening. Can I get you any drinks?" Nikki immediately became their best friend and she invited them to join her on Facebook.

They were onto their next round of drinks when Lara, who wasn't as inebriated as her fellow hens because she had been on spritzers, noticed the bar seemed to get quieter. Suddenly the first few introductory bars of 'Someone Like You' by Adele played, and the voice of an angel started singing. She was note perfect and the whole audience was quiet. Lara had her back to the stage and was compelled to look round. There on the dais was a beautiful teenager, long blonde hair and very long legs, like Lara. Then she blasted out the chorus in a voice way beyond her years. She sung the last chorus in fluent Portuguese and then in English. The bar erupted when she finished with 'encore' and applause. She obviously had a flair for languages, just like Lara. Lara thought she was imagining the coincidences.

The chef came out of the kitchen and shouted at her in Portuguese. She ran back through the bar and disappeared into the kitchen.

Before she could ponder on it, Nikki came over with a massive bowl filled with a mixed cocktail, six straws and an enormous sparkler lit in the middle for the hen. Everyone in the bar cheered when Tori blew the sparkler out, on the second attempt. Lara turned to the waitress as she was taking the sparkler away and asked her who the girl was that had just sung.

"That's our Megan. She lives up in town. She's only

fifteen, would you believe, with a voice like that? She helps out in the kitchen in the evenings as she's still at school. She's our little star. Chef gets annoyed with her when she sings though; she's underage so she's not supposed to be this side of the bar."

Lara's heart missed a beat – Megan was *her* middle name. She couldn't get the girl out of her mind. She decided to act drunk so as not to let Tori think she wasn't enjoying herself, but stay sober. She had some investigative work to do the next day. She was going to leave them all in bed asleep, early in the morning.

Lara managed to get everyone back to the hotel around four o'clock. She managed to sleep for a few hours but her brain was too lively with expectation. In the morning, she went quietly out of the room leaving her sister sound asleep and down to reception.

"Could I order a car to rent for the day please?" She asked the young man behind the desk.

"Of course madam. May I have your driving licence and I can have a car here when you have finished your breakfast." She wasn't sure she could eat any breakfast, but it seemed a sensible idea. Luckily she kept her driving licence on her at all times. She often ended up driving some diplomat from venue to airport because of over indulgence during lunch!

Where to start? She decided to start at the beginning, 'Jilly's'. She drove down the familiar track. The only thing that had changed was a small amount of tarmac had been laid for cars to park outside the two restaurants and two bars. Apart from that it was like a mini time-warp. 'Jilly's' was now called 'Issabel's', but apart from the sign, it hadn't changed at all. Lara parked the car and looked around. It was closed, too early for lunch. A man came out of the kitchen with a bag of rubbish. She went over to him and spoke in Portuguese.

"Excuse me. I'm looking for Senhor and Senhora Simpson. Do you know where I can find them?" The man scratched his head.

"Simpson, ah, yes. We bought this place from them years ago. The Senhora was very ill, I remember, so they had to sell to take her back to England." Lara didn't like the sound of that.

"Do you remember their daughter's name?" The man scratched his head again.

"Issabel." He shouted. "Issabel." He shouted again. Eventually a woman came out of the kitchen wiping her hands on a tea towel.

"What is it you old fool?" she shouted back in Portuguese. She suddenly noticed Lara. "Oh, sorry. Can I help?" Lara explained in Portuguese that she was looking for the Simpsons, and wondered if she remembered the daughter's name.

"Maisy? Or Maggie, sorry it was a long time ago. So sad. She was a lovely lady too." Lara wasn't sure if she understood her own translation.

"I'm sorry, who was a lovely lady?"

Issabel began to speak English to her. "Senhora Simpson. It was tragic and she was so young. Senhor Simpson and the daughter are back now." Issabel wiped a tear away.

"What happened to Senhora Simpson?" Lara instinctively knew the answer.

"She died in England. The husband and child live in Almancil I think." Lara thanked them for their help and got back in the car. She burst into tears. She could have been there for Jill; she should have been there for her. It made her more determined to be there for Rob now. She had to find him, even if it was just to offer her condolences. She went over to one of the bars and ordered a coffee.

The next course of action needed thought and a clear mind. She sat out on their balcony with her coffee, looking at the sea. She couldn't believe the only difference from fifteen years ago was the number of planes flying over her. She had counted at least five in the time she sat there.

Having made the decision to go and find Rob, she went back to the car and drove to Almancil. They could have moved, but her gut reaction would be that Rob would find comfort being where Jill had been happy. She drove up and parked outside the villa. Apart from electric gates, nothing seemed to have changed. It was still a pastel shade of peach, with tiles around the front. Most Portuguese houses had been built with tiles on the outside, it was to reflect the heat of the sun and keep the building cooler. She looked at her watch. It was nearly lunchtime. After a lot of debating Lara had come to the conclusion that she should go back to the hotel and leave the Simpson family to themselves, she had left it too long. She thought she had no right to be there after all this time. She was about to turn the key in the ignition when something caught her eye. The electric gates were opening. The young girl who had sung the previous night was riding on her bike out of the gate and down the road, waving back to her father who had come out into the garden to see her off. He turned and looked at his garden. He was thinking of weeding it, but it was still far too hot, perhaps later. While his back was turned Lara had managed to sneak in before the gate closed. She gave a little cough.

"What have you forgotten?" Rob assumed Megan had come back. He turned and was face to face with his past.

"Oh, my goodness, Lara." He ran towards her and they were in each other's arms sobbing for ages.

"I'm so so sorry Rob. I should have been here for you both." It had been the first time in the last five years that Rob had managed to show his true feelings.

"I miss her Lara." He had put on a brave face for Megan, but he missed his Jilly so much. They didn't say another word, just hugged.

After a few minutes Rob pulled away and took a good look at Lara, smiling. She had hardly changed. Lara was thinking the same of Rob, apart from a distinguished few grey hairs around his temples.

"It's wonderful to see you Lara." Lara smiled. "How did you know about Jilly?"

"I went to the restaurant and the new owners told me. I'm so sorry I left it too late Rob." Rob took her hand and led her inside.

"Come and have a coffee and we'll catch up on fifteen years." Lara looked around, nothing much had changed apart from the 21st century had come to Portugal. Electrical gadgets seemed to be everywhere; Megan's she thought. The furniture was the same, and the kitchen was still as welcoming. She sat at the breakfast bar and watched Rob fill the cafetiere. "So, what brought you to this neck of the woods?" Rob sat opposite Lara taking in the fact she was there.

"My sister's hen weekend. We are staying in Vilamoura,

going back on Monday. Fate stepped in before I left." Rob looked bemused. "We decided to go to Monty's last night, Karaoke evening. From out of the kitchen came an angel. The whole bar was quiet listening to her sing."

"Megan?" Rob knew Megan sung at Monty's, but turned a blind eye. She had brought so much joy to Jill through her singing; he was not going to stop her doing the same for others.

"She's amazing. You must be very proud of her." Lara watched Rob's face. He smiled.

"All this," he pointed to the gadgets around the place, "is Megan's recording paraphernalia. She'd put her songs on CD and Jill listened to them while she was ill." Lara didn't want to make polite conversation. She was trying to work out how to broach the subject of Jill's death without being insensitive. Rob seemed to sense what Lara was thinking.

"It was cancer, back with a vengeance. She managed ten good years with Megan, but she came out of remission very quickly. By the time I got her back to England it was too late, we just had to keep her comfortable and cheerful. That's where Megan's music came in. Jill used to put on the headphones and listen for hours. She said it took her off to a better place." Lara started to cry, quietly to herself. Rob noticed. "In her final days Jill thanked you in her prayers for giving her her own little angel for ten years." Rob went round and hugged Lara. "Jill used to comment that it was like having you back with us, watching Megan. She is very like you." Lara looked up at him and realised he was crying again too. She needed to change the subject.

"So, you came back to Portugal? I noticed that Megan is fluent in Portuguese too." She wanted Rob to speak about Megan, he was so proud of her she knew it would cheer him up.

"Yes, she goes to the local English school where both languages are spoken. She seems to have a flair for languages, don't know where she got that from," he teased, a glimpse of the old Rob was coming through. Rob poured the coffee and placed a mug in front of her. "Lara, without Megan I wouldn't have got through the last five years. I want to thank you. Would you like to meet her? I mean properly." Lara wasn't sure. Megan now needed a mother more than ever. Once she had met this angel, could she walk out of her life again? Rob could see Lara was debating with herself. "You haven't changed, have you? You're still your own worst enemy. Stop thinking things through to intensely. Sometimes you've just got to go with the flow. Meet Megan and we can go from there." Rob was right. She had hidden from responsibility for too long.

"I'd love to. I can be her friend. She may need a female confidante. Does she know anything about me?" Lara didn't want to harm any story that Megan had been told.

"When Jill died Megan became paranoid about her health. She started reading articles on the Internet and found out that you were more likely to be struck by cancer if a family member had been diagnosed. It got to the extent that I had to tell her that although we were her parents, she had been a gift to them from a wonderful, unselfish person who knew Jill wanted a baby more than anything in the world." He smiled at Lara. She looked concerned.

"Did Megan understand? Did she ask who I was?"

"She accepted it back then. Now, she asks questions. She wants to know if she will ever meet 'the lady who gave her away'. That sounds brutal Lara, I know. But you have to understand that she is fifteen years old and her hormones and emotions are all over the place." Lara took a deep breath.

"Well, it sounds like she is not ready to know who I am. Perhaps I could just be a friend of the family, would that work?" Lara would feel more comfortable with that.

"Jill and I were always talking about you, in front of Megan too. We had explained that you were the best linguistic waitress we had ever had. Funnily enough we have followed your career avidly. Jill was very proud of you. So was I." Lara laughed, but was chuffed to bits. "In fact a few years ago Megan and I were watching the news, and I jumped out of my seat and pointed to you. You were in Copenhagen standing behind the Foreign Secretary at a Climate Control conference. I couldn't believe it was you. Megan was so impressed that we knew someone so famous." He was teasing her like the old days, but she loved it. "She tried Googling you after that. She was doing a project on the British Government and I think she was going to see if you could help her. Her teacher told her that you would probably be protected by the Home Office and therefore not be contactable by the public. She gave up eventually. I wish she had managed to find you though. I've missed you." Oo, Lara wasn't expecting that. She had *almost* managed to suppress her memory of them over the years, missing them had been too painful.

"Well, Megan willing, perhaps I could become her friend. I could then be back in your lives to help with school projects and teenage problems." Rob looked relieved. If only she knew how much he had wanted her back in his life. He had very nearly phoned the number he had for her parents hoping it hadn't changed, when Megan was looking for her. But the time wasn't right. He needed her to come back freely, when she was ready. It was one of the reasons he had brought Megan back to that villa. She would be able to find them, and did. "I've had a thought." Lara said jovially. Rob did his old trick and looked worried.

"Oh dear." He had always said that whenever Jill or Lara had ideas.

"Ha ha. I've missed you too." They both laughed. "Anyway. How about all meeting for lunch tomorrow? It is so much easier meeting people in a crowd. Where does Megan like to eat?" Lara was expecting Rob to say McDonalds but he surprised her.

"Nelitos is her favourite." He noted her face. "You forget; we owned our own restaurant and Megan had been spoilt by the chef. She only likes the best." Well, Nelitos was probably the best restaurant in the area. She remembered it from the brochure they had read in the hotel and decided it was too posh for a hen do.

"Nelitos it is. Shall we say 12.30? I'm so excited. I hope she likes me." Insecurity had never bothered Lara before. But then she had never been introduced to her daughter before.

"Yes, 12.30 will be good. Megan isn't working tomorrow. We always keep Sunday free, so she can keep her 'old man' company! Also, so she can get her homework done." Lara realised that Rob was a brilliant father. She didn't want to leave, but she looked at her watch and realised that her hens would be wondering where she was. It was nearly time to organise that night's venue for more frivolities. Rob had noticed her check the time. "Have you got to go?"

"I'm AWOL at the moment. My sister and the rest of her hens will be sending out the search party soon. I'd much rather stay here and catch up, but now we have reacquainted ourselves I'm sure I won't be a stranger." Rob got up and helped her off the stool. They hugged again. It felt natural and strangely comforting for them both.

Lara drove back to the hotel in an ambivalent mood. On one hand she was

glad to have seen Rob again; on the other she wished she hadn't left it so long. She would have been a big help during their bereavement, but perhaps all Rob had needed was Megan and vice versa. She can't change the past, but perhaps she could support them both in the future.

"Where have you been? We were getting worried about you. Have you been crying? What's happened?" If Tori calmed down for a moment, Lara would be able to tell her. She had just got into the bedroom where Tori was getting ready for a few hours by the pool. She obviously hadn't been up for long.

"I've just been with Rob. Oh Tori, it's so sad. Jill died five years ago. I should have been here for them." She had promised herself no more tears, but as soon as her sister put her arms around her, the waterworks started again. This time it was guilt.

"How were you supposed to know? It wasn't your fault you weren't here. Was it cancer again?" Lara nodded. "Poor Jill." Tori hadn't met her, but Lara had always talked about Rob and Jill in her letters from Portugal. She knew they had looked after her sister while on her gap year. Lara composed herself.

"Remember that young girl who sung so beautifully last

night?" Tori nodded. "Well that is their daughter, Megan." Lara wondered if this was the time to confide in Tori, but felt she had left it too late. Tori was about to marry her soul mate, her childhood sweetheart. She was too happy with her wedding plans for Lara to drop a bombshell. Lara also needed Megan to know first or Tori was bound to give it away. Maybe sometime in the future, but she would leave the past where it was, for now.

"Oh Lala, life can be so unfair." Tori hugged her sister and gave her a kiss on the cheek. "Come on, let's go and get some sunshine. There won't be a lot of it once we get home." Tori was right. Lara changed into her bikini, and they both made their way to the pool.

They found their hens hungover on the sun loungers. Tori decided to explain where Lara had been and why she looked sad. Josh gave Lara a quick cuddle.

"So that angelic voice was their daughter?" Josh was still in awe of Megan's performance. "Can we meet her?" Lara was so glad Josh had asked that.

"As it happens, I've organised for us to have lunch with them tomorrow. I hope you don't mind." She looked anxious. "I can go alone if there's a problem."

"It was five years ago since she lost her mum. I'm sure it will do them both good to come out with us!" Tori was a star. Hayley and Kate agreed. Josh looked at Chuck, waiting for a reply. He was giving him a 'look'.

"No probs. I'd love to meet Megan in the flesh. She could be famous one day. I can tell people I knew her when she was just an aspiring starlet." Josh smiled at Chuck. Good boy, he thought.

"There we are then. We could do with an earlier night tonight anyway. Too much debauchery makes Josh a jaded boy, and that jade really doesn't suit me. We keep missing the best of the sunshine clubbing all night too." Josh was right. The girls nodded; then wished they hadn't. Lara thought 'what a state to get into'. She was slightly older and a whole lot wiser, but occasionally she too had felt like the other hens. She was glad she had kept a clear head for that weekend, anyway.

"So, where are we meeting them?" Tori was quite looking forward to lunch out.

"Nelitos." Lara noticed Hayley and Kate glance at each other. They had remembered the brochure. "And it's on me. A pre-wedding present to all the hen's for supporting my sister." They looked relieved.

"How can we refuse such a magnanimous gesture? We cordially accept." Josh was in his element. "Tell me, is it black tie?" They were all laughing. Lara couldn't have hoped for a better outcome. Thank goodness for Josh.

That evening they stayed in Vilamoura, Lara enjoyed herself and relaxed. She was apprehensive about meeting Megan, but she was equally excited at seeing Rob again. She hadn't realised how much she had missed him. Talking to him had made the years vanish. She must keep in contact with him once they leave.

They got to Nelitos before Rob and Megan. Josh and Chuck were impressed to find Luis, the maître d', holding open the door for them. As they got to their reserved table (Lara had phoned ahead for a table for eight) staff were on hand to pull back the girls' chairs for them. Lara ordered water and they waited for the guests of honour.

"Cor, this is posh!" Kate hadn't been in a restaurant with so much cutlery for one person.

"Kate, don't let me down. You start from the outside." Her sister showed her what she meant. Lara's eyes were on the door. Rob walked in alone. Her heart missed a beat. Megan didn't want to meet her. He saw them and went over. Lara got up and they kissed. She introduced him to the hens. He sat next to her.

"Megan not coming?" She tried to make it sound light, but the disappointment came through in her voice.

"Yes, she's outside on the phone. I told her to finish her conversation before she came in. It's rude to be on the phone in a restaurant." He smiled at her and squeezed her hand. "Don't worry, she's dying to meet you." He put her mind at rest.

"Before she comes in, may I offer my condolences Rob?" Tori wanted the lunch to be happy for them, so wanted to get the sad bit out of the way.

"Thank you, Victoria. That's very kind." The others smiled and he acknowledged their unspoken sentiments.

"Please call me Tori. All my family and friends call me that. I feel you are both." Rob was touched. "Now, where's that amazing daughter of yours. We were awestruck on Friday night. Where did she get that voice from?"

"I'm not sure." He glanced at Lara quickly and smiled.

"Sometimes these things skip a generation. Like baldness." Lara couldn't believe she had just said that. The whole table had erupted in laughter.

"What have I missed?" Megan had got to the table.

"Lara was just saying that you might go bald someday."

Rob wiped the tears from his eyes, and noticed Megan giving him a very strange look.

"I'll never understand the adult sense of humour. Hi everyone, I'm Megan." They all introduced themselves and she sat next to Josh. The table was round and so it was easy for everyone to talk and for Lara to see Megan close up without her realising she may have been staring. She hoped Tori didn't look at Megan's features too closely; there were definitely family characteristics obvious to the discerning. Luckily she was sitting the other side of Megan, so only got a side view.

The maître d' took their order and the wine waiter had let Rob choose the wine.

"A meal without wine is like a day without sunshine, except that on a day without sunshine you can still get drunk." Chuck couldn't resist making Megan laugh. "What's your favourite drink Megan?"

"Charles! She's still at school." Josh was mortified. He really didn't want Chuck upsetting Lara's friends.

"I'm rather partial to a white wine spritzer. I find I can drink a little more before I become drunk." Megan was winding Josh up. She took after her father there.

"That's Lara's favourite drink." Kate joined in the conversation. She wasn't feeling quite so intimidated with Megan there. "She says she doesn't like losing control. Don't you Lara?"

"Not when I'm in foreign countries, no. I need to keep sober when I'm with heads of government, someone has to!"

"Wow, you are important, aren't you? Dad and I saw you on the TV, *BBC News* actually. Do you know the prime minister of this country?" Megan was intrigued. "We are doing a project on him at the moment."

"I was in Porto a month ago, and yes, I met him over dinner. He's a very nice man. I couldn't help giggling every time anyone said his name though. It reminded me of the bedtime stories my dad used to read to me." Lara stifled a giggle. That was a major problem with a translator; you ended up translating every word you hear in a sentence, even names by mistake.

"Who is he?" Josh wasn't very good at current affairs.

"Pedro Coelho. Translated into English means Peter Rabbit."

"Ah, our Mum used to read that to us when we were little. Do you remember Kate?" Hayley loved those stories.

"Oh my goodness, yes." Kate still did.

Megan didn't think that was going to help with her course work.

"Any interesting facts about him?" She needed an edge that would impress her teacher.

"I'm afraid if I tell you, I'd have to shoot you." Megan knew she wouldn't get anything else out of Lara. "I will tell you, though, that he was married to Fatima Padinha who was a singer in a girl band called Doce. They came secind in the Eurovision Song Contest for Portugal in 1980. They sang a song of the same name, 'Doce', meaning sweet. There, does that help?" Megan said thank you but she wanted personal details, not things she could read for herself on Wikipedia. But all the same she was secretly filled with admiration for Lara. She was so interesting and clever. No wonder her parents had thought so much of her.

Lunch was a huge success. Everyone enjoyed the food, and the company. Megan was in her element. She winked at Lara a couple of times when she bantered with the waiters in fluent Portuguese. Lara decided she had Rob's wicked sense of humour. Albeit by nurture rather than nature. She was so proud of Megan, and grateful to Jill and Rob for bringing her up to be such a delight.

"So Megan, do you speak any other languages? Your Portuguese sounds fluent." Tori was never any good at languages.

"I can speak Spanish and am learning French for GCSE."

"Lara speaks loads of languages too. Hey Lala, perhaps you could get Megan into government as your junior." Although envious of her sister, she was equally proud of her too.

"It is very boring. You have to sign the Official Secrets Act for a start. That bit is the most difficult." Lara was trying to put Megan off.

"It is for you, you could never keep a secret." Everyone laughed at Tori's revelation of her sister. Only Rob wasn't laughing. He just looked at Lara and smiled a knowing smile.

"But you get on the TV, and meet lots of famous people." Megan was young and impressionable. It was a lonely job; Lara wouldn't wish it on anyone she loved.

"OK, I visit lots of countries, meet loads of important people, but that means I'm in hotel rooms more often than my flat. It's lonely, and I've done it for ten years now and I need to settle down like my lucky sister, before I'm past it." She looked at Tori, who for the first time realised that *she* was the lucky one. She had Adam, and a future. Poor Lala.

"I'm about to find out what loneliness feels like. Megan

is off to England in September next year, for sixth form." Megan got up and went over to cuddle her Dad.

"We can Skype each other every day. And keep in touch with Facebook. I'll be home for all the holidays." She kissed him and sat down.

"Whatever happened to the good old telephone?" Josh couldn't keep up with gadgets.

"You really are a Neanderthal Josh. We don't use smoke or drums anymore. It's the 21st century." Tori bashed him playfully. "What part of England will you be living in Megan?"

"I'm hoping to be in a Dorset boarding school. I have to wait for my GCSE results, once I've taken them." Although her school has a sixth form, most of the girls liked to go to England for the social life, but she wasn't going to tell her dad that.

"You'll be near us then. We can take you out at weekends." Josh was getting excited. He liked Megan. He'd love to hear her voice again. He had an idea. "How about while you are in England you audition for the *Make Me A Star UK*. You are undeniably good enough."

"I'd have to wait until next April. I'm not sixteen yet." She'd already thought of that.

"Oh no you don't young lady. You need to get your qualifications behind you before you even think about talent shows." Rob was not impressed. "How many of those people give up their education and have nothing to fall back on when it's over. No, I want you to have a good education first. Then we will see, ok?"

"Yes daddy." Megan replied with little conviction. What he didn't know wouldn't hurt him, she thought.

Lara needed to catch up more with Rob. She didn't know what he even did for a living any more. The problem was they had only one more night. She couldn't let her sister and the others down. She needed a plan.

"Well after all that food I'm sure I won't be needing dinner tonight. Have you any plans yet Tor?" She tried to make it sound like idle curiosity.

"Hayley and I were thinking of a quiet night in the bar of the hotel. We have to be out of our rooms by mid-morning tomorrow. Is that ok with everyone?" Josh and Chuck nodded and agreed.

"What are you two up to tonight?" Lara looked toward Rob, she was trying to be spontaneous.

"I've got homework. Dad's free though." Good girl Megan. It was almost like she knew what Lara was doing. "Dad hasn't been out for ages. Go on Dad, I'll be ok. I can get Chloe over. We have to get this course work done by the end of term anyway. Or I could go to Chloe's." Megan seemed to have everything planned.

"Please come Rob. Lara needs someone sensible to talk to." Tori was joking, but realised her sister needed some time with Rob before they went.

"Well that rules me out then." He laughed. He glanced at Megan who was already texting on her phone. "I haven't said yes yet." Megan looked up.

"Just in case, I was making sure Chloe was free." Megan smiled at him.

"Talk about being bulldozed. Ok, just for a while. But I need to get back in time to read Megs a bedtime story." They all laughed.

"Oh Dad." Megan saw the funny side.

So it was arranged. Rob would go over to the hotel for drinks, and a longed for catch up with Lara. He took Megan home and organised with Chloe's parents that she'd keep Megan company; but he would take her home at bedtime. It was school the next day and on past experience neither girl would achieve any sleep if they had a sleepover.

"Lara's really nice, isn't she, and very clever." Megan was sorting out her schoolbooks before Chloe arrived.

"Yes. She doesn't sound very happy at the moment though. It'll be nice to catch up with her." He was staring into space.

"I wish Mum could be here to see her again. She missed Lara, didn't she?" Rob wished the same. Megan had grown up very fast over the last few years. He had to be careful; she didn't miss much.

"We both missed her, darling. Are you sure you don't mind me going out tonight?" Megan decided to play it cool.

"I don't mind. You take as long as you like. Enjoy yourself." She thought she'd gone a little too far.

"What have you got up your sleeve? I hope you're going to do your schoolwork. You seem in a hurry to get me out of the house." Rob was suspicious.

"No I'm not. I just want you to enjoy an evening out. You haven't been out socially much recently. Ideal opportunity I'd say. Now, what are you going to wear?" Good manoeuvre she thought. He smiled at her. He wasn't that gullible, but she deserved a bit of fun too. It wouldn't do her any harm to have a girlie night with her best friend.

"Ok, go and choose something that you think appropriate. I need to look hip, bordering on cool."

"Dad, no. 'Hip' and 'cool' are not words that should come

out of a father's mouth. Trendy would be more apt." She was laughing.

"How old do you think I am?" Then he realised she was winding him up. He couldn't be cross. After all, she got her sense of humour from him. It's the one thing that Jill enjoyed telling him. He realised it was easier to think about her these days, happy thoughts of happier days. He was finally getting into a good place. It had taken five years.

He found the hens at the bar. They were having fun, except he could see the worry lines on Lara's forehead. She wasn't looking forward to going home, that was probably it.

"Rob, a beer?" Josh had spotted him. Rob said thank you and sat at the table with them as Josh got the attention of the waitress.

"How's Megan? Did she enjoy this afternoon?" Ah, thought Rob, that's what was worrying Lara.

"She had a fantastic time. Thought you were all phat. That's with a ph not an f, by the way."

"Thank you for explaining, I was about to look up the number for Weight Watchers." Tori thought Rob was such a nice guy, phat even! "So Rob, you know we are all hair and beauty consultants, and Lara works for the FCO…"

"The FCO, what's that? I thought she worked for the government." Poor Kate, Tori thought she'd probably be a junior until she retired.

"Foreign and Commonwealth Office. It's just a bit of a mouthful Kate." Kate nodded in enlightenment. "So, what are you up to these days. No restaurant anymore?" Tori wasn't exactly nosy, just very interested in other people's lives. It came with her job!

"Well, after Jill died, I sold the restaurant and as we'd doubled the turnover, with the help of Lara's brilliant ideas she had set into place before she left, I managed to get a lot more than I paid for it. Megan and I made the decision to come back here. It was the only place she knew. All the happy memories of her childhood were here. Jill had a little life insurance; I've put that aside for Megan's education in England. But I kept the apartments in Quarteira so they've been quite lucrative. The whole area has got so popular with cheap flights from the UK. I also made a bit of a killing, and used my initiative, when I realised that the cheap flights didn't include luggage, or more relevant to my idea, sports equipment." Rob's beer arrived and he took a large gulp. "Ah, needed that. All this talking, I hope I'm not boring you." He was looking at Lara. She smiled. It was exactly what she wanted, to find out how he was, without openly showing concern.

"No, not at all. So what was this great master plan of yours?" The hens moved forward slightly, the bar had filled up and it was getting more difficult to hear each other.

"Well, it cost about £70 to bring over and take back a set of golf clubs. So I bought a few second-hand sets from the local pro, he's a golf buddy, and opened a kiosk in the airport carpark. I paid them a small rent for the space, and charged golfers €30 per week. It totally snowballed after the first season, to the point I now employ the pro's eighteen-year-old son who looks after the shop now inside the airport, and I have another in Almancil itself, which deals with online bookings, so golf clubs are ready when people arrive here. It's proving very profitable, so much so that I am expanding to Vilamoura." He took another swig from his beer. He thought he had talked enough. "So, who's the lucky man Tori?"

"His name is Adam, he's a teacher." Tori was very proud of Adam. "Don't laugh, but he was my first and only boyfriend. My soul mate actually." Josh put his hand down his throat and gagged. Chuck hit him. "You can mock, but I was pure when I met him, more than you could ever say, you biatch." Josh looked theatrically shocked at Tori's accusation.

"I'll have you know, I'm completely pure as the driven snow, ask Chuck." Chuck really didn't want to get into the banter. He always came off worse. He excused himself and went to powder his nose!

"More like the driven slush. You've had more partners than I've had highlights!" Tori and Josh were thoroughly enjoying their playful squabble, so were their audience.

"Are they normally like this?" Rob asked Hayley and Kate.

"They keep our clients entertained. I'm sure that's why most of them come back, for the matinee show." Hayley did love the two of them.

Rob left them all laughing and turned to Lara.

"When are you off tomorrow? Do you need a lift to the airport?" Rob would like to see her alone. He was worried about her.

"That would be very kind. The others are going back to Bournemouth and their flight isn't until the early evening, but mine is at 11.30 a.m. to Gatwick. I've got work on Tuesday. I have to be at London City Airport by 7 a.m. in the morning." She felt exhausted just explaining. Rob gave her a peck on the cheek and got up.

"I'll pick you up from here at nine o'clock, it'll give us time for a coffee at the airport. I better go. Megan won't go to bed without a decree, in triplicate, posted on her bedroom door. I've had a great time this evening. Thank you."

"No, thank *you* for letting me share your life again. I'll see you in the morning. Sleep well." Lara got up and reciprocated the peck on the cheek.

"Do you know, I think I will. You sleep well too, but make sure you set an alarm!" He waved to the others and said goodbye. "And good luck with the wedding Tori. He's a lucky man." Tori got up to say goodbye.

"I'll send you and Megan an invite. Oo, I've had an idea..."

"You can get a tonic for that." Rob couldn't resist.

"Ha ha. No, I was wondering, do you think Megan would honour us by singing at our wedding?" Josh jumped up, clapping his hands.

"What a brilliant idea Tor. You are so clever." They hugged; the making up was the best part of their tiffs.

"I don't know; you'll have to ask her. I'll give Lara her mobile number, and you can ring her when you've discussed it with your fiancé. In the meantime, I have to get the songbird to bed. She's got school in the morning. See you tomorrow Lara." He left the bar feeling more upbeat than he had in a long while.

Rob was in Reception when Lara came down with her case. She'd said goodbye to the others the night before and had kissed a sleepy Tori on her way out of their room.

"Good morning, got everything?" Lara nodded. Rob took her suitcase out to his car. "Ready?"

"Yes, thank you for this Rob. I know you're a busy man

these days." He opened the car door for her.

"Not at all. I always have time for my bffs!" Lara knew what that meant.

"You really have caught on to the Facebook jargon, I'm impressed."

"If you can't beat them, join them. Megan and her friends are always leaving messages for each other on my computer. I just had to learn to decipher them or I wasn't cool." Lara laughed. She had a lot to learn about teenage girls. Hopefully Rob could teach her.

"We've got a little while, let's have a coffee at the airport. We need to liaise over email addresses, Skype addresses, mobile numbers and Facebook profiles!" Lara remembered Josh's simple question, what happened to the good old telephone number? There were now so many communication devices, all so impersonal, but, of course, a lot quicker than the humble letter. Rob got her to the airport in plenty of time; they sat outside and drank coffee. Having swapped numbers and addresses they were ready to say goodbye.

"I hope you can come back very soon Lara. Your job seems to be exhausting you, perhaps you could come for a holiday?" Lara wished.

"I have to admit, work is getting more and more difficult as I get older. Travelling all the time may sound glamorous to most people, but it is just tiring. Most of my time is spent in places like this." She looked around Faro Airport. "The rest of the time I'm in inhospitable hotel rooms, with very few homely comforts, just a mini bar and a kettle if I'm lucky. Don't get me wrong. I've enjoyed my career, but I think I'm well past its sell by date." Rob looked at her. She still looked like that nineteen-year-old girl, without a care in the world, to him. But he understood what she meant. She wanted to settle down, like her younger sister.

"Have you thought about what you'd like to do instead?" Maybe he could help her decide.

"Not really. I thought of working as an independent translator for corporate businesses, but I think that I'd have the same problem, as now most of them have gone global. Perhaps I could become the little spinster woman at the end of the cul-de-sac that teaches French to schoolchildren. I can have a few cats and a budgerigar." They both laughed. "Anyway, for now I have to keep working to pay my credit cards off, then I can decide, when I'm solvent. I better get going. I have to get my case checked in. It's been so special seeing you again. If you do manage over for Tori's wedding, in October, perhaps I could take you and Megan to a show in London? I think she'd like that."

"So do I. I'll have a word with her and give you a ring. Take care of yourself lovely Lara. And this time, keep in touch." He bent over and kissed her on the cheek. Luckily her suitcase was on wheels, so she managed to manoeuvre it through the doors while waving with the other hand. Then she was gone. Rob felt a stab of pain. He'd miss her. What a wonderful person she had become. He was glad she was back in his life.

CHAPTER 4

~~~

Work for Lara was getting more tedious. With flight delays and the world deciding to go to war all over the globe, she could barely get her laundry done before the next summons to a meeting in Timbuktu or wherever.

She did manage to get to her office to clear her post a week after returning to the UK. Unfortunately the low profile she was keeping hadn't worked on the Foreign Office Lothario. She had just popped into the coffee room when he walked in. The annoying prat was called Hugo. He didn't seem to take 'no' for an answer. He had asked Lara out on numerous occasions, and to spare his feelings for the first half dozen, she had said she was busy. But coming up to the milestone dozen, she decided that blunt and brutal was the only way to get through to him. She had said that she would rather watch *Carry On...* films back to back for a whole evening than be in his company. Unfortunately, his hero was Kenneth Williams. Go figure!

That afternoon she was at a particularly low ebb. She had chatted to Rob the night before on Skype and realised how far away he was. They were coming over for the wedding, but could only stay for the weekend as Megan had exams looming. She was disappointed, but still glad they were able to make it at all.

"Salutations, the Luscious Lara. How's tricks?" Why couldn't he be normal? He was so creepy. Lara tried to ignore him, but he persisted. "We're in the middle of something really big 'downstairs'. I'd tell you about it, but I'd have to kill you after. Ha ha ha." Not funny. Why would he think he was funny?

"Goodbye Hugo." She left him pouring a coffee. Hugo worked 'downstairs' as he put it. It just meant that the department he worked in was even more secret than hers. Lara tried to fantasise that he was Q from James Bond to see if she could, just once, go out with him. Unfortunately, she kept picturing Rowan Atkinson in *Johnny English* instead, totally ruining the fantasy.

When she got back to her office she had a message from Tori pop up on her phone. She had received a lovely email from Megan who was flattered and would love to sing at her wedding. How apt, thought Lara. One day Tori would realise that her niece had sung at her wedding. There were only a few more weeks to go until the big day. How to kill the time? She wasn't due to go to Belgium until the end of the week. She was ok at the office; she had a good deal of speeches to translate before she left. But the evenings seemed protracted due to the excitement she was feeling. She needed to fill in the time doing something different or it would just drag on. She was abruptly roused from her thoughts by a head appearing round her door.

"Salutations. Are you trying to avoid me? I was wondering if you wanted to accompany me to the opening of the new French Restaurant in Sloane Street; Le Pied du Cochon. Translated as the foot of the, um, *cochon*. It sounds good doesn't it? What do you say?"

"Pig, Hugo." He looked hurt.

"OK. Point taken." He was about to leave.

"No. *Cochon* is a pig. The foot of the pig, trotters to you!" He got the joke.

"Ah, yes, of course. Trotters. Doesn't have the same ring to it, does it?" Hugo tried again. "So, can I pick you up, around 20.00 hrs." Lara wondered if she needed to synchronise her watch. He didn't know where she lived, and she wasn't falling for that old ruse.

"OK Hugo, it's your lucky night. I'll meet you there at 8.15 normal time. 20.15 hrs if MI5 need to know." Hugo looked baffled. Lara realised it was going to be a long evening, but she had nothing else to do. "You can go now Hugo. I've got a lot to do before I can get home to change for this evening. See you at the Foot of the Pig."

"Oh, right. Yes. Trotters. Ha. I like that. Yes. See you later. Toodle-pip." Yes, thought Lara, a very, very long night.

Lara decided to take a taxi. She lived about four minutes from Sloane Street, but if he saw her walk up to the restaurant, even *he* would work out she lived near. She explained her predicament to the taxi driver.

"Not a good idea, you living on your own. You don't want any Tom, Dick or...?" He left a gap.

"Hugo," she replied.

"Hugo knowing where you live. Very wise. We'll just have a little motor around Belgrave Square and back. Lovely this time of year. Is that ok, miss?"

"Yes, thank you. Just right." She sat back and relaxed. He was right. Belgravia was wonderful, she just never had the time to notice.

She arrived at the restaurant fashionably late, five minutes. Hugo was waiting outside and leant over to pay the driver. Lara noticed they had only clocked up £5 so she whispered to the driver to say £10. He obliged, with a smile. Well, she thought, Hugo could afford it, and it would defeat the object of the exercise if he worked out she'd only been in the taxi for five minutes.

"Enjoy your evening, miss." He drove off highly amused, and £5 richer, a very happy cabbie.

"You look wonderful Lara, and you smell divine." He was so creepy. What was she doing there? She was determined to enjoy the meal, so she took Hugo's offered arm and walked into the restaurant.

The restaurant was rather nice; she had to admit, very French. A waiter showed them to their table. A chill ran up Lara's spine. It was a booth. Intimacy she didn't need. Hugo was smiling and slipped the waiter a note of some denomination. How crass, Lara thought. A gentleman would have sorted that out before she arrived. But then again, Hugo and gentleman do not belong in the same prose. They sat down and read through the menu. It all looked very nice. Hugo hardly looked at the menu. He was looking at Lara. She purposely kept her eyes firmly on the Carte. A waiter started hovering a few minutes later. Lara ordered the "*canard a l'orange, rose*"; her favourite.

"And for monsieur?" The waiter waited for Hugo.

"*Fillet steak garçon. Bien done, avec sauce de poire. S'il vous plait.*" The theatrically camp waiter turned to Lara and tried to stifle a snigger. That in turn made Lara snigger. They both tried so hard not to, but both failed. With a straight face Lara looked at Hugo.

"Did you want pepper sauce Hugo?" Lara thought she'd help out.

"That's what I said." Hugo couldn't find anything funny in pepper sauce. The waiter went off to the kitchen. Lara waited for the explosion. As the kitchen door reopened she could hear laughter coming from its depths. Hugo seemed oblivious to it.

"You ordered fillet steak with a pear sauce, Hugo. The difference was a missing 'v'. *Poivre* was what you meant." Hugo looked puzzled.

"I'm sure that's what I said." He wasn't happy. He decided to look at the wine list. Poor Hugo. A basic schoolboy error. He probably hadn't spoken French since GSCE oral. If you were going to take out a linguist, speak English, it was safer.

Luckily, he just needed to read the name to order the wine. The food took an eternity, or so it felt. It was probably only a matter of a few minutes.

"I'm busy 'downstairs' on something very hush hush. I can't talk about it." Lara sighed.

"Then don't."

"Suffice to say it is very important. But I'd really have to shoot you if you get it out of me." Lara wondered if it was worth knowing even just for the blessed relief of a bullet.

"It's about an important meeting at the end of the week, in Belgium. To do with certain restrictions the EU want to enforce."

He'd make such a useless spy. In interrogation she could offer him a Harrods' Black Points card and he'd cave. In fact, why waste a Harrods' card, a bar of fruit and nut would be more apt, and still have the desired effect.

"Hugo, I've just translated all the documents for that meeting, unless I could do it with my eyes closed and my brain in neutral, I think I know all about the agenda." The food arrived on queue. Please just eat, she prayed. That was definitely the last time she accepted an invitation from Hugo. A book and a cup of cocoa were looking very tempting now; but she had to admit, she was enjoying the duck.

"Did I tell you my brother, Piers, has moved into a very important job?" She continued eating and hoped he'd do the same. No such luck. "Well you know he was in the last government? Well, he's just been moved to the Department of Culture, Media and Sport. He'll get on well there. He has the brains of the family. I, on the other hand, was given all the charm." He guffawed and Lara was sure she felt a food morsel brush passed her arm. Oh, dear God, please let this evening end. Just thinking there could be two of them was a nightmare. She really didn't want to get any more involved in his family.

She'd got home quite early, making her excuses that she had an early morning start, when in actual fact she was bored out of her mind. Hugo had asked if she wanted to share a cab, but Lara declined, saying she wanted to have a quick look in some shop windows, as she didn't get a chance during the day. So Hugo said goodnight and immediately went for a tube so Lara was able to walk home and de-stress. A huge lesson learnt.

Lara had tried to get Rob and Megan to go up to London for a few days after the wedding, but Megan had to get back for some mock exams. It was her GCSE year, very important not to miss any of it. They had managed to take her out for the Thursday and the Friday, but the school had insisted she was back by the Monday. Unfortunately half-term was two weeks later.

The wedding was on the Friday, and Lara travelled down on the Thursday for the rehearsal. She had planned her trip to coincide with the flight to Bournemouth from Faro, and was waiting at the airport for their arrival. She watched the flight come in from the carpark, and wandered in to the arrivals lounge. Summer, although round the corner, hadn't kicked in so there were only two flights arriving that afternoon. Passport Control would not be too busy. They were out within ten minutes, with just hand luggage.

"Lara, how lovely." Rob spotted her and swept her off the ground. Megan came up behind him.

"Hello Megan. Good flight?" Lara could see Megan was quite excited.

"Yes, thank you. Anything is better than being in school." She smiled at her father. Lara got the carpark ticket out and hunted for some change. "Can I do that for you?" Megan took the ticket and the change and went over to the machine.

"It's really good to see you again Lara. Megan is a little nervous about singing tomorrow, although she won't let anyone know that." Megan caught them up and they headed for the carpark.

"Your hotel isn't far from us. I'm sorry mum couldn't put you up. She wanted to, but it'll be mad tomorrow." Lara put the cabin cases in the boot, with Rob's help.

"I wouldn't have expected any of your family to put us up. I'm sure you have enough to deal with. Anyway, Megan and I like staying in hotels. She goes on the websites and marks them on how good or bad they are." Megan frowned at her father.

"I've only done that once. It was a stomach-churning cesspit, and deserved my comments." Megan gave her father a cheeky grin. Lara was intrigued.

"Was this in Portugal?" Megan shook her head.

"No, Brighton. They've pulled it down now. Good job too." Lara knew the hotel she had booked them into was delightful.

"There's a rehearsal at 7 p.m. this evening at the church, where you can have a practice and meet the rest of the family, including the very nervous groom." Lara hoped that Megan would feel better if she knew someone else was anxious too.

As they drove up to the hotel Rob couldn't help but notice how similar it looked to his home.

"This is like home from home with the palm trees, and the beach. No wonder you chose our beach all those years ago, it must have reminded you of here." Lara nodded.

"We live just up that road, and the church is behind this hotel. That chine there leads down to the beach, if you fancy a nice walk." Lara was very lucky having grown up there. "At the end of that road is the hotel where the reception is being held and outside is a chain ferry that takes you over to the Purbecks. Unfortunately the one thing it doesn't guarantee, like Portugal, is the sunshine. Oh, and by the way, after the rehearsal everyone is coming back to our house for supper, I hope you two will?" She was desperate to ask, but waited until it sounded like she had just remembered.

"That's very kind. We'd love to, wouldn't we Megs?" She nodded. Lara realised the reason why she hadn't spoken for a while was that she was busy texting. It was good that she had so many friends though. She had probably needed them. Lara would try to have a chat with her later, to get to know her a little better. They organised that Lara would come and walk with them to the church later, but Tori and her mother needed her for the afternoon. They said goodbye and she left them to get settled in their rooms.

Rob and Megan were waiting for Lara outside the foyer of the hotel. Megan was wearing a coat. She looked cold. There was a chilly breeze coming off the sea.

"Welcome to England! I would imagine we are at least 10 degrees colder here in October than you are used to." Rob nodded. He had forgotten how quickly the temperature changed in the evening. He only had on a jumper. "Let's get moving, that will warm us up." Lara took Megan's arm and huddled her along the road. Megan quite liked it.

"Will Josh and Chuck be at the rehearsal?" Megan did enjoy their company.

"No, only family, Hayley as the other bridesmaid, and the best man, Jeremy. Mind you, Josh may slip in to watch. He was quite miffed when Tori didn't choose him to be a bridesmaid." Megan laughed. "I know we are in the 21st Century, but even my tolerant family may have had something to say about his hairy legs in a frock!" Megan was in stitches. Rob was so pleased that Lara was making Megan feel at ease. She always had that knack. They arrived at the church and Tori ran towards them.

"Megan, my angel." She took hold of her and steered her over to Adam. "Adam, this is the angel I was telling you about. Megan, this is Adam." Adam shook her hand. "I haven't told him what you will be singing yet. I thought it would be a lovely surprise for everyone." Megan and Tori had organised the choice over email. Megan had sent Tori some demos and she then chose.

"I have to admit, I'm a bit nervous. I'm not used to church acoustics. It's a challenge, but I'm happier now I've sung it a few times." Megan didn't know if she was trying to convince herself or Tori.

"Father Michael is dying to hear it, I had to tell him what you were singing, and he's really excited." As they were speaking, Father Michael walked up behind Megan.

"I take it this is your angel from Portugal?" Megan turned round and saw this man in jeans and a jumper. She thought it must be Tori's father. He put out his hand to introduce himself. "Hello, I'm Father Michael." She looked slightly surprised. "I'm in mufti, it's my day off!" She laughed. She was feeling less and less nervous as she met everyone.

Rob and Lara had stayed at the back of the church while Lara pointed everyone out to him. Names were now becoming faces and personalities. He felt he'd known them for years.

"Come on, meet my parents." Lara pulled him over to her Mum and Dad who were standing in the pews, chatting to Hayley.

"Rob. Lovely to see you again." Hayley gave him a peck on the cheek. Lara took over the introductions.

"Mum, Dad this is Rob." Debbie kissed him on the cheek and hugged him.

"How lovely to meet you at last. This if Peter, my husband." They shook hands. "Come and sit next to me. I don't have anything to do until we get back for supper. We can get acquainted." Rob looked at Lara and she laughed.

"I'll leave you in safe hands then. Come on Dad, we have to muster at the back of the church." Lara and Pete went off to find Tori and Hayley. They had to walk down the aisle together. Adam went to stand at the front with Jeremy, his best man and best friend from school. Megan went to join her dad for the moment and was introduced to Debbie, who made a big fuss of her.

"If we are ready in our positions, we'll start." Father Michael decided to get the show on the road. He was quite looking forward to the little girl singing. He did love a good song.

After a lot of giggling and a few minor changes, the wedding party had almost got the ceremony perfect. It was soon Megan's turn to rehearse. She had organised a tape and Jeremy, the techno geek, had put it in the church sound system, and was waiting for his queue to start it.

"If Megan can stand by the pulpit, there. Or would you rather be in the pulpit?" Megan shook her head. She needed to move her arms when she sung. She thought she'd feel trapped actually in the pulpit. "Ok, there will be fine.

Jeremy, are you ready?" Jeremy nodded. "When you are ready Megan." Megan took off her coat; she was feeling quite warm. She then signalled to Jeremy, who started the tape. Suddenly Megan was belting out 'Pie Jesu' beautifully, with the acoustics blending so well with the aria. She had everyone mesmerised.

When she had finished, everyone clapped. Debbie stood up.

"Well that was my rehearsal, I now know I'll need more tissues for the ceremony." Debbie was dabbing her eyes. Everyone laughed and Megan felt happy. It had gone the way she had planned and everyone seemed to like it. Tomorrow won't be so difficult because it will be in front of strangers. She had a harder time when she wanted to please her friends.

They all walked back to Debbie and Pete's for supper. Father Michael had been invited, but he was otherwise engaged having promised the Scouts they could use him as a patient for their First Aid badges.

"I'll see you all tomorrow though." He went over to Megan before she left. "You have a beautiful gift from God there. Take care of it." She said she would, and thanked him.

At the Allen house, the girls congregated in the kitchen while the boys were in the lounge. The reason may have been the football match playing in the background on the TV. Tori took beers into the boys and pecked Adam on the cheek as she passed him talking to Rob.

"So, Adam, you're a teacher. I would imagine that's very rewarding work. What subject do you teach?" Rob took a beer off Tori and thanked her.

"Mathematics for my sins. Rewarding? Pay cheque comes in handy. No, I'm joking. It's brilliant when you see a child suddenly get it. So yes, I suppose it is rewarding." Adam noticed Tori listening.

"My very clever husband-to-be." She cuddled him. "You'll meet his parents tomorrow, Dr and Dr Sinclair. They are both doctors!" She found that amusing, Adam raised an eyebrow at her. He loved her to pieces. "Adam would have been a doctor if it hadn't been for his haemophobia." Rob looked confused. Why would that be a problem in today's medicine? Most prejudices could be repressed in the name of professionalism. "Not to be confused with homophobia." Tori noticed Rob's puzzled look. "He loves Josh, it's blood he's scared of. Not good in a doctor as you will agree." Tori squeezed Adam's cheek and went back to the kitchen.

"Yes, much to my parents' horror, I faint at the sight of the red stuff. Have done since I was very young. So I went into teaching. I just have to keep off playground duty. Always a battlefield." Rob really liked Adam. Jeremy on the other hand was very different. He was very serious. "He's a boff." Adam explained. "He's always been the studious one. It got him the job of Head within five years of leaving university. He's into computers and gadgets. He was dead impressed with your daughter's skills. Apparently, her demos for the wedding songs were very professional. Praise indeed from the master."

"Our house is completely taken over by recording equipment and synthesizers. I've only just mastered the mobile phone." Adam laughed. He knew what Rob meant. Adam and Jeremy had shared a flat and had found it difficult to watch the TV without some gadget being attached to it. Lara came in to find him.

"Hello, supper is ready in the kitchen if you boys can tear yourselves away from the match." They walked through to the kitchen that luckily had an extension into a conservatory. The girls fussed around the men. Giving them plates as they walked in so they could help themselves from the breakfast bar. Megan was chatting to Hayley and Tori in the extension. Adam turned to Rob.

"She's a very talented girl. You must be very proud of her." Rob looked over at his daughter.

"Yes, I am."

"She's beautiful too." Rob instinctively looked towards Lara.

"Yes, she gets that from her mother." Lara smiled. Rob was staring at her. She felt goose pimples on her arms. What was she feeling? Flattered? She wasn't sure, but she had to get the potatoes out of the oven before they were forgotten. She hurried off to keep herself busy.

Tori and Hayley had persuaded Megan to sing at the reception. Tori had watched one of the demos, and Adam had commented that it was one of his favourite songs.

"You've got to keep it quiet though. It's a surprise for Adam." Tori was getting quite conspiratorial. "I can pretend I'm singing it to him." Hayley laughed.

"You haven't heard Tori's voice, have you Megan? Have you ever heard a cat fight?" Tori thought that rude!

"It's not that bad. I know all the lyrics and the tunes, it's just when I let them out of my mouth they sound different. You are so lucky." Megan knew she was lucky. What had that vicar said, a gift from God. She wanted to believe it was a gift from her mother, whoever she was.

"So you have decided you want 'Wherever You Will Go'?" Megan would need to find the right tape to give to Jeremy. Luckily she had brought a few with her in case she had the opportunity to sing more songs.

"I love that one, especially the chorus." Hayley had started singing the chorus and Tori and Megan joined in. Fortunately the boys had gone with their plates back into the lounge, so only Debbie and Lara had heard the impromptu performance.

"That's a lovely song. Who sings that again?" Debbie kept up with most of the current music; after all, it played all day at the salon.

"Charlene Soraia, she's from London. She did open-mic nights at a club while at school, fitting in her homework before her performances. She got into the Brit School, London School for Performing Arts & Technology, with Adele. I think they are both amazing." Megan took a deep breath. "How cool would it be to go to that school?" Lara wondered if she had asked her father about it.

"I thought you wanted to go to school around here?" Megan looked up at Lara.

"I know; it was only a dream. Dad believes in academia before art. He's probably right. What do I know, I'm only fifteen." She was smiling. Lara would say almost cheekily. She had spirit, that daughter of hers.

Lara walked them both back to the hotel. Supper had been lovely. Rob felt like one of the family. Megan had dawdled behind, texting.

"Has she got a boyfriend, do you think?" Lara looked back to check Megan was still moving.

"No, it'll be Chloe. The pair of them are joined at the hip, usually. Thank you for inviting us, Lara. What a wonderful family you have." He squeezed her arm. "I hope you are saving a dance for me tomorrow. I'm a little rusty though."

"You're lucky you won't be wearing high heels. Mind you I might have slipped them off by then. I can't believe this time tomorrow it will all be over." Lara wanted it to go on forever so Rob and Megan didn't have to go home.

"Hey." Rob raised Lara's chin up so he could see her face. She was crying. "Why the tears? This is the beginning, not the end." He looked like he was about to kiss her. He let go of her chin and shouted back at Megan. "Come on slow-coach. Big day tomorrow. Bedtime." Lara pulled herself together.

"You can make yourself a nice cup of cocoa before you go to bed. Or ask room service to deliver." Megan liked Lara's idea. "Good night Megan, sleep well. See you tomorrow."

"Night Lara. Are you coming in Dad?" Rob nodded. Megan went in.

"Goodnight Lara. Thank you for coming back into our lives. See you tomorrow." He bent down and kissed her on the cheek, a little longer than a peck.

"Sleep well." Lara waved as he went into the hotel. As she walked back to her parents' house she wondered if she had been caught up in the wedding excitement and was reading far more into Rob's kindness than she should.

The wedding day had arrived. Josh was in his element. He had been at the bride's house, putting hair up, since early morning.

"I haven't had so much fun since we went to see *Priscilla,*

Queen of the Desert. Do you remember Lara, we stayed at yours in London, and you were late for work the next morning?" Josh was giggling at his memory of the events.

"Ah yes. My alarm clock was mislaid if I recall. Somehow it had managed to get into my freezer." She had to admit, it had been a brilliant night.

"The tick-tocking was driving me mad. It was so loud." Poor Josh had ended up on the floor with Chuck, he swore he could feel the clock vibrating on the floor boards. "Anyway, you said it had been the best night you had had for a long time, so we froze it in time for you." Lara didn't find it that amusing when she finally got into work the next morning, but found it hilarious thinking about it now. They were both in hysterics when Debbie came in with coffees.

"Lara, watch your make-up. Josh, do something with Hayley's hair please. She looks like she's been dragged through a hedge backwards." Josh went to find Hayley. Kate was doing her hair, a little bit too advanced for her maladroit hands. "Your turn next?" Lara realised that she would be hearing that phrase frequently that day, from all the older relatives. Why is it that when the younger child gets married first, everyone thinks the older one will end up on the shelf?

"I've decided to become an old maid, with lots of cats and a budgerigar for company." Her mother realised Lara was joking.

"There's no need to be facetious Lara, darling. I'm worried about you. You don't seem very happy at the moment. Are you taking extra vitamins? With all the travelling you do, it must knock your metabolism out of kilter. Your dad is worried too, darling." Debbie was concerned about her eldest daughter. She had been top of her game for a long time, it was time she reaped the benefits and slowed down.

"Mum, I'm fine, really. You and Dad have no need to worry. As a matter of fact, I was thinking about a change myself. London is for youngsters. I'm getting too old to live out of a suitcase. When I have decided what to do, you'll both be the first to know. I promise." She kissed her mum on the cheek and took her coffee off to find her sister. Debbie stayed in Lara's old bedroom for a few moments. She was thinking that she needed a nice man to swoop her off her feet; someone like that Rob. He was very nice. She won't mention her thoughts to Pete though; he got annoyed when she interfered in the girls' lives. But sometimes a little help from 'Mum' was all it needed.

"Debs, where are you? The buttonholes and corsages have arrived." Pete was panicking. She had better go down and help, Pete was a poppet, but unless it had a stamp on it, or you could chip and putt with it, he was pretty useless. But she still adored him after nearly forty years together.

"Coming." She put Lara's Binky Bobtail back on her bed, she hadn't even realised she was cuddling the teddy, and went downstairs to help.

Debbie, Lara and Hayley had all gone off to the Church. Tori was helping her dad calm down. He was terrified. In a funny way, it kept Tori from being nervous. The irony of role reversal was making her smile. The car came back in no time and Pete helped get Tori's train in without too much trouble. He thanked goodness it wasn't raining. In fact, it was a very pleasant day, apart from a cold breeze. He was so proud of his younger daughter. She looked beautiful.

"Dad, don't you start blubbing. You'll get me started and then my make-up will run." They both laughed.

"You look like your mum, absolutely beautiful." He got in the back next to her and held her hand, more for his nerves rather than hers. He wished he'd taken Josh's advice now and had a quick half before they left. Only he didn't want to arrive at his daughter's wedding smelling like a brewery.

They arrived at the church, traditionally late. The bridesmaids were all fussing as Tori got out of the car, straightening pieces, and smoothing sections, until they were happy. Then they all got into position.

As the organ started playing Wagner's 'Bridal Chorus' Tori was suddenly hit by nerves. Luckily something inside Pete had clicked. Whether it was parental responsibility, or just that he couldn't let his daughter down, he took her arm, kissed her on the cheek, wished her luck and they were off down the aisle. Lara as maid-of-honour walked behind Tori, with Hayley behind Lara.

Lara couldn't help herself, she was looking through the guests as she walked, until she spotted Rob and Megan; she smiled, they smiled back. She looked ahead and saw a very anxious Adam, staring at Tori as she walked towards him. He was grinning from ear to ear, a definite sign of nerves.

The service began. It was a beautiful service, with a subtle amount of humour and a great deal of tears from the female members of the congregation. As the vicar announced, "You may kiss the bride," a feeling of relaxation rippled through the wedding party, all except one. Lara was nervous for Megan. As they went into the vestry for the signing of the Register, she heard the introduction of her aria. With the church's sound system, and the high roof, it sounded hauntingly like it was coming from above – heaven in a way. Instead of the usual chat and laughter in the vestry, everyone wanted to hear Megan, so seemed to whisper to the registrar. The photographer was clicking as quietly as he could, and then Tori asked him to pop out and take a couple of Megan, and the congregation which looked mesmerised.

When she finished the congregation clapped loudly, some forgetting where they actually were, such was the power of her performance. She went to sit with her dad, when Mendelssohn's 'Wedding March' started and out came the bride and groom, followed by Debbie and Dr Iain Sinclair, then Dr Shona Sinclair with Pete. Then Jeremy and Lara, and bringing up the rear was Hayley.

The photos seemed to take an age. Most of the guests had already gone on to the hotel. The breeze had picked up and it had got quite cold. Adam's parents were ushering his grandmother and themselves into a waiting car. Although from Scotland originally, they now all felt the cold. The photographer said he'd got enough and wanted to take the rest in the hotel, with the cake. Tori and her bridesmaids were very grateful. Their frocks were made of silk and taffeta, neither a shield to the wind.

The reception was everything Tori had hoped for. The hotel had done them proud. The chairs were decked in a purple silk, to match the bridesmaids' dresses and boys' cravats, and the flower displays on each of the tables were beyond words. They were larger versions of Tori's bouquet; made from lavender roses, purple lisianthus, and for height purple hydrangeas and delphiniums. The colour mixes were breath taking.

Everyone had found their names and were seated at their tables when the Master of Ceremonies from the hotel announced the bridal couple. Everyone stood up and cheered as Adam led Tori into the room and to their seats.

Speeches done, cake cut, all that was left was the evening dance. Older relatives began to leave and younger guests began to arrive. Lara thought she might change into something more comfortable for the evening, but was persuaded by Rob that she looked incredible and should stay like that for the dance she had promised him. Megan and Jeremy had gone off to talk to the DJ, who had just arrived. The first dance had to be sung by Megan without Adam knowing; a little surprise from Tori to her new husband.

The DJ announced that it was time for the first dance and Megan popped up next to him holding a microphone. Tori found Adam and they both walked onto the dance floor, with everyone clapping. Adam hadn't noticed Megan as the lights had been dimmed. After the first few introduction bars of 'Wherever You will Go', Megan started singing. Tori was pulling Adam around the dance floor, while he was trying to see Megan. Tori whispered that Megan was next to the DJ and after Adam had spotted her, he then concentrated on the business at hand, trying not to tread on Tori's toes. When the song had finished Tori and Adam kissed ending a perfect dance.

The lights went back on and the guests were clapping and whistling. Megan decided she could get quite used to all this. She took a small bow and ran off to find Josh. He'd promised to sneak her a small drink.

"Fabuloso, Megs. That was high class. I think I will be your manager, it'll pay more than hairdressing." Megan found it amusing. A manager would be cool. "Let's go and find the wine before it all goes and we will end up having to buy a drink at the bar." He was fun to be with.

"Megan seems to be enjoying herself. She is very talented, Rob. She obviously loves singing. You should…" She stopped herself. It wasn't her place, or right to dictate to Rob how to bring up his daughter. She gave up that right fifteen years ago.

"I know what you were about to say. I should encourage her?" Lara nodded. "Her language skills are like yours. Her mathematical capability is endless. She is talented in so many ways. If she stopped it all now for just one of her talents how would she ever know if it was the right one?" He was very wise. It came from growing up with Megan, not just coming in at that point. Lara trusted Rob's decisions were for Megan's benefit, not her detriment.

"She is a very lucky girl having you as her dad. I had no right to question your authority. I apologise." Rob thought Lara was getting too serious. He pulled her close and whispered in her ear.

"I may not be right, but with your help we can find out together. I shall call you her guardian angel. Almost good cop, bad cop scenario." He was grinning. "But I get the ultimate say so, because…"

"You're her father?" Lara asked.

"No, because I'm the boss." She playfully slapped him on the arm. He actually hadn't changed a bit. "Are you ready for that dance now?" She smiled and he escorted her to the dance floor.

The evening was enjoyed by all of the guests. Tori and Adam were saying their goodbyes. They were off to an unrevealed destination that night, and then to the airport for a flight to Italy, Portofino, in the morning. Tori had heard from a client about the area and had fallen in love with the description. They could only go for one week as Adam could only manage cover for that long. Term time was a nuisance, but as the Head was his best man, he managed to wangle it.

"Have you had the best day of your life? I hope so." Lara was cuddling her sister.

"It has been fantastic. It's gone so quickly though. I'll come up to London when I get back and we'll have a look at all my honeymoon pics." They hugged for a bit longer then Adam parted them and hugged Lara.

"Bye bye, sister-in-law. I'll take care of your little sister, don't worry." Lara knew he would. It was time for the bride and groom to leave. They were standing in the doorway of the ballroom. Tori made eye contact with Lara, winked, then turned and threw her bouquet. Lara caught it and laughed, as she turned she glimpsed Rob smiling at her. Stop it, she thought. She was reading far too much into his body language. Verbal language she could read, but unconscious gestures were not her forte.

The main lights in the ballroom started going on. The spell had been broken. Rob had managed to find Megan curled up on a window seat. He woke her and told her it was time to find a more comfortable bed.

They said goodbye to Lara's mum and dad, and Jeremy, and then went over to Lara who was staring at the bouquet.

"Well caught. Methinks it was a fix though." Rob was smiling. Lara kissed Megan and told her how proud she was of her. Megan looked shattered. She probably hadn't slept much the night before with nerves. Lara turned to Rob.

"If you haven't any plans for tomorrow, I'd love to show you both the area. We have forests, beaches and castles to choose from. You better get that little lady off to bed for now though." Lara noticed Megan was forcing her eyes open.

"Thank you for inviting us, Lara. We've had a lovely time. A sightseeing trip tomorrow sounds great, but not too early. How about eleven?" Lara agreed, not too early. So that arranged, Rob took his daughter off to their hotel for a good night's sleep. He turned at the door and blew Lara a kiss. She felt like a schoolgirl. Her heart did a somersault. She was going to catch it and put it to her heart like they did in the movies, but she was not sixteen and she wasn't in a Broadway musical. She really had to sort herself out. That man was making her into a quivering wreck, not good for a woman who had to translate for the country's Foreign Secretary in four days' time in The Hague.

Having helped her parents get the presents and the remains of the cake into the car, and round up the stragglers, Lara was fit for nothing else but her bed. She couldn't even remember dreaming that night.

CHAPTER 5

~

The next morning when the rest of her family were feeling anticlimactic, Lara was buzzing. She had showered and changed and had her breakfast before her mum had even surfaced.

"Where are you off to so early? I thought you'd take advantage of a lie-in when you have the opportunity." Her mother had caught her on the landing. Lara tried to sound nonchalant, but it was difficult.

"I'm picking Megan and Rob up for a little sightseeing tour. They haven't been to this neck of the woods before. I thought I'd start with Corfe Castle and work our way back towards Poole Quay for lunch. Have you any ideas where would be nice?" Lara thought her mother was looking at her strangely.

"You like him, don't you?" Debbie was concerned for her eldest daughter. Lara needed a nice young man without baggage. But Debbie had to admit, Rob was a wonderful person.

"Mum, I'm fond of him and Megan. He was very good to me in the past, and life has thrown him some sh…, poo. He needs a friend, that's all. Those wedding bells yesterday have fuddled your brain. You are going to be hearing them for a while, so I shall keep out of the way until they have died down." She went over to kiss her mum. It was, after all, only because she loved Lara that she was so concerned. Lara couldn't fault that.

As she pulled up to the hotel foyer she could see Megan sitting on a massive plant pot, texting furiously. Rob had been watching for her car and was already bounding towards her with a big smile on his face. She had to admit, her heart felt funny, almost fluttering. It was weird, she hadn't felt like that before, with anyone. She put it down to excitement from the day before. Perhaps she was still slightly under the influence of the champagne.

"Good morning, and how are you this fine morning?" Rob had been looking forward to their adventure into Dorset, more than he realised. "Come on Meggie Moo, let's not keep Lara waiting." He was in the car before Lara had time to get out. He stretched across and kissed her on the cheek. She wondered if he noticed her heart racing. She could hear it; she hoped he couldn't.

"Hello Rob, I hope you slept well." How lame was that? Lara had to pull herself together. "Wasn't it a lovely wedding? I just hope mine is as beautiful." Nooo, Lara, she was now cross with herself. Was she trying to scare the man? But Rob just smiled at her.

"You deserve the very best, and I'm sure when it is your turn, you will have the wedding of your dreams." That look he was giving her, was she seeing more than she thought? Megan getting into the back of the car broke the tension.

"Morning Lara. Sorry about that, I was just changing my status on Facebook. My bfs need to know what I'm doing." Lara laughed. She loved the way Megan was so casual about life. Oh, to be a teen again.

"Off we go then. I hope you don't mind some history mixed with a little geography today." She looked in her rear-view mirror and Megan poked her tongue out at her, with a smile on her face. Lara knew it was going to be a good day.

They drove onto the Sandbanks Ferry to start their expedition into the depths of Dorset. Megan got out of the car and went up to the viewing deck while the 'olds' stayed in the car. It was only a five-minute crossing.

"Thank you for this Lara. Megan has actually been quite excited about today. She really likes you." Lara felt relieved, on both counts. She was sure a teenager would think a sightseeing trip would be boring, but on the other hand it was totally different from where she lived. The fact that she liked Lara was wonderful news. Lara loved Megan more and more each time she saw her. She knew that was due to Jill and Rob bringing her up so wonderfully. "There you go again, thinking too much." Rob was laughing. She turned and smiled at him. He leant over, was he about to kiss her? She'd never know. Just at that moment Megan jumped back into the car.

"Wow, have you seen those houses?" Megan was pointing to the beautiful mansions on the Sandbanks Peninsula.

"I'm expecting in a few years, after a couple of Platinum

Discs, you will have one of those, Megan. I hope you invite me to tea." Megan giggled, but was inwardly happy that Lara thought so positively about her singing.

"So where to first? I need a coffee." Rob was eager to get the tour started.

"Well, I thought as we were over on the Isle of Purbeck, we have to drive through Swanage. I used to go there on my Sunday School outings when I was a little girl. They had donkeys on the beach and Punch and Judy. It really was fun." Megan had heard of Punch and Judy from her parents, but had never seen it and donkeys on the beach was another memory her parents talked about.

"We had the same childhood! Brighton Beach was exactly the same. I wonder if they still have things like that today?" Rob was sighing. Lara realised that a lot had changed in England since he lived there.

"I know they still have Punch and Judy in the summer. I'm not sure about the donkeys though. I think that a lot of Animal Rights issues stopped things like that." Animal welfare had advanced greatly in the UK since they were children. As they approached the turning to Swanage Rob noticed a sight he hadn't seen in years. His eyes lit up and he was like an excited schoolboy.

"Train, train!" Rob was positively jumping in his seat. Megan looked over to see what the fuss was about.

"Oh, my goodness, it's like the one from that film, you know, the one with those children that had to stop it with a petticoat. *The Railway Children*, that was it" Megan used to watch the old English films to get a feel for the country she had never lived in. They were both straining to see it before it went behind the hedges. All that was seen then was the steam.

"The station is in Swanage. We'll add that to our stops if you like." Lara was happy her guests were enjoying the day already.

Swanage hadn't changed a great deal since she was younger. The Amusement Arcade was still on the sea front. The Mowlem Theatre still stood proudly by the sea wall, albeit a little older, and the shops were still making the High Street look up-to-date, even without the famous 'Woolworths' landmark where all the children made a beeline for the 'pick-and-mix'. They drove to the end of the High Street and into the station carpark. Rob's eyes lit up to see the train back in the station. He went to watch the engineer stoke the boiler, while the girls went into the shop.

"Lara, may I have a loan of £6? I'll be able to pay you back when my first million is in the bank." She was smiling, how could Lara resist that smile. "It's just that I only have euros, and I want to cheer Dad up, and look they have Thomas the Tank Engine mugs. I know he'd love one of those for his cup of tea in the morning, and it will remind him of this visit." Lara looked at the mug Megan was holding proudly. She knew Rob would love it. Megan and Rob had such a good relationship; she had better tread very carefully so as not to spoil it in any way. She gave Megan the £6 and told her the loan was interest free for five years. Megan liked that. She went off to pay. Lara went back outside to the station platform and watched Rob chat to the engine driver. He was as animated and excited as the driver showing off his train. Did men ever grow out of their boyhood? She thought not, thank goodness.

"Lara, come and look at this. It's fascinating." Lara took one look at the black soot that was falling from the air and shook her head.

"You're alright. I'll stay here and wait for Megan." Rob laughed. Girls, he thought, and shook his head. He'd never understand them.

"How long will we be staying? I was going to have a wander into the town." Megan was as enthusiastic about the train as Lara. It was lovely to watch in the open countryside, but it was noisy and smelly close up. Lara took the package off Megan.

"I'll go and pop this in the car boot, you go and have a wander. I'll get a coffee into your father and we'll be ready to leave in about half-an-hour, how's that?" Megan thought that a good plan. Lara popped some more English money into Lara's hand. "There's a change machine in the arcade, don't spend it all in there." She winked at Megan. How did Lara know that was where Megan was headed? Megan liked Lara more and more. She thanked her and made her way along the High Street. She'd actually spotted a cool clothes shop on the way in, Tilly Whims, she had to check it out first.

When Rob's thirst kicked in he said goodbye to the engine driver and made his way along the platform where Lara was waiting patiently. He tapped her on the shoulder and made her jump.

"Fancy a coffee?" Rob looked around. "Where's Megan?" Lara told him she'd gone exploring and led him into the little station coffee shop. Half-an-hour turned into a full hour. Neither had noticed the time fly by. Catching up and enjoying each other's company made the world go by around them. It was only when Megan burst into the café that Lara looked at her watch.

"I'm so sorry I'm late. It wasn't my fault." Megan was out of breath. She'd obviously been running. She turned to the doorway and pointed at a young man. "It was his fault." She beckoned him over. "This is Willy-Yeo. Say 'hello' Willy."

"Hello." Willy looked completely petrified. "I'm sorry Megan is late. It was my fault." He was about to give them a reason when Megan cut him off.

"It's ok, Willy. I'll explain. You can run along back now. I'll text you later. Bye." Megan almost dismissed him with a wave, but Lara noticed the wink she gave him. He smiled and was gone.

"Well, what a morning. I've had great fun. Where to now?" Rob and Lara looked at each other and burst out laughing. They left the café to some odd looks, and made their way back to the car.

Lara drove on to Corfe Castle, she had a plan and that was where it started. In the meantime, both she and Rob were desperate to know who Willy-Yeo was. Lara didn't think it was her place to ask and was hoping Rob's curiosity would get the better of him. As it happened Megan decided to explain.

"I expect you are wondering who Willy was. Well, after I left you I went to the arcade. I was popping in these copper coins, when this lad came up behind me and told me they were the wrong ones for that machine. I said I was sorry, but I wasn't from this country and am only used to euros. He was very understanding and got the keys to take out the coins I had put in. It turns out he was the owner's son and had been made to work there today as someone had called in sick. He wasn't happy because he was supposed to be out on his boat with his mates. He gave me the coins back and showed me which machine to go on and how to win some money. I thought, since he's the owner, sort of, that I wasn't hurting anyone by winning. In fact, I was helping him feel better by him getting his own back on his parents." Rob and Lara could see the logic – whether they agreed with it was another matter.

"I left with double the money in my pocket and popped over to that lovely shop, Tilly Whims." Lara knew the shop.

"It's named after the caves along the coast, you know." Lara didn't know why she had said that. She was beginning to sound like a schoolteacher. They pulled into the castle carpark.

"Well it's full of some lovely clothes. I'm afraid I couldn't afford much, but I've bought you this Lara, for looking after us. And I've got enough to give you back for the other thing." She leaned over and gave Lara a bag. Lara opened it and it had the most beautiful scarf in it.

"Oh Megan. It's lovely. You shouldn't have spent money on me." Lara was delighted with the thought as well as the very pretty scarf. "You should have bought something for yourself."

"Willy-Yeo bought me this." She produced a t-shirt from another bag. Both bags had been small enough to keep in her shoulder bag so the game hadn't been given away too soon.

"This Willy-Yeo, how old is he?" Rob couldn't help his concern creeping into his voice.

"Oh Dad. He's seventeen years old and he's just started his A Levels. They live up the road from our hotel, and he has his own car." Lara was amused at how much information Megan had gleaned from this lad in under one hour. "Oh, and he has a boat." Well, he was just perfect son-in-law material Lara thought with a smile. Rob was not as amused, but looking at Lara's face he realised he was being a little overcautious. "So, where's this castle?" Megan made an effort to change the subject. From the carpark, all that could be seen was a hill.

"We have to cross the road and walk towards the village to be able to see the castle. Let's go." Lara put on her scarf, locked the car and they were off on the next leg of their adventure.

In the shadow of the castle was a little tearoom. They sat in its garden eating toasted cheese sandwiches and crisps, with a small side salad and coleslaw. Lara was explaining a little of the history of the castle.

"I'm sure you have done some of 17th century English history? The Cavaliers and the Roundheads?" Megan nodded. Instead of being bored, she was actually interested. It may have been because ruins surrounded her and it brought the story to life, or it may just have been the fact that Lara was more interesting than Mr Foster, her history teacher. "Well Corfe Castle was owned by the Bankes family who supported Charles I. During the Civil War the castle suffered from two sieges. After the second it was in government hands and Parliament ordered it to be demolished. Luckily their attempt was only half successful. The family moved out and although keeping the title to the castle, they built a mansion in Wimborne called Kingston Lacy House. The family left both to the National Trust, which is why the public can see history brought to life. Oh dear, I'm sounding like a history teacher." Lara thought she'd gone on a little too much.

"No you don't, I'd have been asleep by now if you *had* been my history teacher, he's so boring. You make it all sound real." Megan stared up at the castle. "How on earth did the Roundheads manage to get in? It's perched right on top of that hill so no one could sneak up without being seen." Lara was glad Megan found it interesting.

"Unfortunately it was a turncoat in the Bankes' household. One of their own soldiers let them in. Simple as that. Poor Lady Bankes was on her own during that siege, as her husband was off with Charles I. The Roundhead's captain thought so highly of Lady Bankes's efforts to protect the castle that he escorted her safely out with her family. Normally they would just have been killed." Rob was watching Megan. He had never seen her sit still for so long. She was genuinely interested in what Lara was saying. "I thought you might like to see Kingston Lacy House next. It is a little boring unless you like old buildings and flowers, but there is a method in my madness." Lara winked at Megan. Megan had no idea what Lara had up her sleeve, but so far she hadn't disappointed her, so she'd go along with it.

"Sounds intriguing! I'm up for it. Dad?" Megan looked at her father.

"Well, I love old buildings, and English flowers, so I'm game." Lara led the way back to the car.

On the way Megan was texting furiously. She had 'checked-in' at Corfe Castle on her Facebook profile and having had numerous comments, had a suspicion as to what Lara had in mind. She wouldn't say anything though, in case she jinxed it.

They wandered around the Gardens with Rob pointing out the English flowers to Megan. Lara realised just how much Megan had missed of England, living in Portugal all her life. But the more she thought about it the more she realised how worldly Megan was compared to some English girls. Her confidence was brimming and her social skills were good, judging on how easily she managed to get around Willy-Yeo. No, she thought, Megan hadn't missed out at all.

"So, where to now?" It was Rob who had exhausted his flora and fauna knowledge and needed an excuse to go.

"Well, we are very near the old market town of Wimborne Minster. I thought you'd like to have tea and scones there." Megan looked at Lara. Lara realised Megan had sussed her plan. Megan went over and linked her arm through Lara's.

"I love it when a plan comes together." Megan whispered so only Lara could hear. Lara smiled at her and squeezed her arm. Rob didn't stand a chance now Megan had an ally.

As they approached Wimborne Town Centre there were a group of schoolchildren chatting and laughing. They were in school uniform on a Sunday, which could only mean they were boarders. Lara pointed out how smart they looked.

"What a lovely uniform. Tartan skirts are all the fashion at the moment." Lara caught Megan's eye in the rear-view mirror. Megan put a thumb up, and smiled.

"Why are they in uniform on a Sunday?" Rob hadn't yet realised the ploy.

"They are from the boarding school just outside the town. It's called Canford." The penny dropped. Rob turned round to see Megan stifling a laugh.

"Well, when did you two dream up this little scheme?" Lara hoped he wasn't too cross.

"Megan had nothing to do with it. In fact, she only cottoned on when she realised where we were heading." Megan kept quiet in the back. She was answering a text message, which was very difficult with her fingers crossed. "I'm sorry if you are upset Rob, but I thought if you saw the school and exactly where it was, it would make it easier for you to know Megan would be happy here." Lara too had her fingers crossed. Rob could see Lara was right. It was a lovely area, not far from the airport, set in idyllic surroundings and the schoolchildren he could see were happy.

"Well we better go and see it then." Megan leaned over from the back seat and gave her dad a big hug. "I haven't agreed yet. But I'll give it a chance." She sat back down, put her seatbelt back on and continued texting.

They drove up to the massive entrance gates, Lara noticed lots of cars in the carpark, so she drove in. As they approached the main carpark it was obvious that a game of rugby was in full swing, thus the cars in the carpark, parents and friends supporting their school.

"A look around would be a good idea, don't you think?" Lara looked over at Rob to gauge his response.

"OK. Let's start with the rugby pitch." He smiled at her. Megan was already out of the car and looking around. Suddenly a voice was screaming her name.

"Megan, Megan, over here." Megan looked over towards the other side of the carpark, near the main entrance.

"Dad, look it's Abi." Megan ran over to Abigail and they hugged. They walked back to Rob and Lara, chatting excitedly. "Lara, this is Abigail. We were at school together. Abi's mum and dad own the gourmet restaurant in Quinta. Abi this is Lara." Lara shook Abi's hand. Abi very politely told her it was very good to meet her. She turned to Rob. Rob grabbed her and kissed her on both cheeks.

"I feel this has been a put-up job." He looked at the two girls.

"I couldn't believe it when Megan told me you were just down the road. Can I take her to my dorm? I'd love to show her where I live." Rob nodded. He thought it would be a good idea. Was he hoping Megan wouldn't like what she saw? He didn't think that was possible, so far he had been very impressed.

"Well, I suppose it wouldn't hurt to have a look around ourselves. And stop looking so worried, I agree, this was a good idea." He took her hand and squeezed it. "And if you had asked me I'd have said under no circumstances would I want to see the school, so I'm glad you didn't ask." Lara felt so much better. "Come on then, at least we may get to see some sport." Rob led the way, Lara followed. It was a wonderful school. The buildings were imposing and the grounds were a delight. There seemed to be a small golf course, games fields, landscaped gardens and a river flowing by the side. Even Rob had to admit it was a good choice of Megan's.

"Abi's parents were very worried when Abi went off to boarding school this term. It was her first time away from home, and also it was abroad. They were even considering putting their restaurant up for sale and moving back to England, but she seems very happy." At least Rob could go back and tell them to stop worrying.

"It's nice to know that Megan has a friend already here." Lara knew how important that would be for her to settle in.

"I know of at least three girls and a boy who came here

this term. Megan said there are a few from her year already nagging their parents for next year. It's such a small community, their school in Almancil, although they are from different years they all know each other and are very close." Rob was watching the rugby. "But I'm not sure whether she'd be happy away from home." Lara knew she would. It was Rob who wouldn't be happy. He needed to take his mind of his loneliness; perhaps that was where she could come in. She had nearly a year to work on it. They wandered a little further round until they came to the front of the main school building. It was an architects' dream. As they were looking around a group of boys went over to them and politely asked if they could help them in any way. Rob explained that he was waiting for his daughter. They said goodbye and left.

"Well, if that wasn't a good advert for the school's discipline and manners, I'd like to know what would be." Lara was very impressed. Rob's phone vibrated. He looked at the screen.

"Megan is back at the car. I wonder if she liked the dorms. I hope she did, but don't tell her that." Lara hugged Rob. "What was that for?"

"You are a wonderful father, Rob. Come on, let's not keep her waiting or she'll go off and we'll never find her." They walked together, Rob putting his arm through Lara's, naturally as they walked.

At the carpark, a group of girls were standing by Lara's car. Megan was telling them about her conquest at the arcade that morning.

"Dad, you'll not believe this, but they know Willy-Yeo. He's a Day Bug here. Isn't that brill?" Megan looked so happy. Lara looked quizzically at her. "Boarders are Bed

Bugs!" Lara understood, but didn't enquire why.

"Say goodbye, Megan. We better get back. Bye Abi, I'll send your love to your parents." He gave her a hug.

"I've given Megs a letter for them, if you can get it to them I'd be very grateful. I know they worry." Rob assured her they would drop it off as soon as they got back.

Goodbyes said Lara decided the quickest route back, and they were off.

"Can we drop the letter off on the way back from the airport please Dad? Abi's worried her parents may get on a plane and take her home." Rob could understand why.

"Of course we can. She was very happy, wasn't she? It's a good school." He said no more, but Lara and Megan made eye contact in the rear-view mirror and Megan again put a thumb up to Lara, and mouthed a big 'thank you'. Lara felt a bond growing between the two of them, but she knew gently did it.

To show their appreciation, Rob and Megan had invited Lara to dinner at the hotel that night. It was a lovely gesture and Lara was delighted to spend more time with them before they left the next day.

The meal was good, but by the time the pudding was served Megan's attention span was diminishing.

"Can I be excused Dad? I need to get on Facebook and pack my stuff." Rob nodded. "Goodnight Lara. Thank you for a super day. I didn't realise history was real; I thought most of it was made up just for kids to have to learn. See you in the morning." She kissed Lara on the cheek and then her father. She went off almost running. Adults were quite boring; Lara couldn't blame her.

"Coffee?" Rob didn't want the evening to end. He enjoyed

Lara's company, there was no pretence and she was very easy to talk to.

"Yes please, just an Espresso though. Hopefully it won't keep me awake." Rob ordered the coffee. The waiter asked if either of them would like a liqueur on the house. They both declined. The flight wasn't too early in the morning, but neither felt they needed an extra buzz.

"Thank you again Lara for today. I don't know when you became so wise, but it's lucky for Megan that you are." He was smiling, almost taunting her.

"Us girls have to stick together." She by no means wanted to take over any parental rights or responsibilities, she just wanted to complement what Rob and Jill had already put in place. The groundwork had been very well laid; she just felt like caretaking it so it stayed in good order. It was her way of thanking Jill. Perhaps when she and Rob were closer she'd explain it to him, but now it seemed a little too soon.

"There you go again, overthinking. Come back!" Lara shook her head and smiled. He knew her better than she thought. "Are you sure you don't mind taking us to the airport in the morning. We could get a taxi and you could have a lie-in."

"I have to be back in London by lunchtime, so it's not a problem." Back to reality, she thought. "When will you be over to England again?" She hoped that didn't sound too desperate.

"In the New Year. Probably not until February half-term. We need to pop down to Brighton but I'm sure we could meet up." Rob was thinking of Jill. It would be the fifth anniversary of her death and he wanted to mark it with a visit to her grave with Megan.

"You'll be going to Gatwick then. Let me help. You can both stay at my flat for a few days when you get back from Brighton. I can book a show for you and Megan. Please say yes." She needed something to look forward to. It felt like an age away.

"That would be lovely. I'll email you the dates, hopefully you can arrange time off and we can do a London expedition. Megan seems to like your treks." He was laughing. "Just no more schools, ok?"

"Ok. Just a few museums and some dungeons then." They were walking towards the foyer. It was getting late and they both had to be up early. Lara was walking the short distance home.

"Let me see you home." He was helping her on with her jacket. There was a distinct autumnal chill in the air.

"That's very sweet of you, but I think you may be needed upstairs to shepherd a little lamb to bed. I'm sure she will still be on her computer." Rob knew Lara was right.

"How funny, you can tell you are from Dorset. Your idioms are characterised by your locale." He surprised her. Now who sounded like a teacher? They were both laughing. Neither wanted the evening to stop, but Lara knew he had a lot to do before he could get to bed.

"Goodnight Rob, see you in the morning. Sleep well." She stretched up to kiss him on the cheek. He turned his face and they kissed gently on the lips. Not a longing kiss, nor a romantic one, more of a peck, but on the lips.

"Goodnight, lovely Lara. Thank you for coming back into our lives." He turned to go back into the hotel, but the light caught on his eyes as he went and Lara realised he had turned just in time. His eyes had filled with tears. He didn't want her to see, so she respected that and walked away, turning briefly to wave as he entered the hotel and waved back. She realised her presence back in his life had brought back memories of their lives together, and how much he had missed them both. Life was unfair. Why did he have to live so far away? She had loved it in Portugal once. Perhaps she could live there again. Anything would be better than the schedule waiting for her on her return to work. She needed another plan. She'd give herself six months to plan, organise and put into motion her new life.

She got them safely to the airport the next morning, giving them both hugs and kisses and hiding her tears. Rob noticed them, and gave her an extra squeeze with a promise that he'd call her the minute they got home. She drove on up to London with a heavy heart. It would be months until she saw Rob again. Why was she feeling like that? She knew the answer. She had fallen for him hook, line and sinker. There was no getting away from it. The only thing she could do in the meantime was to keep busy. That was the easy part as her desk was covered in speeches to be translated and her travel folder had boarding passes for three flights that week. She took off her coat, put her bag under her desk and went off to make herself a coffee. Phase one of her plan underway, she needed to chill to make sure she was healthy enough mentally and physically to enjoy the conclusion of her life change.

Lara was so busy in the weeks up to the Christmas break that the time flew past. She had decided to take a short break over the main holiday and go home. The government stopped until well into the New Year, so she thought she'd follow suit. She was tempted to get onto a plane and pop across to Portugal for the Christmas holiday, but decided her own family had been neglected and Rob had already got his and Megan's Christmas planned. They were going to Abi's parents' restaurant where they were having a Christmas lunch with all the English trimmings. Lots of the expats would be there, perhaps next year Lara would be eligible to join them.

Lara had a good Christmas with her parents and Tori and Adam. She had managed to talk to Megan and Rob on Christmas evening and New Years' Day, via Skype. On New Years' Day she managed a private call to Rob and he assured her that they would be taking her up on her kind offer in February. She couldn't wait. She'd managed to book most of the week off, which fell in with Rob's plans as he wanted to do Brighton first and let Megan visit her grandmother in Redhill too. Although Rob's mother used to get out to see them in Portugal, due to an ear operation a few years ago, she couldn't fly anymore. The journey would be too much for her by boat or train, so she looked forward to having her granddaughter visit her instead. She loved Megan's visits as she could show her off to her neighbours. It's a grandmother thing.

Again, Lara was so busy that January whisked by. February was cold and snow was about, London as usual was at a standstill. Flights were being cancelled and Lara was stuck in the office. All she could think about was that the snow had better be gone by the end of February. It was.

Rob and Megan had arrived at Gatwick safe and sound on the Saturday of half-term. They had taken the train down to Brighton and placed a beautiful tribute on Jill's grave. On their way back, they had stopped at Redhill for a night. Megan dutifully did the granddaughter bit. She sung to the neighbours, and Rob's mum was thrilled. Megan promised to stay with her for a while in the summer holidays, and told her that she'd only be 'down the road' at school so she'd see much more of her come September. Rob explained the school was in Dorset, not that far from Surrey, but certainly not 'down the road'. He had to agree with Megan though she would be in the same country.

Lara met them at Victoria Station on the Sunday. She took them back to her flat where Rob was suitably impressed by the location, just off Buckingham Palace Road. Not many people have the Queen of England as their neighbour. Before they had time to catch-up or unpack, Megan wanted to see the Palace. They walked round and Megan took photos. She had been to London before, but she was younger and didn't remember it very well. Lara still couldn't believe that some of Megan's friends at school, who had English passports as their parents were originally from England, had never been to England let alone London.

The week was jam-packed, Megan had told Lara where she would like to go, Lara had organised a rough itinerary to fit it all in. By the last few days they were all exhausted, but Lara had a surprise arranged, her pièce de résistance. She had booked to see the cast of *Glee* at the O2 Arena. Megan jumped in the air when she was told and rushed over to kiss Lara.

"You are the best. Oh, my goodness. Just wait till the

girls at school hear this. *Glee* is their absolute fav. I've got to go and tell Chloe, she'll be dead jel. Thank you Lara." She disappeared to her room.

"I think she's pleased." Rob understated as usual. "You are clever. Will I enjoy it?" He was teasing her now.

"It depends on where you sit." She was teasing him back.

"Hopefully next to you." He took her hand. "Thank you for a lovely visit, Lara. I think you have a fan forever. She's needed a woman in her life, I hope you realise you are that woman now." He was being serious. She knew what he meant.

"I'm not going anywhere. I'll be here whenever she needs me. That goes for you too." She put her hand on his cheek. He took it and placed a tender kiss on it.

"I'll be here for you both." They were just staring at each other. Lara was willing him to get closer. He moved closer.

"Dad, you'll never guess what. Chloe is so gutted. She's promised me €100 if I get Puck's autograph." Megan was so excited.

"Puck? Is that a person?" Rob had stepped away from Lara. Lara began breathing again.

"Oh Dad. You are a Neanderthal sometimes. Puck is short for Noah Puckerman, the character Mark Salling plays in *Glee*. Der! I want Matthew Morrison's, he plays Will Schuster, the Spanish teacher and director of the Glee Club. Oh, my goodness Lara, I can't believe it. When are we going?"

"This evening, we'll leave here around sixish and pop into my favourite Italian restaurant at Westminster for a bite to eat, then catch the tube from there to North Greenwich. The arena is opposite the station, so it should be easy." Megan disappeared back into her bedroom worried she had nothing to wear to meet that calibre of celebrities. Lara and Rob had stifled their laughter so they didn't burst Megan's euphoric bubble. The moment had passed, but Lara hoped there would be more moments like that.

"Cup of tea?" Lara asked in as normal a voice as possible.

"That would be lovely." Rob answered in as normal a voice he was able. The tension was electric. He followed her into the kitchen.

"Dad, it's no use. I've nothing to wear. Can Lara and I go out and find something at least from this century for me to wear." She was pouting at the kitchen door. Rob and Lara couldn't help but laugh.

"Portugal does have modern shops, young lady, and you have plenty of clothes." Rob was a typical man.

"Rob, can you pour the tea, I'll be about twenty minutes. Come on Megan, have you heard of the famous Kings Road? Well it's five minutes away. If we hurry my tea will have brewed just nicely by the time we get back." She turned to Rob and winked. He was actually grateful. He hated shopping, and knew that Megan did need some up-to-date clothes. He smiled at her, without Megan seeing.

"You better get me a tie while you're there if it's a posh do!" Rob was winding Megan up.

"Oh, Dad." Megan despaired of her father sometimes. But she loved him to pieces, his teasing and all.

When they got back, nearly an hour later, Rob had fallen asleep on the sofa. Megan and Lara had had a wonderful shop. Megan had got some very cool things. No one in Portugal would have them yet. She would set a trend. They seemed to have the same taste in colours and styles. Perhaps that was nature rather than nurture Lara thought. Wishful thinking, but it didn't hurt anyone.

Luckily Lara had a small en suite so she left the larger bathroom for Megan to get ready in. Poor Rob had to cross his legs until one of the ladies finished titivating themselves.

"Well, you two have scrubbed up well." Megan thumped him.

"Do you realise how long this takes us? It's not like you, with a quick shave and change of trousers. We have to create this appearance before you. It takes artistry and finesse." Lara was teasing Rob for a change and Megan was enjoying every moment.

"Well come on then, or we won't have time to eat." Rob had got to the front door and was tapping his fingers on it.

"You're going like that then Dad?" Megan asked, with her eyebrows raised.

"Yes, what's wrong with the way I look?" He looked himself up and down, then realised what he'd forgotten. He disappeared off to his bedroom. He came back with his shoes. Megan and Lara were laughing as they walked out onto the road. Rob did see the funny side, but he would sulk for a while just to keep their camaraderie going for a while longer. He was so pleased that they were getting closer.

They had a wonderful evening. Lara had managed to call in some favours, and pulled a few strings. Although Megan hadn't got to see the cast backstage, she was given two posters signed by the whole cast. She was completely made-up.

The next day Lara had to go into work and left Rob and Megan to enjoy London on their own. They had only two more days before their flights were booked back to Portugal, and Lara certainly didn't want to spend them at her office. She managed to delegate quite a few speeches for translation to her juniors, but there was one that was highly confidential that she had to do herself, as the juniors didn't have the necessary security clearance. Taking it home to do was out of the question. If caught the reprimand would be severe. So she sat down and got on with it. By four o'clock it was done and on its way to the Foreign Secretary's Office. She checked her emails and calendar, which she had purposely kept clear, and found she had been booked in, in her absence, to go to Rome on Saturday, their last day. She made a few phone calls, to no avail. She could throw a sickie, but her conscience wouldn't let her do that. She was mortified. Was it too much to ask to have a life of her own, not dictated to by the upper echelons of the government? She had made herself indispensable through her own brilliance for language. But the novelty had now worn off. She wanted to be normal, to have a nine-to-five job. She decided to accelerate her plan to leave the rat race; she'd talk to Rob that evening.

By the time she got back to her flat Rob and Megan were busy in the kitchen. The smell that hit her as she opened her front door was to die for. It reminded her of walking into her home in Poole, with her mother in the kitchen cooking dinner, a warm feeling of belonging.

"Dad, she's back." Megan ran to Lara and kissed her. She grabbed her hand and walked her into the lounge/diner where the table had been set and a glass of wine poured. Lara was touched. She was trying to get her coat off at the same time but got her hand stuck. Before she realised, Rob was helping her and gave it to Megan to put on the hook at the front door.

"Madam, dinner is served." He motioned for her to sit, pulling out her chair. He took her napkin, shook it and placed it gently on her lap. Megan was giggling; Rob gave her a raised eye brow look, she stopped. Rob went into the kitchen to bring out the first course.

"Oh, my goodness, you remembered." Lara couldn't believe her eyes. Rob had made Lara's all-time favourite starters from his restaurant. It was a prawn cocktail, but done on a flat plate, with the prawns in a Marie-Rose sauce in the middle with avocado fanned out at the top, small olives made into eyes and a nose, and a slice of tomato for the mouth, finished off with a garnish of water cress made into a bow tie, well, more of a clown's ruff.

"Believe it or not, it's Megan's favourite too. I've kept in practice because she always asks for it when she brings friends home." Rob smiled at Lara as she tucked in. She didn't realise how hungry she was, she'd worked over lunch to get it finished.

"I've always known it as Lara's starter since I was a little girl." Megan didn't realise the significance of what she had said. Rob and Jill had kept Lara's memory alive to her own daughter all her life. She looked at Rob who just nodded. Tears were starting to form in the corner of Lara's eyes. Megan noticed. "Don't you like it any more?" Megan had been told that tastes change as you got older.

"Sorry, I've had the day from hell, and this has been the best surprise. Thank you both." She hadn't got a hanky so dabbed her eyes with her napkin. Rob picked up her wine glass and handed it to her.

"A toast. To Lara the perfect hostess. To Megan the almost perfect daughter, and to me, the perfect chef. Cheers." Rob had tilted his head and was smiling at Lara. She couldn't help but smile back. After all the work and effort Rob had put into the evening's fare, she was not going to ruin it for him. Her problems could wait until later.

The meal just got better. For the main course, he had chosen another of Lara's favourites, Moroccan lamb tagine with cous cous; also another favourite of Megan's. To round off Lara's reminiscent dinner, dessert was a banana and Bailey's crepe. Megan informed Lara that the dessert was known as 'Lara's Pudding'. Megan left her father and Lara during coffee. She'd never liked coffee and was sure she never would. Anyway, she had things to do. Lara had let her use the scanner in her bedroom (which was usually Lara's home office) and she was trying to download the poster with all the autographs, to show her friends on Facebook.

"What can I say? You definitely haven't lost it!" Lara was teasing Rob for a change.

"I take it you mean my culinary skills?" Lara laughed. She was beginning to feel very comfortable in his company. The alcohol had probably helped too. "Well at least it seems to have cheered you up. You didn't look this happy when you first got home." Rob had seen through the brave face Lara had put on for the evening.

"Can't fool you, can I? I have to say I've had better days. I've been called away to Rome tomorrow, and it's your last day. I've tried to get out of it but unfortunately it's unofficial, which means they don't want the press finding out so I couldn't make too much noise about it." Rob leant over and took her hand.

"Megan and I have had the best holiday since Jill died. And it's all thanks to you. Don't beat yourself up over one day. There'll be plenty more now you and I are back as a team." Lara wanted to read more into his words, but knew Rob was just being caring. "Now, we've stacked the dishwasher but I'm not sure how it works!" Lara got up and walked to the kitchen with the empty coffee cups. She couldn't believe how tidy the kitchen was considering the amount of food that had been prepared in it. "Tidy up as you go along. Jill would repeat that over and over when we sold the restaurant. I had got so used to staff cleaning up for me that poor Jill couldn't even get into the kitchen at home. So we came to an arrangement. It actually was easy once you get into the habit." He'd just washed the wine glasses by hand and was drying them while he talked. He put them into the cupboard he had found them in, and then closed in on Lara. He put his arm around her and pulled her close. "I wish I could take all your worries back to Portugal with me and leave you happy." That was it. The floodgates opened and Lara just cried and cried. It probably wasn't just work. She was tired, and she didn't want Rob to go. He lifted her face up and got out his hanky. He wiped her tears away and led her back to the lounge. They sat on the sofa and hugged. Eventually she was all cried out. "There, do you feel a little better now?" He squeezed her and let her go. He wanted to talk to her so faced her. "You are not happy at work, are you?" She shook her head. "There must be other employers who would snap you up with your skills?" He was so kind.

"I was thinking about teaching." The longer holidays would be nice, she thought. "I have to give three months' notice, it isn't that easy once you've signed the Official

Secrets Act. I have to play down my position, and promise that I won't tell my new employers that I'd even signed it. I am only allowed to give my job title, which is only half of what I do." Rob had the answer.

"If you have to give three months' notice, why not hand it in now? You will easily find something in three months. Then while you are working your notice it will be easier as there will be a light at the end of the tunnel for you." Lara knew what he meant.

"Do you know, I *will* hand in my notice on Monday." Lara felt strong for the first time in ages. Rob shook her hand and patted her on the back.

"Congratulations, this is the beginning of your new life." Which hopefully would involve Rob and Megan, she thought. "Let's drink another toast." He got up and was about to get the glasses from the kitchen.

"Rob, I've got a flight early in the morning." She looked at him with a smile painted on. Rob went back and sat with her.

"What time will you be back? We can wait up for you." He held her hand again. She liked the feeling of him being so close.

"As it's unofficial I'm not sure what airport we will be leaving from, but on past experience it won't be a civil one. The car is picking me up at seven thirty tomorrow morning and I'm scheduled to be dropped back home at seven in the evening." Lara looked at her watch and realised that she should be making tracks to bed. Rob got the hint.

"Megan and I will do a spot of sightseeing, she's desperate to have a ride on that frog-looking monstrosity." Rob shook his head. "Bloody ridiculous if you ask me."

"Ah, you mean the Duck Tours. I think it's quite unique, road and river in one vehicle. It'll be fun, honest. You'll enjoy it." She wished she could go with them.

"Well, I'll let you know tomorrow evening. If you are back at seven then we have the whole evening to go out and enjoy." He kissed her on the cheek. "Now you get off to bed. I'll see you tomorrow night."

"Thank you for a lovely evening. The meal was amazing. I can't believe you remembered all my favourites." She tried to stifle a yawn. "Oh, sorry. I'm exhausted. I'll be as quiet as I can in the morning. No point in getting you up too early. I'll see you in the evening. Any change of plans I'll text or ring you. Good night Rob." She walked into her bedroom, closing the door gently behind her. She leant on it for a few seconds, willing it to open with him pushing her onto the bed. What was she thinking, she was too tired even to undress herself, let alone engage in carnal activity! She moved away from the door, smiling to herself. She set her alarm before she forgot, got ready for bed and was asleep before she had time to collect her thoughts of the evening.

Rob finished in the kitchen, looked into Lara's study where Megan was on a bed/settee and checked Megan was in it, and went off to the guest bedroom, passing Lara's bedroom door and hovering for a moment. He would have loved to have opened her door and sneak in beside her, just to feel the warmth of her body close to his. It was the main thing Rob had missed when Jill had gone. For five years he had been celibate, but Lara was waking up feelings in him that he thought had died with Jill. He didn't think he was betraying Jill, feeling like he did. In fact, he thought Jill would approve. He shook himself out of his musing and went to bed.

Lara had been right. She was taken to a private airfield in Kent and from there flown to Rome. In the old days her adrenalin would have kicked in and she would have flirted with the pilot looking so handsome in his uniform. But she wasn't feeling well, late nights and early mornings took their toll on her. She had the evening to look forward to though, which was something. She just hoped the meeting would go as planned and she would be leaving Rome at 3.30 p.m. that afternoon.

All went well and she arrived at the Italian airfield a little after 3 p.m. on the homeward journey. London traffic wasn't too bad; it being a Saturday the offices were mainly closed. They made good time and she was at her front door by 6.30 p.m. Rob and Megan were very pleased that she was back safe and sound and early. They told her about their day, knowing she wasn't allowed to speak about her own. Rob had booked a table at the restaurant around the corner called Le Pied Du Cochon. Lara had giggled.

"Do you not like the restaurant? Megan looked it up on the internet and it had good reviews." Rob looked worried.

"No, it's just that I went there the other day with Johnny English." Megan and Rob looked at her as if she had gone slightly mad. "I'll explain over dinner. I think it would amuse you both. I need a shower. What time is it booked for?"

"Eight o'clock. I'll pour you a drink, it will help you unwind." Rob went into the kitchen while Lara decided what to wear. Megan had followed her in and was helping her chose. Rob coughed at the door. "Oh, thank you Rob." She took a glass of red wine from him. He chinked her glass with his. She could so get used to family life. "Now out you two, or I'll never be ready in time." They went off to change. Lara watched as they went. Yes, she thought smiling, she could really get used to it.

The evening went too quickly. Lara explained about Hugo, much to Rob and Megan's amusement. Megan thought it hilarious that Lara had caught a taxi for the three-minute journey from her home to the restaurant. Rob felt for Lara's vulnerability. She laughed with them, but he could see how much she wanted a normal life, which her job wasn't allowing. He would ring her on Monday to check she had handed in her notice. The sooner they got the ball rolling the sooner Lara could have a normal social life.

All too soon they were at Gatwick Airport saying goodbye. Megan thanked Lara for the best time ever. Rob held her tight.

"You take care of yourself. And make sure that letter goes off tomorrow. I'll ring you in the evening." He kissed her again on the lips, but not lingering, just a peck. To her it seemed a little more than on the cheek, but not enough to call a proper kiss. She leant over and kissed Megan. They had become firm friends.

"Safe journey you two. I'll be over soon to see you." She waved as they disappeared through the North Terminal doors. She walked back to her car very downhearted. She'd miss them; on a positive note though, tomorrow was Monday, and as Rob said, the beginning of her new life.

CHAPTER 6

~~~

For the sixteenth time Lara remembered Megan's birthday. This was the first year she could actually celebrate it. She telephoned Rob a week before to make sure he wouldn't mind if she bought her a present.

"Of course I don't mind." Rob was just pleased to speak with Lara. They hadn't contacted each other for a few days with Lara having been exceptionally busy, interviewing numerous applicants for her own replacement. "What did you have in mind?"

"Well, I know it sounds daft, but I'd love to get her a little scooter. I just thought with all her jobs and school activities, it would be useful for her to have less time travelling and more time to do her homework." Rob knew exactly what Lara meant, but wasn't enamoured by the idea. She'd have to sell it to him. "Obviously you would have to put ground rules in place first; like no going on the major roads. Always wearing her helmet. No taking anyone else on it." Rob got the gist.

"Ok, you've won me over. She'll be thrilled. Thank you, Lara. So, how's the interviewing going?" That was easier than she thought. She thought she'd have a battle on her hands persuading him. Perhaps he was mellowing, or he realised that Lara had Megan's best interests at heart. Either way she was grateful.

"I cannot believe how young the applicants are, and how eager. I was just like them when it all began. The idea of a job that took you to all the corners of Europe and beyond was a dream. How can I tell them that they will have no social life to speak of? That they will be burned out by the time they reach thirty. Just interviewing these kids has made me more positive that I am doing the right thing in getting out now." Rob agreed with her.

"Leave it to the youngsters. Us oldies need more sedate life styles." She knew he was teasing her, but she agreed with him. "Anyway, changing the subject back to Megan's birthday, we're having a quiet day with a few of her friends. But the first weekend of the Easter holidays I am throwing her a surprise party, with the help of Chloe. I'll email you the dates. I hope you can make it over. Your old room will be waiting for you. Please say you will come." Lara didn't need to think it over.

"Of course I will. I wouldn't miss it for the world." She had an ulterior motive for going over to Portugal. She wanted to look at the cost of small villas over there. Her Portuguese was still fluent so she could use that to her advantage. "I'll book my flights and let you know when they are. Not sure whether I'll be coming from Bournemouth or Gatwick." She had been visiting her parents more often and had arranged to see them over Easter. "I'll get onto the bike shop in Almancil and organise delivery of the scooter. Thank you for letting me do that Rob. I hope she likes it." Rob laughed.

"Of course she'll love it. What teenage girl wouldn't? She'd have to wait another year in England of course. Not sure if that's a good thing. At least they are private roads all round here, not sure I'll allow her out on the major ones. It's very generous of you Lara. You are a very thoughtful person. I haven't even thought of what to get her yet. I was thinking some jewellery. What do you think?" Lara was flattered that he was asking her opinion.

"I think that a wonderful idea. Those charm bracelets seem to be all the fashion at the moment. Thomas Sabo are to die for. Adam has just bought Tori one for her birthday. She won't wear it though, says it's too good to wear." She could hear Rob laughing.

"I do love your sister. She is a one-off." He thought Lara was unique too. "That's a good idea though. I'll go on the internet and see if they deliver over here. She has always loved jewellery. She's had most of Jill's over the years, but something special of her own would be nice. I'm glad I asked you." So was she. It made her realise that Rob was including her in his family. She went back to work with a happier heart.

Lara had organised a pink scooter with matching pink helmet to be delivered during breakfast on Megan's birthday. Megan couldn't wait to phone her and thank her. She caught Lara as she was going out of the door. Lara promised to talk to her properly that evening, and wished her a very happy and safe birthday. She told her to post a photo of herself on her scooter on Facebook so she could see how grown up she looked. Megan promised she'd do it as soon as she'd finished her breakfast. Again, Lara wished she had been there to see Megan's face, but perhaps in the not too distant future she'd be nearer them both.

Lara arrived in Portugal on the Friday evening, the day before the surprise party. Rob had gone to pick her up and told Megan she was coming over for a few days' rest. As she got through passport control she caught sight of Rob on the balcony above waving frantically. She waved back and rushed through the automatic door. Rob ran down the stairs from the gallery and swept her off her feet in an affectionate Rob cuddle.

"Hello stranger." He put her back down and looked at her. "You are a sight for sore eyes. Come on, let's get out of here." He took her case from her and led the way to the carpark. "Megan is waiting at home. She wanted to come but Chloe had popped over to give me final numbers for tomorrow and Megan thought she'd come to see her. So Chloe had to make up a problem for her to solve." Rob was glad to get out of the house. "How's finding your replacement going?"

"Well, so far so good. I've narrowed the candidates down, now it is up to William to decide." Lara realised Rob was looking puzzled. "Hague? Our Foreign Secretary?" Rob nodded.

"Sorry, I forgot you were on first name terms with

government ministers." He laughed. "Are they annoyed that you want to go?"

"Not really. I think they understand that I need some life after government. They are married and have their families; I started straight from university and haven't had time to get a social life let alone a family of my own."

"Hopefully things will change now. You have the rest of your life to enjoy." Rob had moved his hand off the gear stick and squeezed her hand. She looked up at him and he was smiling. "First social event of the year, Megan's Sweet Sixteenth Birthday Party. Only the elite of Portugal will be attending." She laughed. She had missed Rob and his sense of humour.

They arrived at the villa, with Megan, having heard the gates open, standing on the doorstep. She rushed out to meet Lara.

"It's so lovely to see you. Did you get my thank you letter? Would you like to see my scooter?" She had Lara by the hand and was leading her towards the garage.

"Megan, Lara is here to rest. You can show her tomorrow. She's been at work all day and then travelling, leave her to at least get a glass of wine inside her." Megan looked apologetic. She was so excited that she hadn't thought why Lara needed to rest. Perhaps she was ill. But then she wouldn't have been at work. She'd never understand adults.

"I did get your thank you letter, Megan. It was very thoughtful of you to include the photo. You looked very trendy on your scooter. You reminded me of the models in the sixties." Megan liked that idea. "Let me have that drink your father promised me, then I'll have a quick look at your scooter." Megan took her hand and led her into the villa. Lara had been diplomatic as always, thought Rob. He followed with the case. He couldn't fault Megan being so excited about Lara's visit. If the truth be known, he was just as excited.

Lara took Megan out for the afternoon in Rob's car, on the pretext of choosing some new curtains and matching cushions for the lounge. Rob had said it was a woman thing, and he had no idea of interior design. Lara knew that to be untrue. Rob had a brilliant eye for colour but it did the trick. Megan was totally unaware that it was a ruse to get her out of the villa until Lara got the all-clear phone call from Rob. Lara looked at the properties for sale as they drove off to Faro. She'd taken a mental note of the name of the agents and would check on the internet for the prices later. They'd managed to get fitted curtains, exactly the right size and beautiful cushions from Faro by 6 p.m. Megan wanted to get home to show her father what they had found. Lara text Rob to see whether they could start making their way back. His text back was simple 'ok'.

As they drove up, Lara couldn't see any cars, people or movement. In fact, the villa looked empty. As the gates closed behind them Chloe and another friend came from round the back garden holding a banner. It read, 'Happy 16th Birthday Megan – The Party is Here!'

Megan looked round at Lara who was smiling. Suddenly people spilled out of the front door blowing whistles and waving flags. There must have been at least fifty adults and children coming out of the house. Chloe led Megan round the side to the back garden, where Rob had set up the bar-b-q and the pool had beautiful lilies floating on the top, with candles lit in the middle of them. The whole garden looked like something from Hollywood. Megan ran into her father's arms.

"Thank you, Daddy." She was crying with happiness. She then turned to Chloe, knowing she had to have something to do with it. "Thank you, Chloe, you're the best." They were hugging when suddenly the whole party erupted into a chorus of 'Happy Birthday to You.' Lara went over to join Rob and was introduced to Chloe's parents and Abi's. Everyone was so friendly. That would never happen in London, Lara thought. Neighbours didn't do more than a civil nod of recognition while putting out the wheelie bin.

The evening ended with karaoke, where all the guests insisted on hearing the birthday girl sing a few numbers. She didn't disappoint. Lara noticed that the atmosphere when Megan sang changed. She had captured the whole audience within the first few bars of each song. No one talked over her singing. Most even stopped drinking and eating. The power her voice had over anyone who listened was phenomenal. Lara wiped a tear from her eye. That little girl over there singing to all those people was hers. Rob crept up behind her.

"I hope you are proud of your daughter." He whispered into her ear. "You deserve to be." Lara turned to face him. She noticed his eyes were welling up too. For a split-second Lara thought he was going to kiss her, but he smiled at her and turned back to the bar-b-q. It had been at that moment that Lara realised she loved that man very much. Would he ever love her back?

Megan slept most of Sunday morning, while Rob and Lara tidied up. They chatted about Lara's future. She'd told him that she was still thinking of teaching. She thought it would be fun. What she hadn't said was where. She had been busy during the party, the previous night, talking to a number of expats who agreed life would be easier if they could speak at least a little Portuguese, but they were lackadaisical about learning, as most of the people in that area spoke English. They told her that the classes all seemed to be either in Faro or the other end of the Algarve in Lagos and Portimão. There was obviously an opening for a small set-up run from home in that area. She'd have to see what the legality of the idea was on the internet. Different countries had different working laws. Hopefully it was feasible, but she'd not say anything until she'd developed her plan in detail.

Rob and Megan took her to the airport that evening. Although Lara was sad to go, she went knowing in her mind that she'd be back. Megan gave her a hug and thanked her for coming. She wandered off to buy a magazine in the paper shop. They were more up-to-date at the airport than in town. Rob took hold of her.

"We always seem to be saying goodbye. It doesn't get any easier, in fact it's getting harder." He placed a kiss on her lips, this time for a little longer. Lara could hear her own heart thumping. He pulled away too soon.

"Goodbye Rob, take care. Thank you for inviting me over. I'll speak to you soon." She wanted to go and not prolong the farewell. She looked at Rob and couldn't work out what his face was saying. He looked really sad. "Hey, it's normally you telling me to cheer up. We will see each other soon. I promise." There wasn't time to tell him her plans then. Her flight was being called.

"Are you sure you can't stay for a bit longer?" He knew she couldn't.

"I'm in Brussels on Tuesday evening for a conference on Wednesday, and not quite so bad I have a lunchtime meeting to attend in Dublin on Friday, but should be back by the early evening, as long as it doesn't drag on. It depends if alcohol is served. I'll ring you on Friday evening and we can have a lovely chat." She was smiling. Her flight was called again. Megan got back in time to say a final goodbye and Lara was off through to Security. She turned to watch them leave. Megan had grabbed her dad and was steering him back to the carpark. At least he had Megan.

On Friday night she didn't get back until quite late. Alcohol had been served at the lunch, which drew out the speeches, as usual. She pressed in the passcode on the front door, checked her mailbox and then moved on to her flat. She walked up to her front door where she found a crumpled body leaning against it. It wasn't normally an area for homeless people. Her jangling keys disturbed his slumber. It was Rob. Before Lara could say anything, he took her key off her, unlocked her door. Put in the alarm code. Pulled her gently into her hallway, and kissed her passionately for what seemed like hours. Eventually he let her go.

"Good trip?" He said nonchalantly, hiding the fact very well that he had been petrified of that moment all day. What if he had read all the signs wrong and she had slapped him across the face? After all he was totally out of practice where dating was concerned. He looked into her eyes; she had said nothing to him since her arrival back at the flat. She was absolutely mesmerised by his presence. "Earth calling Lara, come in Lara." He helped her off with her coat, steered her into the lounge, and placed her gently on the sofa. He sat next to her. It was then he noticed the tears. Oh dear, he thought. Maybe he had misread her signals. He wanted the floor to open up and suck him back to Portugal. Lara took a deep breath, grabbed his hands and looked into his eyes.

"Oh Rob. Do you know how long I've waited for you to do that? I love you so much. I've wanted to tell you on loads of occasions, but the timing never seemed to be appropriate." He snatched her up into his arms again.

"I've felt exactly the same way. After I had got over the guilt of betraying Jill I then had to protect Megan. But now you are best friends, and I've made my peace with Jill, I feel able to let my true feelings out and shout from the rooftops 'I'm falling for Lara Allen'." She put her hand gently over his mouth. It was very late and her neighbours probably need not know all the details of her personal life.

"Where're my manners? Would you like a drink? You must have been waiting outside a while. I'm afraid the meeting went on longer than scheduled, but when it's in Dublin you have to add on at least an hour. The Irish are very sociable and friendly, to get them back to the matter in hand is challenging at the best of times." She realised she was wittering. She did that when she was nervous. Rob had the best answer, covering her mouth with his. This time he was passionate, and slightly forceful. Lara loved it. She was beginning to think that all their kisses were going to be friendly but phlegmatic. Rather like a kiss from a great aunt. Without spoiling the moment, Rob stood up, pulled Lara to her feet and led her to her bedroom. He took one more look for assurance that it was what she wanted too, and his query was confirmed by a simple smile.

Having had a very late night, both Lara and Rob stayed in bed most of Saturday morning. Lara had anticipated a lazy day after her travels, and so she had stocked up on croissants, pains aux raisins and fruit juice, positively her favourite weekend breakfast.

They had a lot to talk about. Firstly for a few months Rob had been soul-searching and had told Lara that Jill would have been pleased with his choice of girlfriend. His conscience was appeased by a conversation he had had with his own mother. She loved Jill like a daughter and knew that she would have wanted Rob to be happy. She also knew of the sacrifice Lara had made to the couple when they needed a child. Who better to help mend Rob's heart than the one person Jill loved unconditionally, Lara.

Rob had held Lara close to him as he explained to her his inner most worries. Lara just listened. She knew he had to dispel all feelings of guilt before he could move on.

"I know in my heart that Jill would want us both to be happy. If that means having you by my side for as long as we both shall live, I'm hoping she is looking down smiling. As for Megan, she already respects you and as far as I can judge, likes you enormously." He noticed Lara's demeanour change. "Can you see a problem?"

"My only concern is that Megan has had you to herself for a long time now. What I don't want to do is to make her think she is losing you. We will have to move very slowly, making sure she is happy with each step." Lara knew only too well how jealous a teenager could get over her dad. She and Tori had quite a few battles vying for their dad's attention.

"What's your suggestion? Shall we tell her who you really are? Maybe that would stop her feeling left out." No, thought Lara. What part of 'move very slowly' did Rob not grasp?

"On no account must we overwhelm her with that, while she is getting used to us being together. She is by no means stupid Rob. If she hasn't picked up on the closeness between us already, I'll be very surprised. We will have to gauge her reactions to us wanting to be together more often. But we can balance it with me having time alone with her too. She's the age where she'll need a mother figure in her life. I'll be proud if she accepts me in that role. She'll have plenty of time off when her exams are over, I'll invite her and Chloe over for a girlie sleepover in London." Lara already liked the idea.

"How brilliant you are. Will the government survive without you? Now we have all that sorted, what about you?" Lara took a deep breath.

"When I've worked my notice, I'm thinking of renting in Portugal until I find somewhere. From there I'm considering giving Portuguese lessons to the expats, and English lessons to the business community in the area. That should keep me busy for a while. What do you think?" Rob looked ecstatic.

"Why not stay at mine? It will be cheaper for you, and I can be near you all the time." Again, Rob hadn't listened. Lara rather liked the 'little boy' quality about Rob.

"Not the best idea, Megan may see through that one. Softly, softly approach until we are sure she is ok with the idea, remember?" Rob looked like he was sulking.

"I wish I was as clever as you." He smiled. He was

teasing her again. "So when will you be moving to Portugal?" Now Rob had her, he didn't want to let her go.

"Hopefully before the summer holidays. I have to tell my parents yet. Let's just enjoy this weekend." She snuggled down under the duvet. "Now, where were we?" Rob joined her.

Monday morning was bleak, well, bleaker than usual. Rob had caught an early train back to the airport and Lara had to be in the office early to arrange the tests for the shortlisted applicants. They had to translate four speeches of different languages into English in the time allocated then they had to translate one back to the original language orally in a special booth. This was to make sure they could work in confined spaces without feeling claustrophobic. Many times Lara had to work in the language booths in different countries and it took some getting used to. She felt like a fish in a bowl as they were normally glazed for the speaker to be able to see his or her interpreter.

While waiting for her 'lambs to the slaughter' arrive, she checked her emails. She had set up a website to see how many takers she could get for her language tutoring project in Portugal. Much to her surprise and delight she had had quite a few hits. There were hits from English, Irish and Germans and a few from Belgium which suited her a great deal as that would keep her French, German and Portuguese up to scratch. More interestingly, there was also an enquiry from the European High School in Almancil, which was where Megan was at school. They taught parallel to English schools up to A Level certificates. They needed a language teacher for French and Portuguese, other languages a bonus. She thought that very exciting. With her university qualifications, she had a teaching certificate that she had never used. Until she built up a client list for her home school a more regular income would be brilliant. She emailed them immediately for an application form. Her future was looking very optimistic. Maybe Mondays weren't quite so bad after all.

There was one other email from her sister and it needed an urgent response. She was asking Lara down next weekend to a family meal on the Saturday night. Why hadn't she just telephoned her? Actually, she probably had. Lara had put her phone on silent so her and Rob didn't get interrupted with calls from her work. She checked her phone; there was a voice message and text message from Tori. Both said the same thing, well that hadn't given anything away. Lara didn't have time to ring so emailed her answer. She would go down at the weekend, see what Tori had wanted the family for, (she's probably pregnant, thought Lara) and tell them about her plans.

She Skyped Rob when she got home and told him about the European High School's job. Megan would have left by September so it wouldn't embarrass her. Rob thought it was fate. How often did those jobs come up? She was chatting to Rob for so long that it was bedtime and she still hadn't called her sister. At least she would have got her email so that should do. Guilt got the better of her. She picked up the phone and rang her sister.

"Tori, is everything alright?" She could hear the television in the background so knew she hadn't rung too late.

"Lala, am I glad to hear your voice. I've been trying to get

hold of you all weekend. Where have you been?" Lara wondered if she should lie, a little fib wouldn't hurt. She could say she was in Mozambique where the signal was crap. She couldn't do that to her sister.

"Sorry, I had my phone on silent so the office couldn't get hold of me. I was entertaining a gentleman caller." Tori screamed. "Ouch!" Lara smiled. She was glad she'd told Tori the truth, but she needn't say any more until next weekend.

"Anyone we know?" Tori was fishing. Lara changed the subject.

"Well, tell me, what is so urgent?" Lara nearly said 'apart from being pregnant' but that would have stolen Tori's thunder.

"I'm pregnant!" She was screaming again. *"It's due before Christmas. Are you coming down for the weekend? Mum and Dad are over the moon and want to celebrate. Mum's so excited to be a grandmother at last."* If only she knew. Lara said she'd be there. It would be an ideal opportunity to tell them all her news. But for now, it was Tori's moment.

"That's wonderful news, sweetie. I can't wait to see you on Saturday and give Adam a pat on the back. We'll be able to catch up on all our news." She said goodnight to her sister, and went off to bed. At least now she had her daughter back in her life so she could enjoy Tori's euphoria.

Megan had been staying at Chloe's house for the weekend. They had been very busy but unfortunately not on their revision. Knowing where her father was made her more determined to defy him. But on reflection, she realised she was being a spoilt brat and her father deserved some happiness. It was the teenager in her that was jealous. She'd had her father to herself for a long time, she felt resentful to share him. She was off to boarding school in September, would her dad even miss her once Lara moved in? But she liked Lara. Her emotions were everywhere, which was why she resorted to the one thing that helped her escape, singing. Megan had taken Chloe to her house and had set up her recording equipment.

"Are you sure about this Megs? Think of the repercussions when your dad finds out." Chloe was concerned for her friend. She knew how Megan was feeling, and was sure when she got used to the idea all would be fine.

"I'm not doing it out of spite, Chlo, I'm doing it for myself. Just think how wonderful it would be if I got through and became famous. We could do anything we wanted without having to ask all the time." Chloe wasn't sure it worked like that, but she would support her friend. Megan set up the video recorder, fed the backing track through, did a couple of practice runs and then she was ready. She queued Chloe with a signal and the track started. Megan had chosen 'Make You Feel My Love', originally Bob Dylan's, but to make it more current she used Adele's version for the backing track.

"That's a wrap." Chloe felt so important. She switched off the recorder and video, rewound them, and played it back. "Oh Megs, it's brilliant. Right, now what do we do?" Megan got out the page she had printed off the internet. She had to load her video onto her computer and then send it to the Official *Make Me A Star UK* web page. With the video, she had to tell them something about herself. They also wanted a copy of her birth certificate.

"I don't have a birth certificate. Mum said it got lost and

she hadn't bothered to get a duplicate because I have a passport. If I photocopy that, do you think it will do?" Chloe nodded enthusiastically. She seemed more excited than Megan. Her best friend may get to meet Mason Morgan, chief executive of record and entertainment company Mamo, and judge on reality TV hit shows *Make Me A Star UK* and *USA*; she could barely contain her emotions. She realised she was screaming. Megan gave her a look. Chloe calmed down. Megan laughed.

"Oh Chlo, you are funny. Besties forever." She hugged Chloe and then got on with the job in hand. They managed to download the video and application and received an acknowledgement via email almost immediately. They both screamed and hugged. The waiting began.

Lara got to Bournemouth on the Saturday morning, near lunchtime. Tori was in the kitchen with her mum.

"Cooee, I'm home." Lara always entered the house with that utterance. Her mum and dad loved it. She'd done the same ritual since she was a little girl home from school. Tori rushed out of the kitchen.

"Lala, you're going to be an auntie. Isn't it exciting?" Lara cuddled her sister. Her mother came out of the kitchen and joined in the embrace.

"I'm going to be a grandma. Isn't it wonderful" Lara felt a little guilty. Her mother had been a grandma for sixteen years, if only she'd known.

"It's brilliant news. I've just bought the book *Etiquette of Modern Aunts*, to make sure I get it right." Tori looked at her sister, never quite knowing when she was winding her up. Lara was grinning.

"Oh Lala. You shouldn't tease me. My hormones are all over the place, I may cry at any moment. Be gentle with my feelings." Lara saw through Tori's attempt for sympathy, it wasn't going to work.

"So, are you being sick yet?" Debbie decided to leave the sisters to their warped sense of humour. She put the kettle on and busied herself getting lunch. It was so nice to have the whole family together; she'd missed it.

"Luckily I seem to have a period of the day around six in the evening that I'm not at my best, but it soon passes ready for dinner. I have to say my appetite has got massive. Adam says I've already put on a few pounds. But he says it's cuddly. He's an angel." Tori sighed. She was still very much in love. Long may it be so, thought Lara.

The men came in from the garden. Lara gave her dad a big kiss, and then congratulated Adam. Debbie had made a roast, as it was the girls' favourite, and she knew Lara wouldn't bother cooking one for herself. They sat down and caught up on all the gossip. Pete wondered why Lara was so quiet; not like her, he thought.

"You ok darling? You've been very quiet. Anything you want to divulge at the dining table?" She looked up at him. He was probably the only other person, apart from Rob, that actually got Lara. She looked up from her plate. It was time to drop the bombshell.

"I've handed in my notice at work. It's been getting too much for me recently, I decided I needed to settle down." Lara watched their faces. They all looked shocked apart from Pete.

"And what brought this turn of events to fruition? Could

it be a lad?" Debbie laughed.

"I think you mean a man, Pete. Lara is a little old to be with a lad." Thanks Ma thought Lara. But she knew what she meant.

"If you must know, I'm courting, yes." She loved winding the family up.

"Courting, get you." Tori hadn't heard that old-fashioned term used since her grandmother was alive. "Come on then, tell us who the bloke is?" Debbie suddenly drew in a sharp breath.

"It's not Rob, is it?" She was sure there was chemistry between them at the wedding. "Not that that's not good. He's a lovely chap. Is it?" Lara looked to see if they were judging her. All she could see in their faces was anticipation laced with love for her.

"Yes, it's Rob." She needed to explain while she had their undivided attention. "We've got very close over the last few months. It'll be difficult with Megan, but hopefully we can bring her round to thinking it's a good idea. I want her to think of it as gaining a mother rather than losing a dad. Not easy, but we are working on it, slowly." The irony was that she *was* gaining a mother, *her* mother. "The only problem is that I'd like to move to Portugal. We won't be living together. Not yet anyway, I'll be renting for a while. But that means you can come and stay whenever you like." Everyone was quiet. She continued. "My plan is to teach English out there to the expats. I've even been offered a job at the local school teaching French and Portuguese. Someone say something." Pete got out of his chair and went over and hugged her.

"Well I for one will be glad you are out of that job. And as long as you live near a golf course I'll be over as often as the planes are running, now I've opted for early retirement." Tori wasn't quite so forgiving.

"What about your auntie duties? You'll miss your niece or nephew growing up." She was pouting and sniffing. But a smile came to her face when Lara looked at her. Lara knew Tori was happy for her really.

"Well there is another option." Lara was on a roll. "There are plenty of empty shops in the neighbourhood out there, crying out for a hairdressing salon. The expats and holidaymakers would much prefer English speakers for the gossip. Dad could help Rob in the golf shops, and Adam could teach at the school. Baby Sinclair would grow up bilingual and with a healthy outdoor childhood." Tori and Adam were thinking about it, she could tell by the looks they were giving each other. Pete was all for it.

"Well after twenty-five years of delivering the post in all weathers, that is my idea of heaven. What about you Debs? Just think, hardly any cancellations because it's raining!" Debbie looked very pensive.

"I'd have to work out some figures. I suppose I could put feelers out to the local agents to see what the business is worth. It's not insurmountable." She got a big hug from Pete. "I'm not promising anything." She got another hug from Pete. She smiled. "So, what are you doing about Megan?" Debbie could see that if the situation wasn't handled properly all the plans would be for nothing.

"I'm going to invite her over to London for half-term with her friend Chloe. I'll spoil them and hope that she realises I love her as much as her father." Debbie admired Lara. To take on another man's child was problematic in itself, but when you weren't used to children yourself, that was one nightmare waiting to happen. Debbie didn't envy her daughter. Of course she didn't know the whole truth, and may never.

It was about two weeks later that the email arrived. Megan was through to the live auditions. She tried to contain her excitement so her father wouldn't ask any questions, but once at school she couldn't keep it in any longer.

"Chloe, I'm through!!!" They jumped up and down holding each other's hands. Jeremy Dixon from the swimming-pool shop gave them a very strange look.

"I always thought you two were lesbians!" Megan turned her head towards him and poked out her tongue. Nothing could upset her that day.

"What's next?" Chloe needed to act as manager, she had the practice, and after all she had been in charge of Megan's bookings at Monty's for months. Well, Megan let her think that. Bless Chloe; Megan wanted her to share in her euphoria for as long as it lasted.

"Well, I put Lara's address down as my English home. So now they have got me into the London auditions, which are at the O2 Arena. Luckily, I know where that is now. Anyway, it's at the end of May during half-term. Our next objective is to get an invite over to Lara's. Any ideas?" Chloe took a deep breath.

"Well I know this is pretty unorthodox for you, but why don't you just ask her?" Megan laughed. The simple solutions were normally the best.

What Megan didn't know was that Rob and Lara wanted to encourage Megan over for a few bonding days. She had played straight into their hands. The ulterior motives were flying backward and forward from London to Portugal more often than a budget airline!

Lara had spent the previous few days stocking up on what she thought teenage girls ate. From wraps and bagels, to coke and crisps. She was looking forward to their visit. Unfortunately, due to the fact she would be leaving her post very soon, she had only managed a couple of days off toward the end of their stay. She had organised some Oyster cards for them so they could explore London, and had bought underground and street maps to help. Megan had told her that they had their first day organised and were meeting friends across town. Lara thought that so grown up; maybe she was worrying too much. She didn't want to fuss or she would alienate Megan. At least she had Chloe with her, safety in numbers.

She picked the girls up from Gatwick airport and drove them straight to her apartment. They had time to change before she took them to a fantastic restaurant, where the picture of the food to be ordered was projected onto their table so they could decide what they liked the look of before they ordered it. The girls were entranced. While waiting for their food, there were a few games on the device. They could also watch the chefs in the kitchen prepare their meal. It was amazing. While eating they could project a theme to enhance their table, they chose palm trees swaying over a beautiful warm beach. The whole table was bathed in sunshine, while outside it was windy and growing dark. It was definitely a hit. Lara gave herself an imaginary pat on the back. So far so good, she thought.

The next day Lara had gone before the girls got up. That helped their plan. No one left too early to go shopping as most of the shops didn't open before ten o'clock; thus Lara's suspicions weren't aroused unnecessarily. But as soon as they heard the flat door close they were up. They needed to be away around eight. Megan remembered which Underground they needed and made their way to Victoria. From there they took the Tube to Westminster and changed to the Jubilee line to North Greenwich. As they walked up the stairs from the Tube into the daylight they could see the O2 Arena opposite. What they also saw were streams of people heading the same way. The queue was already massive. After a few hours, they managed to get to the desk holding all the entrants names and numbered labels to be stuck on each contestant. Megan proudly gave her name, showed them her passport and was assigned a number that she stuck on her t-shirt. They were then ushered into a holding room.

People were singing to themselves connected to iPods, oblivious to all around. Megan had decided to sing another Adele song, for luck, as the first one had paid off. She had chosen 'Chasing Pavements' as Chloe had said it brought out the versatility of her voice. Megan knew it made her cry and she felt the judges would see she was one with the lyrics.

It had already been a long day. They were both tired and thirsty. They had taken a few cans of coke with them, but Megan needed water. Chloe went off in search of a machine;

she'd seen one on the way through, in the foyer. Megan's voice was paramount. She went into the ladies and warmed her voice up with a couple of scales. She felt a little silly, but it was easier than doing it outside in front of everyone. Chloe found her as she was coming out of the loo. She had managed to get two bottles of water and a Mars Bar to share. Just as Megan had taken a bite her number was called. She gulped down some water and followed Chloe towards the girl with the headset who had been calling her number. She ushered them into the backstage area.

"Oh, my goodness, Megs, there's Sean O'Shea." Chloe was awestruck. Megan had to push her on a little further until they got to where the girl was pointing. In front of them were loads of screens, all playing the scene on the stage at that moment. Sean walked towards Megan.

"Hi 3365, how are you?" Megan laughed. He was very clever. He'd seen she was in a trance and had pulled her back. "That's better, a smile. Now, no point in telling you not to be nervous, but try to relax a little. Enjoy your moment. So, what's your real name?" Megan relaxed, a little.

"Megan Simpson." She was nervous, but excited too.

"Well Megan, good luck." Megan turned and said thank you as a sound engineer signalled for her to climb up the steps towards the stage. He thrust a microphone into her hands and pushed her gently to the back of the stage.

"Just keep walking until you see the cross marked at the front of the stage, that's where you need to stand. Ok?" She mouthed 'ok' back to him. He put his thumb up to her and smiled. She thought even a small gesture like that was so kind. He must have done it thousands of times already that day, but it was still kind. He counted down from five with his fingers and gave her another gentle push on one. She walked into an eerie glare and heard applause. She kept looking on the floor for the marker she'd been told to stand on by the sound engineer. It was hard to see anything until her eyes adjusted to the beam of the spotlights. She found the spot, looked up and she could actually see the judges in front of her.

Chloe was grasping Sean's arm as she watched on the screens. Sean didn't seem to mind, he was smiling.

"Hello, what's your name?" Eamon Maguire had just spoken to her. Another big record producer and judge. It was real and she had to block all other thoughts from her mind.

"Megan Simpson." She took a deep breath and looked at the audience. It was difficult to see them, but she knew they were there. She smiled.

"And where are you from Megan?" Why is he asking all these questions? She just wanted to sing.

"I actually live in Portugal at the moment." She hoped that was it. Now can she sing, please! Mason had other ideas.

"How old are you Megan?" Megan replied that she had recently celebrated her sixteenth birthday. Judges Emma P and Tamara Mills, both from iconic girl bands, looked at each other and smiled.

"And what are you going to sing for us?" Megan said Adele's 'Chasing Pavements'. "Good choice. Best of luck Megan, this is your moment, enjoy it." Megan smiled at him. His voice alone had relaxed her. She closed her eyes as the introduction started and wiped the audience out of her mind. She was now standing at Vale Do Lobo, singing to the children dancing in the square. She started singing. The audience were quiet. No one wanted to miss a note from this young girl. Eamon looked over the girls to Mason and smiled. He was smiling too. Emma P looked behind her to check to see if there was anyone in the auditorium, it was so quiet. As she turned back she noticed Tamara had tears in her eyes. By the last verse Emma P had joined Tamara, dabbing her eyes, trying not to smear her make-up. As the last note faded the whole arena erupted and the audience were up on their feet. The judges were up on their feet too. Mason turned to see the audience and was nodding his head in agreement with their ovation. It was the first time that season that the audience had all shown so much pleasure. After a few minutes, when the audience had taken their seats, Mason spoke.

"Oh, my goodness, Megan you are what this show is about." The audience erupted again. He tried to talk over them but had to wait. Megan was crying. The emotion of the song and the atmosphere had got to her.

"Megan, why are you crying? You have just done a wonderful audition." Eamon was trying to cheer her up. But they weren't tears of failure they were tears of joy. Idiot, thought Chloe, who was watching on the monitors.

Megan smiled. She didn't want to play the sympathy card, so she wasn't going to explain she was singing it for her mother and hoped she was listening. Emma P wanted to speak. She held her hand up to silence the audience as best she could.

"Girl, you brought that song to life. You felt every word you were singing. That song obviously meant a lot to you, tell us why you were crying."

"I used to sing to my mother before she died, it always made her smile. I was just hoping my mother is smiling now." Megan thought that was enough information. Tamara Mills tried to hold back her tears again.

"Oh, my goodness, your mother would be so proud of you. I know she's watching now. Well done." Tamara Mills managed to say leaning forward speaking into her microphone, with her voice shaking. She was trying not to cry again. "I can't even put into words what your voice did to me, apart from giving me goosebumps all over." She smiled at Megan. They voted. There was a 'massive yes' from Eamon; a '100% yes' from Emma P; and an 'Absolutely Yes' from Tamara Mills. Then Mason spoke.

"Megan, at sixteen you have probably had to grow up quicker than most through your mother's illness." Megan realised he had read the blog on her audition video. "But you have a massive talent which I want you to share. It's a big yes from me too. Megan, you have four yes's, well done." He winked at her and smiled. There was a roar from the audience so Megan had to mouth a big 'thank you' to the judges, as they weren't able to hear her. She left the stage, handing the microphone to the sound engineer. She was lucky Sean was waiting at the bottom of the steps. He caught her as she almost fell off the bottom few. He hugged her.

"Well done Hun, see you at bootcamp." Another hurdle to get over, she thought, but she was determined. Chloe joined in the hugging. Megan felt on top of the world. She didn't realise the buzz she had left at the judges' table. She looked at her watch. It was dark outside. They had to hurry, Lara would be getting anxious. They ran through the doors and across to the Tube, they were laughing and screaming as they went. The adrenaline was still pumping through them. Hopefully they would have calmed down after two Tube journeys and a short walk.

Lara was home when they got in. They had concocted a story between them as to who they had met and where they had been. The funny thing was that they were both talking excitedly over each other so Lara couldn't understand any of it, but was pleased they'd had such a good day.

Megan and Chloe agreed that it was lucky the auditions weren't live as they watched TV with Lara. The earliest they'd be aired would be September, by then the cat would probably be out of the bag if Megan got through bootcamp.

Lara had managed to get the next two days off so she took them sightseeing and shopping. They enjoyed themselves, and Megan was beginning to see what her father could see in Lara. She was funny, generous and very caring. What was not to like. With her music career taking off it would be nice not to have to worry about her dad being lonely. She'd have to give him her blessing when she got home.

Lara took them to the airport on the Sunday. They said their goodbyes and she told Megan that she'd be out to see her soon. Chloe hugged Lara and told her she'd had the best time. Lara had said it had been a pleasure. Any excuse to go shopping, she said.

"Just make sure you bring bigger suitcases next time." Megan hugged her and thought Lara was ok; a true accolade from a teenager.

CHAPTER 7

~~~

Megan knew immediately that she was in trouble. Rob was standing on the arrivals balcony at Faro Airport. There was no smile or wave.

"Your dad doesn't look very pleased to see us. Do you think he knows?" Chloe was glad at that moment that she couldn't sing a note.

"I don't see how? I thought we'd covered our tracks brilliantly. Lara would have said something, or at least given it away, if she'd suspected anything. Can I stay at yours tonight, Chlo?" They were through baggage collection and out into the street. Megan spotted Rob at the carpark ticket machine. He hadn't even waited to help them with their cases.

"Hi Dad. Did you miss me?" Megan thought it best to act as if nothing had happened. Perhaps she had just left her room in a mess. Or maybe he'd noticed the scratch on her helmet when she'd taken a tumble without telling him. How could he know about the *Make Me A Star UK*?

"Hello Chloe, Megan. Good trip?" Chloe looked at Megan for support, her mouth contorted. Megan had to brazen it out.

"Brill thank you. Lara showed us loads of good places. We went to Harvey Nicks, Harrods, Selfridges and all the best shops. And we went to fantastic restaurants. There was one where you saw your food projected onto your plate before you ordered it. It was cool, wasn't it Chloe?" She looked at Chloe for help. They had both got into the back of the car. Rob put the cases in the boot and got into the front. He started the car.

"So, meet anyone famous?" Megan looked at Chloe, who was wetting herself. Her eyes were closed. She was being no help at all, thought Megan.

"We saw a couple of people from the TV in the sushi restaurant in Harvey Nichols. Don't remember their names though." Should she confess? It would look better in the long run. But what if he didn't know, what if it was something else that had upset him entirely?

"Chloe, look round and give me some support," she muttered under her breath. Too quietly for Chloe to hear, or she didn't want to hear. The rest of the fifteen minutes to Chloe's house was in silence. It had to be the longest journey from the airport Megan had ever had. It felt like an hour as they pulled up outside Chloe's. Her parents must have been watching from the window. They were out at the car before the engine stopped. Rob got out and kissed Chloe's mum and shook her dad's hand. He got her case out of the boot as Chloe got out of the car. She turned back.

"Good luck, Megs." She smiled encouragingly at her

friend. "Ring me later." Megan nodded. Should she get out and sit in the front next to her dad, like she normally did? No, she felt safer in the back. Rob got back in the car and promised to thank Lara for them. He drove off, Chloe waved but Megan just smiled, nervously. Poor Megs, thought Chloe. Should she tell her parents the truth? Maybe they could help. It wasn't fair that Megan didn't have a mum. Chloe was sure she'd have been on her side. She turned and went into the house with her mum's arm around her. She'd missed home.

Megan wondered whether to break the silence. They were pulling into their road. She'd wait. Her dad couldn't ignore her forever.

Rob was angry. When he was angry he had to think about what he wanted to say. He knew he was both parents and therefore couldn't come down too hard on Megan. There was no good cop, bad cop scenario so he had to be both. At that moment he could only be bad cop, so he waited for his rage, no that was too harsh, more his disappointment to subside a little.

"Megan, when you go inside, I want you to go to your room and unpack. While you are doing that, I need you to think about your time in London, and if there is anything you deem important enough that I need to know, come out and talk to me." Megan had tears in her eyes. She had never seen her father so cold towards her. She realised that he knew, and that she had totally gone against his wishes. At first it was to spite him and Lara, but then she wanted to do it for herself. She knew her mum would have been proud of her, why wouldn't her dad? Perhaps he would have been if she had asked him. But she already knew the answer; he wanted her education to come first, like most fathers. What a mess. She got out of the car and went into the house, following him as he carried her case to her room.

"I don't need to think about it Dad." She grabbed her father's arm. "Please don't be so mad with me." She said through her tears. "I wanted you to be proud of me." She sniffed, and carried on. "Mum would have been." That hurt Rob. He was just mellowing slightly until she threw that at him.

"Your mother would have agreed with me. We've had this conversation before. You need to get qualifications before you go off looking for fame. I agree you have a wonderful gift, Megan. But so have many young girls your age, but by the time they grow up and are no longer cute, they are dropped and they have nothing to fall back on. Unless you marry a footballer, you will end up on the pile of 'has-beens', broke and unemployable." Megan stomped into her room. She was crying and it broke Rob's heart. But he had to be firm. She was just a teenager, and there were a lot of people out there ready to exploit her. He had to protect her. As he turned to walk to the kitchen, Megan called after him.

"Dad, how did you find out?" Rob stopped and looked round. Megan noticed Rob's eyes were very clear, too clear to be dry. She really had upset him.

"Your pals have been phoning wondering when you'd be home, so they could congratulate you on a brilliant audition. Apparently, it's on YouTube. I really don't want to talk anymore about it tonight. Your dinner will be on the kitchen table in half an hour, I will speak to you in the morning." He turned and left Megan feeling ashamed that she had defied her father. She went into her room, threw herself onto her bed, and sobbed into her pillow.

"Why did you have to die?" She needed her mum now more than anything. After wallowing in self-pity for what seemed hours, but was only half an hour, she walked to the kitchen where her father had left her a note. Her dinner was keeping warm in the oven. She wasn't hungry, but she'd upset her dad enough for one day, so she took it out and ate as much as she could. While eating she opened the laptop and went onto YouTube. Should she put in *Make Me A Star UK*, or her name? She tried her name.

"Oh my God." She said aloud. There was her audition video she had sent in to ITV. It had had so many hits, and wonderful comments, why couldn't she share that moment with her dad? She shut the computer and scraped off the remains of her shepherd's pie, into the bin. She put her plate into the dishwasher and went back to her room. She phoned Chloe.

"Chlo, have you been on YouTube yet?"

"As soon as I got in. Mum told me that everyone was talking about it, and that your dad had been over and they'd checked to see when the auditions were. I wasn't allowed to phone and warn you. Mum has only just given me my phone back; she saw it was you ringing. How did YouTube get hold of that video?" Chloe had been so anxious that she hadn't been able to relax until she'd heard from Megan.

"I would imagine the producers of the show probably leaked it. The publicity wouldn't do the show's ratings any harm, but it's done me loads. Dad isn't talking to me, well not properly. Oh Chloe, he's so cross with me. I've never seen him so cold. Why did I disobey him when I knew how he felt about it? Don't say it was to get back at him; I'm cool with Lara now. Please say something." Chloe had drawn breath twice, but hadn't managed to get anything out because Megan hadn't stopped her tirade.

"Well if you want my opinion, phone Lara. She knows your dad well enough to give you advice." Chloe was right. But she didn't want to phone her. She'd go to London and stay with her until her dad had cooled down.

"Thanks Chlo, brilliant idea. I'll talk to you in the morning. Night." A bit abrupt, thought Chloe. But she knew Megan needed to sort the mess out. She was probably phoning Lara at that moment.

Actually, at that moment Megan was on the laptop, checking to see the earliest flight to Gatwick in the morning. She'd get up really early and leave before she had to confront her father again. She'd hurt him, she knew, but he'd also not bothered to see her side. After all, she was sixteen, not six. Her sorrow had turned to anger. The teenage emotions had kicked in. She looked in her bag to see how much money she had, just enough for a taxi. She went on the airline web site and got a cheap flight paid for by the credit card her father had used for the last trip over to London. She'd pay him back when she was rich and famous. She'd show him. She set her alarm and luckily hadn't unpacked. She undressed and lay on her bed. The tears came again. She turned over and grabbed her ted – 'Little Ted' – she'd had him since she was a baby, curled up into the foetal position and dropped off to sleep.

Rob hadn't slept much at all. He hated being cross with Megan. He had missed their bedtime ritual of hugs and 'love yous'. He woke up quite late and wondered if Megan was up. He'd punished her enough, and himself more, so he wanted a big make-up cuddle and that would be all that was said on the matter. He went to knock on her bedroom door, only to find it open, and no Megan. He called out to see if she was in the shower or kitchen. No answer. He checked around the house and garage. Her scooter was behind his car, but she was nowhere to be seen. He went back into his bedroom and picked up his mobile, pressing speed dial to her phone. It went straight into voicemail. It was either turned off or out of signal. He started to panic. He went back to her bedroom and looked on her wardrobe where her little cabin case sat for sleepovers. It wasn't there. He took a deep breath and tried to think logically. His brain wasn't working as well as it would have done on a good night's sleep. His thoughts went straight to Lara. He looked at Megan's bedside clock. There was no time difference between London and Portugal. She was probably already on her way to work, but it was worth a try. Hopefully she'd know what to do.

"Hello, Lara? It's Rob. I'm glad I've caught you." He had phoned her landline on the off-chance she was still home. He worried about ringing her mobile while she was at work.

"I have caller display Rob, I know it's you. How are you? You sound rattled." Understatement thought Rob. He explained what Megan had done whilst in London. He immediately put her mind at rest, he wasn't criticising her skills *in loco parentis*, Lara couldn't have watched her 24/7. That would have defeated the object of becoming her friend ergo trusting her.

"Where do you think she's gone Lara? I'm at my wits' end. Perhaps I did come down too heavily on her. But I was so cross. After all I'd said on the subject, she still went off and defied me." Rob tried to calm down. It wasn't helping.

"She is a teenager, with a very special gift. Yes, you want to protect her, and she needs some boundaries, but put yourself in her position. So many people have told her how good she is, she needed to prove it to herself. Don't tell me when you were younger, you did everything your parents told you, unfortunately, her little rebellion was on a rather large scale. I'm not siding with her, I'm just trying to see it from her point of view."

"Like a mother. Yes, I know you're right. Now I need to cuddle her and get past it. Where is she?" Rob was panicking. She'd never run away before. He could phone Chloe.

"Before you do anything, I have a hunch. Check the computer for the last page accessed on the internet." Rob opened the laptop, went into Google and checked 'History'.

"You're right. She's been on the airline web page. I'll just go on ANA website for live flights out of Faro." He hoped the page wouldn't take forever to load. It was like a kettle boiling when you needed it to be quick, and it always took forever. "There, a Gatwick flight left twenty minutes ago. Do you think she's on it?" Lara didn't want to take any chances. She'd phone work and tell them she had a family emergency.

"I'll leave in a moment. I'm not having her wandering around Gatwick airport on her own. She probably won't have any English money to pay for a train or a taxi. I'll ring you when I get to the airport. And Rob, don't worry, she's brighter than you give her credit for. Just look what she's achieved over the last few days, apart from causing her dad a nervous

157

breakdown." She laughed. Rob felt so much better now Lara was on the case. He realised how much he'd missed the logic of a woman, she'd make a calculable good cop in future scenarios.

Megan realised she hadn't thought this through. What was she going to do once they landed? She had no English money, no credit card, and no means of transport into London. She wasn't stupid enough to hike, but was stupid enough to go to a country without their currency. She wondered how much it would cost Lara if she turned up in a taxi from the airport. Not a good start to get her on her side. The plane landed with a slight bump, she got out her passport and waited for the seatbelt light to go out.

Lara waited in the North Terminal for the Faro flight to disembark. If Megan was on that flight she wouldn't take too long. She had probably just got the cabin case from the previous day, so no need to wait for luggage.

Megan couldn't believe her eyes. There, the other side of the barrier was Lara. She ran into her arms, crying.

"Oh Lara, I've been so stupid. Dad hates me." Lara calmed her down.

"Your dad doesn't hate you. He cares about you very much. Come on, let's go home and you can tell me all about it." Lara kept her arm around Megan until they got to the car. On the journey back to London, Lara telephoned Rob on her hands free. Rob answered immediately.

"I have someone here who wants to talk to you." Lara signalled to Megan to talk.

"Dad, I'm so sorry. I've acted like a spoilt brat. Can you forgive me, please? I hate it when you're cross with me." Rob could hear the remorse in Megan's voice. He was just pleased she was ok. He didn't care about the *Make Me A Star UK*, or her clandestine audition, he just wanted her home, safe and sound.

"I'm not cross any more. I just want you home for a Daddy cuddle. I've missed them." Megan laughed. She hadn't given her dad a 'Daddy cuddle' for ages. She thought she was too old now, but she'd never be too old for her Dad's love.

"I'll take her home and feed her, and put her on a flight tomorrow, if that's ok, Rob." Rob agreed that would be fine. "I'll ring you this evening, bye Rob."

"Bye Dad. I'll be good this time." Megan meant it.

"Bye you two, see you tomorrow Meggie Moo." The phone went dead. Megan knew he had forgiven her.

"Well, let's get you some breakfast, I don't suppose you've had much since you left here?" Lara was right. She was very wise, thought Megan.

"I'm sorry if I got you into trouble with Dad, Lara. I just wanted to make him proud of me." Lara sighed.

"Oh Megan, he is so proud of you, he's fit to burst. He's just worried about you. You are the most precious thing in the world to him. No one will ever take that place in his heart. And no one should." Megan knew what Lara was getting at. She smiled at Lara.

"I do love singing though, it makes me happy." How can Megan get her to understand?

"No one is telling you to stop singing. Please don't ever stop. You have the most wonderful voice. But you will have that same wonderful voice in a few years' time. Perhaps there is a compromise with your father, if you can meet each other halfway? Go into the sixth form and get your qualifications. As your dad says, fame may not last; there could be another Megan with a great voice leaving school now, with no business sense. She could be taken for a ride with unscrupulous entertainment moguls. You, on the other hand, could go back to the *Make Me A Star UK* in a few years' time, having a business management certificate, manage yourself and demand star treatment. Your dad and I will be in the front row as your biggest fans. We'll be the ones wearing 'Megan Rocks' t-shirts." Megan was laughing out loud. At that moment, she was in awe of Lara. There was something about her that made Megan feel secure. She hadn't felt like that since her mother had died. She was so glad she decided to run away to Lara's.

With father and daughter reunited and Lara back at work, she was able to do one more thing for Megan. She went 'downstairs' to find Hugo. She had remembered Hugo bragging about his brother Piers, having been promoted to something in the Department of Culture, Media and Sport. Having found Hugo she'd ask a favour of him. If it meant another evening out with him, so be it.

"You've lost your chance, Luscious Lara. I'm now in a relationship with M, no names, hush hush, in the Ministry of Defence." Lara was devastated... Not.

"Hugo, I need a favour. For old times' sake." She thought she'd throw that one in for effect.

"And what can I do you for." His humour was as old as his fashion sense.

"Is Piers still in the Ministry of Fun?" She couldn't be bothered with the full title, and the DCMS wouldn't have wound Hugo up as much!

"You mean the Department of Culture, Media and Sport? Yes, quite high up actually, rising all the time." She was sure he was.

"Could I give you a note to pass to him? Perhaps you are free for a coffee so I could explain." Hugo checked his diary. He really was a prat. First opinions usually weren't far off the mark, thought Lara.

"Yes, ok, I'm free for a few hours. Busy afternoon though. Top secret, you know the score." He tapped his nose. She played along; after all she needed that favour.

"Absolutely, don't say anymore, I don't want to be shot." He laughed.

"Quite so." He was such a pillock.

Megan found the letter when she got home from school.

"Dad, Dad." She shouted. He was washing his windscreen. The birds had had a field day and his wiper bottle had run out of water.

"I'm out here poppet. What's up?" Megan couldn't believe her eyes.

"It's a letter from Mason. Look, Mason Morgan himself." Rob acted surprised, but was expecting something like that, after his conversation a few weeks ago with Lara.

"What does it say?" Rob could see it was a letter from Mason's own Record Company.

"He says 'to do what your father says, he knows best'. He says, 'you have a gift, but the music business is so cut-throat that you have to be ready mentally too, otherwise you do not survive.' He mentions Amy Winehouse and a few names from the past. He's trying to put me off." She looked up at Rob, had he something to do with it? She read on.

"He says, 'when you're ready, and your dad has given his consent, in writing!' he put an exclamation mark there, he would be very happy for us to contact his office to talk about my future in the music industry. Oh Dad, he liked me." She hugged her father.

"Of course he did. There's no question that you are a marvellous talent. You do understand now though, don't you? Even Mason Morgan agrees with your old man." Megan laughed.

"Did you have something to do with this?" She waved the letter in the air. "Hang on a moment. It was Lara, wasn't it? She pulled some strings, didn't she? Wow, a letter from Mason Morgan. I've got to show it to Chloe. I'll be back later." She kissed her dad and scootered off to Chloe's. Rob went in and phoned Lara to thank her. He knew she had managed to get a government official to contact the *Make Me A Star UK* producers, who forwarded her letter to Mason personally. But it was Mason's good nature that meant Megan wasn't too disappointed at not going to bootcamp that year. A personal letter from Mason Morgan would suffice until she could sing in front of him again.

Megan had telephoned Lara that evening thanking her for organising the letter. She passed the phone over to her dad, who was hovering. She then disappeared tactfully. After all she really didn't want to hear her father being sentimental and romantic. He was far too old for that.

"Thank you again Lara. I don't know what I'd have done over the last few weeks without your womanly wisdom." He meant it too. "I have some good news for you."

"Ooo, sounds intriguing."

"Do you remember Christine and Martin, Chloe's

parents?" Lara had met them at Megan's sixteenth birthday party.

"Martin's the one with red hair? Yes, I remember them. Christine wants to learn more Portuguese to be able to talk to the builders, if I remember rightly."

"That's them. They run a building firm in Almancil. Well, they normally let out one of their villas for the summer, but this year they are going to find it difficult so have offered it to you for a greatly reduced rent for as long as you need it. How's that?" Lara wasn't sure. Why would it be so cheap? Summer was when the rentals were extortionate.

"Ok, what's the catch?" Rob had his fingers crossed. He wanted her near. There was only a minor problem with the villa.

"They have finally got permission for the plot next door to be built on. So the villa will be next to a building site for about one year. It's not as bad as you think though. With all the religious holidays in Portugal and weekends, it won't be every day. What do you think?" Please say yes, he thought.

"I'll leave it up to you. Is it near you?" The one advantage she could see would be that it was walking distance of Rob and Megan.

"It's literally around the corner. I'll send you the map reference and you can have a look on Google Earth. Then if it gets too much you can just pop in and stay with us." She knew that was his ploy, but she didn't mind now. Megan was obviously ok with the arrangement with her father. Lara still needed her own place for business, but for social times, their villa would be handy.

"I've only two more weeks at work, then a week with my family, then I'll be on a plane and with you. I had four weeks

leave left, so I've tagged it onto my notice, which means I can leave a month early. They've been really good about it as they have fresh blood now! I can't wait to be over there with you. I miss you." Rob missed her too. Even Megan kept asking when Lara would be out.

"I'll phone you when I have squared it with Christine and she'll have the keys ready for when you get here. It's furnished and in good condition, so you shouldn't need to do much to it." He was beginning to sound like an estate agent. Lara thought it amusing.

"Has it sea views, with private path to the beach? Restaurants on the door step and a stone's throw from the shops?!" Rob realised what she was doing.

"Oh, ha bloody ha!" There was a second of silence. "Lara, hurry over. I love you." Lara's heart missed a beat. Why had he said what she had been waiting for, on the phone? Typical man, they had no sense of occasion. That should have been said with soft music playing in the background, roses in vases all around, and champagne in the glasses. Rob misunderstood the silence. "Sorry, I shouldn't have said that."

"Yes, you should. I've wanted to hear that for a long time. I love you too Rob, very much. I'll be over as soon as I can. I promise." They said their goodbyes and Rob put the phone down.

"You really are an idiot, Dad." Megan was walking passed him into the kitchen. "Next time you tell a girl you love her, try doing it in a more romantic setting than in the hallway, on the telephone. Men!" She left Rob speechless.

Lara had a very busy few weeks ahead of her. She'd

managed to get her replacement to start a few weeks early so she could show her the ropes. She was a pretty thing, with freckles. Lara wondered if she'd bring in a satchel or a briefcase. She looked so young. She was actually twenty-two, and had been working for the Ministry of Defence for over a year. She was very able and multilingual, and deserved the position. She also had the advantage of already having a life, being engaged, but of course that came with its own problems as the security search had to be extended to his family members as well as her own. All came back clear, which was why she was sitting next to Lara, watching her accessing the main frame and giving her passwords and codes to set up her own department personal folder and email account. She was called Emma, but known as Em to her friends. The irony hadn't been lost on Lara. Having worked in the Ministry of Defence she was sure she would have had the Micky taken out of her with that name. She must introduce her to Hugo. He thought of himself as the Foreign Office's answer to 007. They'd get on very well.

"Now Em, I'll leave you my mobile number for emergencies. Hopefully it will all become clear after a few weeks, but just in case, you can text me with a question and I'll try to help." Lara knew how difficult it would be for Emma. Many a time she'd wished she could ask someone for help, but being in charge meant there was only the foreign secretary or the prime minister to ask on security issues. But looking at Emma, she knew that with her mates in Defence, she'd be fine.

"That's really kind of you Lara. I'm sure I'll be ok. My fiancé works downstairs, so he'll be around to help me." Lara looked like a light bulb had just gone on in her head. It couldn't be. She was too pretty, too intelligent, surely.

"Your fiancé, he works here?" Emma smiled; in fact, she beamed. Oh dear, thought Lara, she had it bad. She was in love. It couldn't be...

"Yes, his names Hugo, and he's a dream." Lara tried to keep a straight face. All she could think about was Judi Dench getting it on with Johnny English; it just didn't work.

"How lovely. Yes, Hugo certainly is a dream." A nightmare, but still it wasn't Lara's anymore, each to her own.

Lara left her job with a smile, and a slightly guilty conscience. Leaving the country in the hands of Em and Hugo, she was glad she would be living abroad.

She stayed with her parents for a week. Debbie needed her advice on Portuguese law, and Pete just wanted to see his daughter. Lara was surprised that the whole family had rallied and were actually thinking of moving to Portugal with her. It was more than she expected. It was amazing. She couldn't have been happier.

"So, this chap of yours, Rob, do you think he'd employ an old man like me?" Pete was a little worried about leaving his job as a postman. He knew it was time, they were cutting jobs left, right and centre, and he wanted to get out before he was pushed out. People didn't seem to send letters nowadays, emails and conference phone calls seem to have taken their toll on the good old paper correspondence. Even birthday cards and other special occasions were done on line. No, he had done the right thing taking early retirement. He just didn't want to potter around the house in his slippers until it was time to go into a Home.

"He's already got you a stall on the market Dad. You can still shout, can't you?" Pete looked up from his paper. The horror in his eyes made Lara laugh. "Got you!" He smiled. His daughter was more like him than he cared to admit. "He's waiting for you to get out there so you can tell him how many hours you want and on what days. You might find the heat a problem, especially in the summer." That was one of the things Pete was looking forward to. "Anyway, I promised Mum I'd pop in the salon to look at some papers for her. See you later." She went over and kissed her dad on the cheek. He'd missed having Lara about, that was the other thing he was looking forward to in Portugal.

"Lala!" Tori saw her sister through the window and ran to meet her. Before she managed to get through the door Josh was pushing his way past her.

"Lara, come on in my lovely. Look at your hair." He was shaking his head. "Not the best advert for your mummy." Lara laughed. She'd just Washed and Went, more times than she cared to remember recently. There just hadn't seemed enough hours in the day for hair titivation, as Josh called it. Deb came over to reception, clapping her hands and shooing.

"Away, away, back to your clients. Shoo." She was trying to look strict, but Lara knew better. "There'll be plenty of time to catch up at six o'clock, in your own time." Josh walked off sulking.

"Josh, if you have a moment before then, perhaps you could run a comb through my hair?" Lara felt sorry for him.

"I'm yours from five o'clock hun. You'll look marv when I've finished with you." He strutted off with a happier gait.

Deb ushered Lara into the office/kitchen where the relevant documents were. Lara had printed off some guidelines to buying property in Portugal, and renting business premises. Between them they should be able to work out exactly what it entailed and get further along with Project Portugal as Deb had headed her notes.

The figures she had been given by local agents for selling the salon as a going concern were very encouraging. She would be adamant that all the staff went with the sale, or at least given the opportunity of finding something else before completion. They had been loyal to her and therefore deserved the same from her. None of the staff knew of the impending move, but Lara wondered if any of them would want to work in the Algarve. Opening a salon with staff already in situ would be a worry off her mother's shoulders. When the time was right she'd get Tori to ask them, in the meantime, walls have ears; especially in the hairdressing habitat.

That evening the whole family dined together. Adam had already put feelers out at the European High School and it looked like he could fill in until a permanent place became available. Luckily being a maths teacher up to GCSE standard, he could fill in from juniors to seniors so was very versatile. He also doubled up as a PE teacher at the school he was at, which would come in very useful in Portugal. They were very big on football, not so cricket, but perhaps he could convert them.

The only problem Tori and Adam had was that Adam's parents would like the baby born in England. They were worried that if Portugal still had conscription and it was a boy, he'd have to go back at eighteen and be in their army for two years.

"Conscription in Portugal was abolished in 2004. It's also much easier now to register a baby's birth in Portugal and get a British passport. The British Embassy in Lisbon is able to register the birth if you want, but it isn't essential. Nowadays you just apply for a British passport online with the birth details and your own passport details to prove you are British citizens and a photo of the baby, and Bob's your uncle, the baby has its own passport. Simple." Not like in her day, she thought. Was it really only sixteen years ago? Times had changed so quickly. Tim Berners-Lee had a lot to do with it, where would we be without the www dot?!

"How do you know all that stuff Lala? You are a mine of useless information." Tori was actually quite impressed. "Funnily enough Adam and I were going to look up the ins and outs of giving birth over there. But I'm inclined to trust the good old NHS and pop back in November, and go back in the New Year. What do you all think?" Debbie was worried that everyone was getting carried away.

"We haven't even sold the salon yet. That may take months. We may be looking at Christmas or into the New Year before we even get out there ourselves. I wouldn't worry just yet where the baby will be born." Good old Mum, thought Lara. Bringing everyone back to reality with a jolt. She'd make sure everyone's feet stayed firmly on the ground until the time was right. Lara was leaving her family in safe hands.

"That doesn't mean you can't all come over this summer and enjoy a holiday, with a little business thrown in? I can have property details ready and business premises to view.

Just in case." Lara looked at her mother with an enquiring brow raised. Everyone was looking at Debbie.

"Ok, perhaps a look wouldn't do any harm, but no promises until we have a buyer for the salon." Pete punched the air.

"Yes!" He was more excited than his wife. Golf, sunshine and his whole family around him, what more could a semi-retired postman want. "Can we get a dog when we move out there? I've always wanted a dog." Lara and Tori tried not to laugh. They knew he was winding their mum up. Debbie was not amused. She gave Pete the look she reserved for the girls when they had been very bad. He looked down to the ground, suitably chastised.

"I give up. Peter, pass your plate." She put an extra helping of pudding on it. She couldn't stay cross with him for long. He looked up and saw she was smiling.

"Does that mean I can have a dog?" He was pushing it.

"DAD!" Both Tori and Lara stopped him before the joke backfired. They all laughed and Debbie joined in. Lara would miss them all. She hoped the salon sold quickly, then her family in Portugal would be complete.

The day had arrived. Lara was checking-in her suitcase at Bournemouth International Airport, praying it wasn't over the weight limit. She had decided not to take any electrical items with her. She could buy them out there, which meant not overloading the sockets with European adapters. So basically the weight was shoes, clothes and toiletries. Her laptop was in her cabin bag. She'd also decided to alleviate any embarrassment by throwing her Rampant Rabbit away. After all, she had the real thing waiting for her in Portugal. Was it really only months ago that had happened? It seemed like longer. Her life had totally changed from that Hen Weekend forever. She would never be able to thank her sister enough for persuading her to go to Portugal instead of Brighton. One day she hoped she could tell her the real reason for her hesitation. So, there she was, standing in Duty Free choosing aftershave for Rob and a fun watch for Megan. It was the least she could do for them after all the trouble they had gone to, getting the villa ready for her. She had seen the before and after photos and their improvement made the difference between a rental property and a home.

Lara sat in Departures, watching the early holidaymakers looking excited and nervous at the same time. She surprised herself when she considered her own emotions. She was calm. In fact, she had to admit to herself that she was totally relaxed. Was it because for the first time in her life she had someone who cared about her waiting? Or was it because for the first time in her life she knew she was doing the right thing? Perhaps it was a bit of both. All she knew was that she was looking forward to the challenges and the problems that entailed, without any fear or trepidation, because she knew at the end of the day Rob would be there to reassure her.

Financially she was ok. She had paid off her credit cards, which was the main undertaking before her job with the government had ended. Her dad and Adam were selling her car for her, proceeds of which would be put into her bank account. Christine and Martin had wavered her first month's rent, until she was settled, as a thank you for having Chloe in London. That was a big help for Lara as she had one more month left on her flat in London that needed paying for.

She'd given Tori the keys so she could make use of it, even if it was only for a month. She was sure Tori and the gang would enjoy a few weekends up in Town. The icing on the cake was the amount of replies she'd had to her advert for teaching Portuguese, any level. She hadn't booked any classes yet though, she wanted a few weeks of Rob and Megan bonding. She actually realised that apart from a few days here and there, she hadn't had a proper holiday in years. With a total change in lifestyle, from the bustling, fast pace of London, to the laid-back, 'mañana' attitude of The Algarve, every day was going to feel like a holiday to her.

She was brought out of her musing by the intercom announcing the boarding of her flight. There was no turning back now. Sixteen years ago, she boarded the plane to an adventure of a lifetime, now she was doing the same journey but this time it was for a lifetime of adventure.

Megan had finished her exams, and so was at the airport with Rob to meet Lara. They helped her to the car with her luggage. Rob gave her a kiss while Megan got in the car.

"Get a room, you two!" Megan thought it quite sweet, actually, but didn't really want to watch. Her dad was far too old for that sort of display in public. Lara laughed. She'd probably feel the same in Megan's shoes. Mid-thirties must suggest that she was practically drawing her pension in Megan's eyes.

Lara asked Megan how her exams had gone, on the journey to her new home. Megan grunted at the back.

"Too many late nights and cramming just before each exam probably isn't conducive to good results, but we'll see, eh Megan?" Rob was being serious. Oh dear, thought Lara, wrong question to ask, obviously. She turned to the back to give Megan a sympathetic smile. She remembered how her own father had given her the same smile after her mother had told her she'd fail her exams, as she hadn't structured her revision properly. Lara had passed every one. She had every faith in Megan. After all, Megan had her genes. If only she could tell her. Megan smiled back, and winked. At that moment Lara realised she'd done fine in her exams. She'd probably just enjoyed winding her father up about them.

They drew up outside Lara's new home in the Algarve. Rob was watching her face for any apprehension. There was none. Lara thought it was very Portuguese. Very like Rob's. It had tiles on the outside, and was brightly coloured. Megan got out of the car and opened Lara's side.

"Come and have a look at the back garden." Lara followed Megan round to the back of the house. To her surprise there was a swimming pool. Well, more a plunge pool, but cool water in a hole all the same, a wonderful relief after a hot day. "Isn't it brilliant? You can have pool parties, one person at a time though." Megan was laughing. Rob and Lara could see the funny side too. Lara didn't mind the pool not being on a grand scale. She'd only want a dunk after all. For swimming she could go to their house, or even down to the sea. Megan ran round to the front with the keys to open up for her.

"Happy?" Rob took hold of her. Lara nodded. She actually was, for the first time in a very long time. The only thing that troubled her was that she wanted Megan to know who she really was, but that could ruin all that she now had.

Megan opened the patio doors into the back garden. Lara went in to have the guided tour. The little things that

Megan and Rob had obviously bought for her, like cushions, vases, lamps and a few pictures, had made the villa feel like her home already. As she walked into her bedroom she gasped. There, on the wall, was the cartoon of Jilly's Restaurant, which had hung over the bar all those years ago. Lara turned round and looked at Rob. He had a cheeky look on his face.

"Just in case you had forgotten you used to be a waitress! How you've exceeded my expectations!" He was teasing her again.

"That was the best year of my life. I'll take very special care of it. Thank you, Rob." She reached up and kissed him. They continued on the tour, a single bedroom with bed/settee had been made into a study for her, with a dressing table as a desk and a leather chair under. There were two other bedrooms, a lounge/diner out onto the back patio, and a kitchen with a dishwasher. In the garage was another surprise. To her delight Rob had bought her a small runaround car. It was quite old, but hadn't done many miles. He had bought it from one of his friends whose wife had left him and moved back to England.

"Every cloud." He said to Lara with a smirk. She felt sorry for the bloke who'd lost his wife, but was very grateful. Behind the car was a washing machine, and utility area.

"My goodness you two. What can I say? I wasn't expecting so much luxury. Thank you both." She kissed Megan and gave her a hug.

"Our pleasure." Megan replied for them both. "We have a few other surprises for you, but I'll let Dad tell you them. I'm off, Chloe will be waiting for an update."

"Can you thank Chloe and her parents for me? I'll pop

round there another day and give them a bottle of something to thank them." Megan said ok and was gone. Lara had got her bearings as they drove there and realised she really was just around the corner from Rob and Megan's.

"I'll leave you to settle down, but I hope you will come over as soon as you are ready and have dinner with us?" Rob didn't want to leave her, but realised that Lara would probably need time alone to unpack.

"I'd love to. Give me an hour and I'll be bashing your door down with hunger." Rob left and suddenly the enormity of what she had done hit her. It was quiet, and she was alone. But in her flat in London when she was alone she felt cold and isolated, here she felt warm and loved. She really was happy.

Over dinner, Megan told Lara of another surprise they had planned. Rob had organised for them to go to Lisbon for a few days. He had to go to a golf wholesaler up there and decided to mix business with pleasure. He'd booked them into a very nice hotel, Megan had asked if she could bring Chloe, as she didn't want to play gooseberry. Lara was delighted. She'd been to Lisbon on numerous occasions, but hadn't actually seen the city. She'd been to the airport, stayed in hotels, and translated at the Palácio de São Bento (Portuguese Parliament in Lisbon) but she had never managed to go to the shops, or tourist areas. She knew she'd need good walking shoes; Lisbon was built on seven hills.

"I've moved over here to start a business, not gallivant all over the country!" Lara was quietly relieved that she had a while to relax and enjoy a holiday. Rob read her mind.

"You have burnt yourself out working every hour in such

a highly stressful job. You need a holiday, admit it. And before you answer, tell me when you last enjoyed a meal and a drink in the evening, without worrying what time you had to be up in the morning?" He was right. She'd been drinking a wonderful Dão red wine, not checking her watch or refusing that last glass, in other words she was totally relaxed. "So after a few days R and R in Lisbon, then you can think about new clients and teaching. But until then, you are under my strict instructions to chill and enjoy the spoiling." Megan raised her glass.

"Well said, Father." She was a little giggly. They realised that she had been filling her glass too. "And if the pair of you don't mind, I'll retire to my boudoir and pack for the capital." She walked off to her room, slightly unsteadily. "Hic! Oops, pardon. Night night."

"Night night Megan, and thank you for all your help." Lara was trying not to laugh.

"My pleasure. Anytime." She shut her door. Lara looked at Rob and they both laughed.

"I wouldn't want her head in the morning. Talking of which, what time did you want to leave?" Lara was looking forward to their trip. It would be a novelty she could get used to, browsing around the shops of a capital city without the constant worry of being late for a meeting.

"I'll pick you up about 11 a.m. We'll let the train take the strain. The stock I'm looking at has to be ordered, and they'll deliver down here, so all we will be bringing back will be shopping bags. Most of Lisbon has been pedestrianised so cars aren't very welcome. We don't need the car anyway, the taxis are reasonable, and there's the Metro." Lara was tired. She tried to stifle a yawn. It had been a long day. "I'm sorry, you must be tired. Let me walk you home." Rob looked at her. He wished she'd stay, but knew she was right about Megan. The last thing he needed to do was alienate his daughter when he was hoping they'd become a family soon. He wasn't even presumptuous enough to book a double room at the hotel, but had managed to get two singles adjoining. What Megan didn't see, didn't hurt her.

He walked Lara home. She'd quite forgotten how balmy the nights were in Portugal. It was lovely and warm, with an equally warm breeze that felt pleasant on her skin. Rob had put his arm around her as soon as they had reached the end of his road, out of view of his house. Was he being overcautious? Megan seemed to be cool with the dating thing. The overthinking thing was catching. Lara thought she had gone to heaven. Could she be any happier? She didn't think so. They had walked almost all the way in silence. Rob finally broke the tranquility.

"I wasn't quite sure what to book in the hotel tomorrow, so I've booked us a room each, but they have a communicating door." Lara watched his face; it was like a naughty schoolboy's, she giggled. "I take it I've done the right thing?"

"If it was for Megan's benefit, I'm sure you have acted correctly. For my benefit, I hope one of the rooms has a double bed!" They had reached her house and he unlocked the front door for her. Once in the hallway, with the front door shut, he pulled her into his arms and kissed her passionately. He had wanted to do that all night. All of a sudden she didn't feel that tired anymore. He walked backwards as she maneuvered him towards her bedroom, still locked in a kiss. Lara hadn't quite worked out the lay of the land, so had to break from the embrace to see where the bed was. He'd taken control in seconds and had spun her round and thrown her, gently, onto the bed. She didn't know if it was the wine, or just their newfound love for each other that had caused the giggling childish behavior, but whatever it was they were both enjoying it.

CHAPTER 8

~~~

The train to Lisbon wasn't like the trains in England. Lara was feeling decidedly sick. It seemed to sway from side to side, and she was sure it was faster too. Lunch was served which didn't help her at all. The smell of chicken was the last thing she needed.

"I thought you were used to travelling. Don't tell me you get train-sick." Rob could see Lara had gone very pale.

"I've not noticed before, but I usually travel in planes and taxis. The only trains I normally go on are underground, and they don't sway." She made her excuses and walked as best she could to the toilet, grabbing the backs of chairs as she went. She was not enjoying herself. Thank goodness the torture only lasted for another hour. Megan and Chloe had been watching the TV on the overhead screens. It was in Portuguese, which they were both fluent in. Rob could pick out quite a few words, if they spoke slowly, but understand a little more than he could converse. Megan used to laugh when he tried, his verbs were all over the place, and his tense was worse; but he tried. Lara made her way back to her seat and sat down. She looked just as pale, but had a smile on her face. She wasn't going to let a bit of travel sickness ruin their break away. She'd just try and keep as still as possible until the train stopped.

Nearer the capital the train's speed decreased and the swaying stopped. Lara began to feel more human and was enjoying the sights. From the station, it was a quick trip on the Metro and they came out opposite the hotel they were staying in. The girls ran off up the stairs to their room when the receptionist had given them their key, and Lara and Rob followed in the lift with their respective keys. Once everyone was settled into their rooms, Lara decided to have a quick shower and change. She was feeling much better, but was a little apprehensive about the journey home. She'd find a chemist and see if they had some travel tablets to settle her tummy before they go. Rob tapped on the adjoining door.

"You OK?" Lara unlocked the door. "You still look a bit pale. Let's get you out into the fresh air. We'll find somewhere for a nice cup of tea." Lara laughed.

"How long have you lived in Portugal? As they say, you can take the man out of England, but you can't take England out of the man." Rob saw the funny side.

"Well I still miss my scones and strawberry jam, with a spoonful of Devonshire clotted cream, but I suppose Madeira cake is a good second best." All of a sudden Lara was hungry. "Megan and Chloe have gone exploring, we'll catch up with them this evening for dinner. The afternoon is ours. Where would you like to go?"

"That cup of tea sounds good, and perhaps a little

pastry?" Rob realised that Lara hadn't eaten since breakfast.

"That's probably why you're pale, you haven't eaten anything. Tea and scones it is then." He linked her arm and escorted her out of the hotel and on into the centre of Lisbon.

They had a wonderful afternoon, playing tourists. Rob was checking out some menus on the way to find out where they could have dinner. He found an Italian restaurant that was in a cellar and looked good. Looking at the menu there was something for everyone. He popped in and booked a table for that evening for the four of them and found Lara looking in the window of the shop opposite. It was a shop selling beautiful lace Christening and Confirmation dresses for children. She was miles away again when Rob joined her.

"Penny for them." Lara shrugged. "We had Megan christened in Brighton when she was nearly a year old. Jill wanted to contact you to be there, but she respected your wishes and wrote down all the details, with a photo of the day and put it in a bottle and threw it in the sea by Brighton Pier. She thought it might travel down the coast and someone would find it and tell you. Unfortunately, the wind was in the opposite direction and had more chance of taking the bottle to France or Belgium than along the south coast of England, but it was the thought that counted." He squeezed her. "Anyway, one day we may need to buy one for *our* child." Lara turned to him to check the look of sincerity on his face that she saw reflected in the shop window; it was there, no mistake.

"Oh Rob, I love you so much." She reached up and kissed him.

"In that case shall we go back to the hotel for a little

siesta before we go out tonight?" He winked at her.

"Obviously siesta in Portugal has a different meaning to that in England." She raised her eyebrows at him.

"What does it mean in England then?" He was teasing her now.

"Well, not hanky-panky I can assure you. I think I actually like the Portuguese translation though." They were both laughing and held each other's hands as they made their way back to the hotel, for their siesta!

Megan and Chloe had been shopping. They'd had a brilliant afternoon, and were holding a fashion show in their room. Megan had knocked on Lara's door to invite her to see what they had bought. Luckily her father had gone back to his own room for a shower. Megan was modelling a pair of purple shorts with a pretty pink top. Lara loved the fact Megan had her figure. Shorts looked so good on long legs.

"Blast." Megan had undone a button on the top and it fell off. "I'll have to take it back." She picked up the button off the floor. Lara stretched over and took the top and the button from her.

"I've got a travel sewing kit in my bag, it will take two minutes to sew it back on, don't worry." Megan smiled. She had forgotten what it was like to have a 'mother' around. She could get used to it.

"Thanks Lara. I'm going to wear my trousers and the t-shirt I bought in London for dinner, so there's no rush." Chloe was going to wear a pretty summer dress she had just bought. Lara looked at her watch.

"Your father will be calling on me in twenty minutes, I better get under the shower. See you girls down in the foyer. Cheerio for now." Lara left.

"I really like her Megs. She's not even trying, she's being normal and that's good, isn't it?" Megan knew what Chloe meant and had to agree.

"Yes, it's good. I like her too. But she's not my mum." Megan looked sad. Chloe looked her friend in the eyes,

"She's not trying to take the place of your mum, she's trying to be your friend." Megan smiled. Chloe was very wise.

"You're right. She has been a good friend to both of us. Come on let's get ready. I'm hungry." The girls went into panic mode putting on their make-up, straightening their hair, getting on their clothes and being ready within half-an-hour. No mean feat but they did it. They were both in the Reception when Lara and Rob got out of the lift.

"Well don't you two look lovely? Rob, do you agree?" Rob turned and looked at the girls.

"Bit overdressed for the chip shop." He smiled.

"Oh Dad." Megan punched him. They went off down the road towards the restaurant like a happy family.

The meal was as good as Rob had predicted, and the cave-like atmosphere was made even more authentic by the rumbling of the Metro, running underneath. Megan and Chloe were animated about what they had seen and done that afternoon.

"Well we did a little sightseeing, and stopped for a cup of tea." When he described their afternoon like that, it sounded quite boring, but was anything but, thought Rob.

"Oh dear, Dad, you are feeling your age aren't you." Megan looked at him with a sympathetic expression. Rob threw an Amaretti biscuit at her, which she caught brilliantly.

"Oh, thanks Dad. Yums." She opened it and ate it. "Sorry, did you want it back?" She and Chloe were giggling. Megan looked at Lara who had been quiet for a while. "Are you ok, Lara?" Megan thought she looked awful, but it would have been rude to say that. Rob turned to look and had to agree, Lara looked very pale. Perhaps she was tired. They hadn't exactly slept during their siesta.

"Let's get you out into the fresh air. It is a bit hot down here." He left the money on the plate the waiter had brought over earlier with the bill on, and put his arm through Lara's and walked her to the stairs. Megan and Chloe had gone ahead. There wasn't room on the stairs for two abreast, so Lara went up first. A blast of wind from above made her realise her arms were bare. She turned to Rob still at the bottom.

"Sorry Rob, I've left my pashmina on my chair." He signalled for her to go on up and he'd fetch it.

As he walked towards the table they had just vacated he heard a commotion. Two waiters and the maître d' were at the bottom of the stairs in seconds, helping someone up. Rob had a terrible feeling about it. Even before he got back to the foot of the stairs he realised it had to be Lara. One of the waiters was dabbing her head where blood was seeping out of a nasty gash. The maître d' was on the phone to an ambulance. Rob knelt down and called Lara's name, but there was no response. The Italian waiter who was trying to stop the bleeding looked up at Rob.

"It's ok mate, I am first aider. I have certificate. No problems, eh?" He smiled at Rob. If that was supposed to put his mind at rest, it hadn't. Megan and Chloe were at the top of the stairs, Rob told them to wait outside for the ambulance. He turned back to Lara who was opening her eyes.

"Hello beautiful. Are you back with us? You'll be fine, just stay still for a bit." Rob held her hand.

"I'm so sorry for ruining your evening Rob. Everything suddenly went dark. I don't know what happened, but my head hurts." She tried to smile, but it hurt.

"Dad, it's here." Megan shouted in Portuguese at the paramedics; Rob was quite proud of her at that moment. She told them what had happened and pointed down the stairs. The paramedics took over. They turned to Rob and asked if Lara had insurance. Lara nodded, that hurt too.

"Ok then, we can take you to Hospital Santa Maria, very nice hospital." Thank goodness she had taken the option of continuing her employment insurance when she left the Foreign Office. She had an idea that the state hospital wouldn't be up to NHS standard.

They had managed to get Lara into the ambulance but couldn't take them all. Rob signalled a taxi and told the girls to go back to the hotel. He left in the ambulance with Lara.

"He's got to be joking. '*Ao Hospital Santa Maria agrada, motorista.*'" The driver nodded and pulled away, following the ambulance. Megan wondered how her father thought they could go back to the hotel as if nothing had happened. She realised she was very fond of Lara.

"I hope your dad isn't too mad when he sees us." Chloe remembered how unhappy Megan was the last time she went against her dad's wishes.

"He's too worried about Lara to be mad with us." Chloe couldn't quite work out when it became 'us'. But she'd stick by her friend.

Lara was perfectly lucid by the time the ambulance dropped her off at the hospital. She wondered what all the fuss was about. Apart from a headache, she was fine.

"You were unconscious for a few minutes, plus the gash on your head is going to need sticking together by some means, plus, why did you collapse in the first place?" Rob wasn't cross, just exasperated. He'd felt useless, and realised he didn't want to lose Lara. "Just humour me for a while and let the doctors do their job, please?" Lara nodded and smiled. It was nice to have someone who cared.

The doctor at the hospital started with a CT scan in case she had damaged her skull. Followed by blood tests, to check why she had blacked out in the first place.

Lara was put into a private room while the scan was read and the blood tests were carried out. Rob sat by her side holding her hand while she dozed. Unfortunately, the whole scenario had brought back the times he sat in the same position with Jilly waiting to know if the cancer was back, and how far it had spread. He was thinking Lara could have a brain tumour, or worse. A gentle knock on the door brought Rob back from his nightmarish thoughts. Megan popped her head round. Rob took one look and quietly ran to the door and hugged Megan. Megan thought some dreadful news had been given to them.

"Oh God, Dad. What's wrong with her?" Rob realised he'd frightened the life out of Megan.

"We don't know yet. I'm just so pleased to see you." Megan turned to Chloe and winked. "Come on in, but be as quiet as you can, Lara is asleep."

"No I'm not. Come in girls. It's lovely to see you both. Sorry I've ruined your evening." Lara leaned forward while

Megan kissed her. Megan and Chloe had been wandering around outside the hospital for a while. It was positioned in the centre of the expensive shopping area in Lisbon. They were actually building up their courage to go in, by window-shopping.

"You haven't ruined our evening, it's been quite exciting. Our taxi driver thought he was playing Grand Theft Auto on an Xbox. He wound round the cobbled streets trying to keep up with your ambulance. It was so exciting." Megan was out of breath just telling them.

"It was actually very scary, and I nearly wet myself." Poor Chloe. She didn't look as happy as Megan. They all looked at her and laughed. Chloe tried to look hurt, but the laughter was infectious and she had to join in. Rob finally understood the quote 'laughter is the best medicine'. He'd almost forgotten why they were there. Through their laughter they didn't hear the knock on the door; it was the doctor. They all immediately sobered up.

"Miss Lara, may I speak freely?" Lara didn't want any of them to go.

"Yes, they are all family." Rob smiled. Megan sat on a chair with Chloe.

"It is good news. The CT scan came back clear. You do not have any fractures of your skull, which is what worried me. I think you may have a little concussion, so we'd like to keep you in overnight to watch you. Otherwise you can leave first thing in the morning. We've put a little glue on the cut, and that seems to be fine." He looked at her head and nodded. "No need for stitches." Rob breathed a sigh of relief. "Now, for the reason you fainted. You are anaemic." He looked at her as if to inform her the reason by facial expressions only. He smiled.

"Do you mean?" Lara had worked it out. She hadn't been travel sick, and the fainting due to anaemia all added up to the symptoms she had sixteen years ago. The doctor nodded. Rob and Megan looked puzzled. Chloe smiled.

"Ahh." Megan looked at Chloe wondering what she meant. Chloe pointed to her stomach and rocked her arms as if nursing a baby.

"Oh my God, Lara, you're pregnant." Megan sounded excited. That was a good sign, thought Lara. Now to see how Rob was coping. She turned to Rob. He was staring at her, tears rolling down his cheeks. He couldn't say if it was relief that Lara was healthy and not dying, or the fact that the baby he hoped he'd have with Lara eventually, will be coming a little sooner than anticipated. Everyone started hugging each other; the doctor smiled and walked out. Just as he was shutting the door he coughed.

"Just to let you know, it will be due in the New Year. Congratulations." He shut the door and left them to their obvious excitement.

It was getting late and Rob needed to get the girls back to the hotel, but he didn't want to leave Lara.

"Dad, Chloe and I are quite capable of getting a taxi to the hotel. It's not like there is a language barrier. Why don't you stay a little longer and we'll see you back there?" Rob was tempted.

"We promise to go straight back. We know you don't need any more worries today." Chloe swayed him.

"Ok, straight back. You two are on your honour, don't let me down." He looked at Megan. A shiver ran through her. He'd still not totally forgotten her London debacle.

"We promise. You can trust us you know. We've learnt our lesson." Again with the 'us and we', thought Chloe. It's a good job she's Megan's bff, or she could take offence.

Rob gave them some money for a taxi, and Megan kissed Lara goodnight. The girls left, leaving Rob holding Lara's hand.

"I've worked out it was that wonderful first night, when I got back from Dublin and you were on my doorstep. How romantic." She looked at Rob. "Are you pleased?" She had misunderstood his concern for disappointment.

"I'm over the moon. It looks like Megan is excited too. But I want the baby to be born into a family. I want Megan to know it is her real sibling, and I want you to be mother to both." He was shaking his head. He knew it would be a difficult road ahead.

"That's a lot of 'I Wants', Mr Simpson." She laughed. He wanted to ask her to marry him, but he remembered the telling off he got from Megan when he told Lara he loved her, on the phone in the hallway. Megan would have a field day if the proposal was in a hospital bed in Lisbon. He decided to pave the way for a future proposal.

"I'm going to let you sleep. I'll be here first thing in the morning to pick you up so we can enjoy a few more days in Lisbon before we get back to normal life. Then we can make plans for our future, together." Lara snuggled down in the bed. She was very tired. The relaxant they had given her for the CT scan hadn't worn off so she knew if she closed her eyes she'd drop off. The problem was the nurses would be waking her up at intervals during the night, to make sure she wasn't concussed.

"Goodnight Rob. Thank you for staying with me. I'm

going to sleep now." Rob smiled and leant over to kiss her. By the time he got to the door she was asleep. He stood watching her for a moment and blew her a kiss.

"Night night, my Lara. Sleep well." He left feeling happier than he thought possible with a baby, hopefully a wife, and a new future. He better make sure the present was ready for it. He'd have a talk with Megan in the morning, when the shock had subsided and the reality had kicked in. He wasn't going to make her feel left out. Perhaps he could involve her in the proposal arrangements.

Both girls were asleep by the time he got back to the hotel. He could tell as there were no giggles or chatter from outside their door. Their key was gone from the Reception, so he knew they were in. He'd have loved to talk to Megan but it would have to wait until the morning. He went on to his room. For the first time since Jill's death, he prayed. He asked Him to keep Lara safe, and to make sure Jill understood his loneliness over the last five years, and that he still loved her very much. He slept better than he thought he would; his mind was at peace.

"What are we going to call it?" Megan was straight in there. She was buttering a croissant and smearing it with jam. "Chloe and I thought if it was a boy he should be called Justin and if it was a girl, Adele." Chloe was giggling.

"You wanted Adele, I wanted Beyoncé." Rob was glad they found the whole thing amusing. He had telephoned the hospital earlier and had spoken to Lara. They were to pick her up after breakfast.

"Are you ok with the news that you will have a little

brother or sister?" Megan looked at Rob with a mock disgusted expression.

"At first I thought it was pretty gross that my dad had made a baby, at his age. But on reflection, it'll be fun." Chloe looked at Megan.

"I've always wanted a brother or sister." Megan put her arm around Chloe.

"You've already got a sister, me! But you can share mine too if you like." Rob was still reeling from the insult Megan had thrown at him, but managed a smile. At least Megan wasn't opposed to the idea. That had to be a good sign.

"Well if you two can get a wriggle on, I'd like to go and rescue Lara from the hospital and take her out for a nice quiet lunch." Rob smiled at both the girls and left them finishing their breakfast and going through all the names in the Charts Top 100. He would have to put his foot down on a few, Snoop Dogg and Wiz for a start, Rihanna and Madonna; he breathed a sigh of relief when he heard the girls burst out laughing as he got into the hallway. It had obviously been for his benefit, and he was quite delighted with himself for not rising to the bait.

Lara was feeling much better. She had a lump on her head, but under her hairline. Her headache had gone, and her nausea was giving her a stay of execution, so she was fit to go. Armed with iron tablets and paracetamol, she was ready to continue their holiday. Rob had decided that sightseeing was out, but that didn't mean they couldn't hit the shops, gently and sedately. His arm stayed firmly round her, which made her feel very secure. How different this pregnancy was going to be. From the moment she heard, she wanted this baby so much, and this time circumstances were in her favour and she would keep it.

Lying in the hospital bed, she realised that there would only be a matter of weeks between her baby's birth and her sister's baby. She wouldn't tell any of them yet though. She'd want to tell them face-to-face. Perhaps when they visited in the summer. She probably wouldn't get away with hiding it by then. Her concern with Megan's reaction seemed to be unwarranted. She had told Lara of the names they had been discussing, and winked at her out of Rob's sight; the wind-up Master had a prodigy, poor Rob, she smiled.

The visit was a huge success. Lara and Megan had managed to fill a wardrobe, Rob had ordered enough stock for the coming season, and Chloe had just enjoyed being with them all. Rob was going to hire a car for the journey back, but Lara insisted that she would be fine on the train. Megan and Chloe watched the TV while Rob made sure Lara was comfortable.

"Rob will you stop fussing. I'm pregnant, not ill." She loved it really.

"You've had a bang on the head, so you need looking after for a while." He wanted to look after her forever. "Are you happy about the baby?" Lara wondered where that had come from.

"Of course, over the moon. Aren't you?" Rob took a deep breath. Oh no, thought Lara, he's not.

"I'm afraid I can't put into words how I feel right at this moment, but yes, I'm ecstatic about the baby. As long as you are happy and healthy then that is my priority at the moment. I thought I'd lost you when I saw you at the bottom of those stairs. I thought 'what had I done in a past life for all this shit to be thrown at me'. Then you came to and smiled and at that moment I vowed I'd protect you for the rest of my life." He wasn't anticipating a speech, but he just voiced his thoughts out loud.

"For someone who couldn't put into words how he was feeling, you did remarkably well." She wasn't mocking him, she knew men found it very difficult to show their vulnerable side, but Rob had done exactly that, she was so proud of him at that moment. "I'm afraid you are stuck with me and this little one now, so I'm glad you feel like that." He pulled her close and kissed her.

"Yuk, get a room you two." Megan had wandered back to where they were sitting, looking for some change for a drink. "It's that sort of behaviour that got you two into trouble the last time." She was teasing them. Lara burst out laughing.

"Oh Megan, you certainly are your father's daughter." Rob joined in the laughter.

The next few weeks Lara was quite poorly. She'd had a scan and everything was fine with the baby. Unfortunately she was told that being a 'geriatric mother' (anyone over the age of thirty seemed to be drawing their pension according to the Family Clinic in Vale Do Lobo), hormonal imbalance and thus sickness is more prevalent. Rob wanted her to move in, but Lara was adamant that she'd stay put, at least until she felt more human. Megan popped in and checked she was ok, and dropped off fresh fruit and homemade soup from Rob.

It was during her twelfth week that the sickness went as quickly as it had started. Lara was so pleased, it lasted a month longer with Megan. She had managed to start up some classes before she ran out of money and energy. She had contacted six people all at the same level, beginners, and was able to designate two mornings a week to them. By the afternoon she was already getting tired. She contacted six more clients, Portuguese business people from the area, to teach them English on two more mornings. That left her free from Thursday lunchtime until Monday morning. Perfect. With the sickness gone she was able to enjoy the lessons. They had paid until the end of July, when Lara was expecting the summer holidays to disrupt the arrangements. She knew her family would be over, and the business clients would be too busy. In September she was to start at the school, so would adjust her private work accordingly.

In the meantime, Rob had written to Pete, asking for his daughter's hand in marriage. Pete had written back with enthusiasm, telling him that 'mum's the word' and he'd have to keep it from Debbie and Tori or it would not be a surprise.

That done Rob engaged Megan in 'Operation Proposal'. Megan was thrilled to be asked. They had chosen a beautiful white-gold diamond ring with sapphires to match Lara's eyes. For the proposal itself, Megan had some brilliant ideas, but they included white horses, miles of golden beaches and an orchestra. Rob was thinking more in terms of an evening meal, a bottle of champagne and then the old 'get down on one knee' scenario.

"Done to death, Dad. Lara deserves more excitement, romance and a hint of mystery." Megan was thinking of Arabian nights with Bedouin tents, and mysterious men on camels with daggers glinting in the moonlight bearing the ring on a velvet cushion.

"What if I pop the question on a Ghost Train at a fairground in Brighton?" Rob was amused but Megan was not.

"If you are not going to take this seriously, I'll not help you." Megan was trying to keep a straight face. She'd just pictured her dad on the dodgems trying to keep up with Lara.

"Well I suppose I could dress in black and ride on a helicopter which dropped me into the sea where I got onto a Jet ski pulled up alongside a jetty, run up the garden, up to the mansion, shinny up the drainpipe, enter the bedroom quietly, leave the ring on the box of Milk Tray and scarper before I leave a damp patch on the carpet." Both of them were laughing so much they didn't hear the knock on the kitchen door.

"Well you two are enjoying the afternoon. What have I missed?" Lara loved seeing them so happy.

"Dad was saying he was going to buy you a box of chocolates." They both burst out laughing again. Lara couldn't see the funny side, but it didn't matter, she just smiled until they calmed down. "I've got to go, I'm singing tonight. It's starting to get busy at last." Megan disappeared into her room to get ready. She shouted out of her door. "You two can come down if you want. I'm trying out a few new numbers." Rob looked at Lara. She wasn't looking as tired as she had been. Lara was feeling quite bright. She'd taken her iron and some extra vitamins and it would be nice to get out.

"I'd love to come, what about you Rob?" He nodded.

"Good idea. We'll have a meal while we watch her. Ok Megs, we'll be there in a while. If it's getting that busy can you reserve a table for us at seven? Text me if that's a problem." Megan was right, the season was starting to take off which meant the locals had to get used to booking everywhere if they wanted to go out.

"Right, I'm off. Table at seven in the front so you can watch me." She beamed at them. "Bye." She was gone.

"I better go and change. I'm lucky the summer is almost upon us. I can get away with flowing skirts and frilly blouses without people noticing I'm getting fat." Rob put his arms around her waist. He snuggled his face into her neck.

"You look adorable. Perhaps we should say nine o'clock for the table." She pushed him gently away.

"Behave. Megan will be waiting for us. Come and get me when you're ready." She kissed him and stared at him for a moment.

"What's the matter, changed your mind?" He raised his eyebrows in anticipation.

"No, I was just realising how lucky I am. I love you, Robert Simpson." Before he had time to respond she shut the back door. He opened it and shouted after her.

"I love you too Lara Megan Allen. With brass knobs on." He heard her giggle and shut the door.

By the time Lara and Rob reached Vale Do Lobo, the music and dancing was in full swing. Children were dancing with each other while their parents and older siblings watched from the restaurant terraces around The Square. It was safe, and secure. Parents were able to enjoy their meals and keep their children within eye and verbal contact. Megan spotted her dad and Lara and waved as she sung. Fernando had spotted them too.

"Senor Simpson, your table." He pointed to a table right at the front of the decking; with a full view of the dais

Megan was performing on and the sea. He removed the 'Reserved' sign and flicked his tea towel across the table-top.

"Thank you 'Nando, looking busy." Rob looked at all the tables mostly full with a few reserved signs on the rest.

"We're expecting at least two covers tonight, perhaps three. It is good for my pocket." He smiled and Lara noticed a big gap between his two front teeth. She couldn't believe that she was thinking of braces and orthodontists for her baby. Megan had perfect teeth though. They sat down and Fernando gave them a menu each. He put a thumbs-up to Megan and disappeared onto the next table to clear their starter plates.

"Did Megan ever have a brace?" Lara was still bothered. Rob burst out laughing. He realised that she had seen 'Nando's teeth and was worried about their baby's.

"Oh Lara, you are so funny. In answer to your question, no, Megan has perfect teeth and always has. I, on the other hand, had a brace and glasses as a child. One to correct an overbite, and the other to correct a lazy eye." She looked at Rob and sniggered. "Which are you laughing at?" He sounded quite hurt.

"I'm not laughing at your imperfections, I'm laughing at your ability to guess what I'm thinking. It could be dangerous for a relationship to flourish with a mind-reader as a partner." Rob had only heard the last word. She was already referring to them as a couple. That was a good sign to a man who was going to propose shortly.

The wine waiter took Rob's order, and brought Lara a bottle of still mineral water. No point in them both suffering he told her. One of them needed to keep the Portuguese economy going by buying their wine. Lara had been told that a small amount of red wine would be good for her anaemia so the waiter poured her a little. The singing had stopped and a tape was playing. Megan went over and sat with them.

"I'm on a break. I've just got time to have a starter before I go back. 'Nando!" She caught Fernando's attention. "Can you get me a quick plate of tempura prawns with sweet chilli sauce? I've got ten minutes, tell chef. Thanks." He ran off to the kitchen. They loved Megan so she had them around her little finger. He was back in seconds, with a plate of prawns in a light batter with the sauce. "Blimey that was quick."

"They were for Table 14 but they can wait." He winked at her. Rob was impressed by the hold his daughter had over them. "Now, Senor Simpson, have you and your lady decided?" They had. With the ordering over and Megan enjoying her prawns, Lara relaxed and sipped her wine. The sun was just going down and a red hue was radiating from the horizon. The sea was calm and the evening was warm. Lara wondered if it got any better than that. She had the love of her life and her daughter sitting at the table on a lovely evening. She realised a tear was running down her cheek. Megan and Rob were in full conversation so hadn't noticed. It must be her hormones, she thought. She wiped it surreptitiously with her napkin and watched her daughter devour her last prawn.

"Right, must go. My public awaits!" She kissed her dad on the cheek, and as she passed Lara she bent and gave her one too. "See you later. I'll be back for a pudding in half-an-hour." As she walked towards the dais the audience of diners started clapping and cheering. It was hard to believe that she was only sixteen. She coped very well with the fame. Rob was beginning to think that she'd be fine in the industry, in fact he could feel quite sorry for the 'moguls' after seeing the way she has the waiters and chef trained there.

The evening did get better. The meal was delicious, and as the sun fell into the sea the moon shone brighter giving the whole area a very romantic ambience. Megan interrupted the singing.

"Ladies and Gentlemen, this next song, before my break, is dedicated to the two people sitting over there." She pointed to her dad and Lara. "Lara and Rob." She winked at her dad, and started the backing track. It was the Michael Bublé version of 'The Way You Look Tonight'. As she sang the words, 'Nando went over to Rob and placed something in his hand. He whispered in his ear.

"Message from Megan, 'Good luck'. She said you'd know what she meant." 'Nando stepped away, Rob didn't need to open his hand, he knew what it was. Lara was staring at Megan, tears were rolling down her cheeks now; she couldn't stop them. Rob got up as slowly and carefully as he could so as not to let Lara see him. He moved behind her and waited until the final chorus. Megan finished singing; the audience were clapping and cheering. Lara turned to tell Rob what a wonderful evening it was but he had gone. He tapped her on the shoulder from the other side. He got down on one knee.

"Lara, I love you so much, I never want you to leave me again. Please will you be my wife?" Lara had almost stopped crying, she took a deep breath but didn't want to risk talking; she nodded her head and positively beamed. "Is that a yes?" Rob was teasing her.

"Yes, yes." She threw her arms around his neck and then realised the cheering and clapping had started up again. They were the stars, not Megan. Megan had jumped down from the stage and was hugging them both. 'Nando and some of the other waiters had brought over a few bottles of champagne and corks were popping, Rob's back was being pounded and Lara was just sitting staring at the most beautiful ring she had ever seen in her life. She turned to Megan.

"Thank you for the song, it was beautiful. And I'm sure you had something to do with this magnificent ring too." She leant over and kissed Megan. Megan smiled.

"You are very welcome, future stepmother." Ouch, all of a sudden those words that Megan had meant in jest stung Lara. Rob noticed Lara's face change. Maybe it had been too much for her. She was probably tired. He'd try to get her home when the excitement had died down a bit. He took her a little glass of champagne.

"Happy?" He asked her, but watching her face he knew she was. She had had a momentary wobble, but she was over it. She was smiling and took the glass from him.

"One sip, but no more, I've had a little wine already tonight. Better to be safe." She touched her stomach. "Don't want the little one coming out and going straight into rehab rather than the nursery." Rob laughed. Megan had managed to get a chocolate brownie smothered in chocolate sauce, with a dollop of ice cream and was tucking into it. Where she manages to store it was a mystery to Rob, she didn't have an ounce of fat on her. But she did have long legs like her mother. Perhaps she fills one at a time. Rob realised he was being silly, but he'd had the majority of a bottle of wine and the champagne was going straight to his head. He chuckled to himself. He was going to take Lara out for a quick bite to eat and then have an early night. Instead, he's betrothed and can't fathom why he had been so nervous. It was simple. He was very grateful to Megan though. He could relax and leave the wedding planning to the girls. The difficult bit had been done, and Lara had said yes, plain sailing from then on.

Lara looked at Rob sitting giggling to himself. She loved seeing him so happy, but the morning after may not be as much fun. She'd have to be a party pooper soon as she was very tired.

"Megan, I think I'll take your father home, if you don't mind." Megan looked at her dad, still sitting giggling to himself.

"Good idea. He does get embarrassing when he's been drinking. We are lucky he's forgotten about the microphone. I was half expecting him to be on the stage by now." Lara hadn't seen that side of Rob. He had always been too busy in the old days to let his hair down. She would enjoy the 'embarrassing' side of his personality when she wasn't quite so tired. She took Rob by the arm and gently got him to stand.

"Hello my fiancé." Unfortunately he then broke into 'The Way You Look Tonight', crooning as if Frank Sinatra but sounding more like Frank Bruno. He took her in his arms and finished with a flourish with Lara almost on the floor. The restaurant patrons and staff all cheered and clapped. Megan, meanwhile, continued eating her dessert. She didn't actually know that man who was singing. Lara told Rob to say goodnight to the people and steered him in the direction of the taxi rank. There was no way she was going to be able to escort him home along a residential street. It had been quite an evening, but Lara had enjoyed every minute of it. Looking at Rob, she knew he had too.

It was near lunchtime before Lara heard a tap at her kitchen door. She opened it and standing there was Rob.

"I'd never seen a dream walking until now." She really shouldn't compound his misery by joking.

"Oh ha, bloody ha. A coffee would go down a treat." She moved out of the way for him to enter the house. He sat at her little round kitchen table and put his head in his hands.

"Well I could take offence, the fact you had to get so tanked up just to ask me to marry you." She knew she should stop with the teasing, but it was a rare occasion that she was one up on him, so she'd enjoy it while it lasted.

"Oh my God. I didn't, did I?" He looked distraught. Lara watched his face for signs of breaking. His eyebrows raised and he smiled. Her heart started beating again. "Never bullshit a bullshitter!" She playfully slapped him and turned to put the cafetière on the hob.

"What a wonderful evening. Megan got home alright, did she?" Rob nodded and immediately wished he hadn't. What a state to get into, he thought. "I've been on the phone to my parents, they are over the moon. My dad said you asked him for my hand, you romantic fool, you." Rob looked up with an inane grin on his face. "My mum couldn't believe he kept it from her. He'll be in for some grief now. Mum wanted to know when we were actually going to get married. I told her we hadn't even discussed it yet. I'm afraid I chickened out telling her about the baby, but they'll all be over soon so I can tell them then. Rob, are you still with me?" He'd collapsed into his arms on the table. He slowly lifted his head and nodded gently again. Lara put a cup of coffee under his nose and it seemed to revive him. Either that or he was worried if he slipped back down on the table he'd burn his nose. "We'll leave the details till later, yes?" They sat in silence, Rob trying to pick up his cup with his eyes half closed, Lara trying not to smile too broadly. Poor Rob.

Lara didn't see Rob until the following morning. He'd managed to sleep through the afternoon into the evening and on until the dawn chorus. He woke up feeling good. His headache had gone, and the nausea had left. He needed to go over and apologise to Lara. He wasn't used to drinking, so armed with that excuse, he walked round to her house.

Lara was in the garden, she had been sipping tea and eating a pastel de nata , her favourite. They were similar to English custard tarts, made in puff pastry with vanilla, sugar and egg yolks blended and cooked inside. She'd bought enough for Rob, as he loved them too. "You look much more human today. Are you feeling it?" She was smiling at him affectionately.

"I am so sorry Lara. I'm not used to alcohol. Mind you I think someone may have spiked my drink." He knew that wasn't true, but he needed an excuse that wasn't his fault.

"Let's forget about it. It's water under the bridge now. Or should I say champagne! No, sorry, enough of the jokes. Let me get you a cuppa." He sat out in the sun and devoured two tarts. He realised he hadn't eaten for thirty-six hours. Lara brought out a cup of tea and sat back down. "Now, what are the wedding plans?" She knew he wouldn't have any, but needed to tell him what she wanted.

"I was hoping you and Megan could go off and plan it all." Lara laughed, and shook her head. Men, she thought. His face was like a little boy lost. He was totally out of his depth.

"Don't worry, I'm sure Megan would love to help me. I would have liked to have waited until the baby is born. It's just that it will be the best day of my life, and I didn't want to hurry the arrangements to fit it around the birth. I'd have liked to get my figure back first and then wear a beautiful dress so you'll look at me and think 'wow'!" Rob took her hand.

"I do that now. You are the most beautiful woman in the world to me. Big tummy, or slim, it doesn't matter. But if it matters to you then waiting will be ok with me." Lara could feel the tears welling up again, bloody hormones, she thought.

"No, that's not fair to the baby. I want it to be born into a family, our family. Somehow, when the time is right, Megan needs to know that it will be her blood sister or brother. I haven't a problem with her not calling me mum, that will always be Jilly, but if I am honest, it hurt me when she called me stepmother the other night." Rob looked horrified. He was sure Megan was over her jealous thing. "It's ok, she said it in jest. The problem is that the longer we leave it the harder it will get." Rob nodded. He had been thinking the same thing. "I just feel with the wedding and then the baby, she would enjoy it much more if she knew we were all truly family. What do you think?" Rob had dreaded the question being asked. He shook his head.

"I really can't predict her reaction, that's the problem. On one hand, what you say about belonging is true; but on the other she may feel we should have been up front with her from the beginning. Let's start the wedding plans and see what happens. With all your family coming over, she's beginning to see them as hers already. Does that make sense?" He was going round in circles. The main worry Lara had was her judgement being put into question sixteen years ago.

"You're right. We will play it by ear. Now we should concentrate on the wedding, firstly where, here or England?" Rob didn't hesitate.

"Here of course. This is where our lives together started. All Saints in Almancil should be the venue, and Father Kevin will almost certainly give up his golf on a Sunday afternoon for something this important." He was chuckling to himself. Lara suddenly thought 'the old boy network' was still going strong in the Algarve. Luckily her Doctor was new to the area and didn't play golf; but as Rob had remarked after her first appointment, early days. Most of the men seemed to succumb to the golf magnet once they had been there a while. Lara thought the inducement was more likely the nineteenth hole rather than the other eighteen, especially in the summer months when the course was too hot and the cold beer was on tap.

"So the Anglican Church in Almancil, followed by a meal somewhere, or a party?" Lara wondered if it was at that point she should phone her mum and sister for advice.

"It depends on how many people can make it over. If it's just your family and my friends here, then we could have a garden party and buffet. It would keep it personal and relaxed. But if you would rather a massive affair in the five-star Quinta Hotel, then that is what you shall have." His fingers were crossed behind his back. He wanted a small, intimate wedding.

"Don't be daft. I'll be showing majorly by then, so a pretentious venue would only be embarrassing." She looked at him and smiled. He wasn't enjoying the details at all. "I'll tell you what, you get a list together of everyone you want to invite and we'll go from there. But just so you know, the idea of a garden party sounds fab." He got up and cuddled her. She sniggered inwardly, having noticed fleetingly that he'd had his fingers crossed. She did love him to bits.

CHAPTER 9

~~~

On hearing the news about the impending wedding, Debbie decided to get the ball rolling. She had a suspicion that a baby would probably follow due to Rob's age, and Lara's body clock was running late for a first baby. To her and Tori's delight, the salon was snapped up. It was hardly surprising looking at the turnover, especially through a recession. Debbie put it down to loyal staff and Tori's new ideas. The next problem was to break it to the staff. The new owners were very keen on keeping them. Debbie had decided to leave it up to Tori. Which was why Tori had invited Hayley and Kate and Josh out for a meal that evening. Josh had bounced back from depression from being (as the girls comically put) chucked by Chuck, which he found amusing now, but was suicidal for a week, until Steven came into his life. He was dark, handsome with a sombre almost melancholy appearance, but a very dry sense of humour. Hayley had joked that he would make a brilliant mortician. He was actually at Bournemouth University studying to be a photographer.

"Can't believe your sister is getting married. How long has she been in Portugal now?" Hayley was thinking if Lara can marry after all that time, there was still a chance for her.

"She hasn't been over there long, but she's known Rob for years, remember. We're off on our holiday there in a month. Probably stay there for a while. How's your pizza?" Tori had backed out. She was going to invite them all over for a holiday to see what their reaction would be. Then ask them if they'd like to stay indefinitely.

"It's fine. You are so lucky. I'd love to go over there again. We had such a good time last time." Hayley looked at Kate. "You've been going on about it too, haven't you?" Kate nodded while sucking some spaghetti into her mouth. "That really isn't very attractive Kate." Kate looked up and wiped her mouth on her napkin.

"You tell me anyone who eats spaghetti attractively, and I'll show you a person who really needs to get a life." Hayley realised her sister had a point.

"Well said Kate. So, Tori, do you think we could come over for a holiday and stay with Lara?" Josh had warmed to the idea of Portugal again.

"Well I'm glad you all like Portugal so much, as there is a little proposition I need to put to you all." They all seemed to move forward, or it could have been Tori's imagination. "Mum and I have sold the salon. But before you all start weeping and wailing..." She knew what drama queens artistic people are prone to be. "You have two options. Firstly, the new owners are happy for you to stay at the same pay as you are on now. They are lovely people. Husband and wife hairdressing team who have inherited money from a relative and want to open their own business, and know it'll be easier to buy a going concern." The gang were unusually very quiet. It unnerved Tori a little, but she decided to go on. "The second option, and the one Mum and I hope you take, is for you all to come to the Algarve and work for us over there." Before she could finish they had jumped off their chairs and were rushing round cuddling each other. "Hang on, I haven't finished." It was their cue to sit back down. "We haven't actually found anything out there yet, but Lara has a few premises for us to view in a month. It shouldn't take long to get the ball rolling out there, so to speak, and in the meantime, we are delaying the completion of the sale here, unless you want to stay with the new people?"

"No, I want to come with you." Hayley was the first to scream.

"Me too, where will we live though?" Kate was a little worried about actually living abroad. "And what about Mum and Dad, Hayley?" Hayley realised that Kate wasn't very old. She'd need more time to consider her options.

"We'll talk about it later with Mum and Dad. Ok Kate?" Kate nodded. Josh had been remarkably quiet.

"What about you Josh? It wouldn't be the same without you. But it's wrong of me to pressure you." Tori gave him an encouraging grin. He took a deep breath.

"I suppose I'll find another Steven out there, or a James, or a Toby or a Ben." He was laughing. "Do you really need to ask? How on earth do you think you can run a salon without me, my lovely? You'd go under within the first week.

You know you would." Tori couldn't have had a better response. Three of her dearest friends were going to start a new life together with her. She was crying. "You really should have gone to stage school, darling, not hair and beauty. Those hormones of yours are playing silly buggers at the moment, aren't they?" She looked up at Josh and smiled. He was right. There was no way the salon would have been the same without him in it. She just wondered if the imminent clients in the Algarve were ready for him.

Lara and Megan had been busy planning the wedding to coincide with her family's visit to the Algarve. It would be a total surprise for them. Her mother was anticipating another autumn wedding. The bump growing under her dress would be another! Lara had wanted to keep it small, especially because of her condition. If her family had known about the wedding in advance she knew her mum would have wanted extended family plus neighbours and friends, which would have been far too exhausting. She would compromise and have a party for friends in England when she and Rob next visit, probably after the birth. She had been very grateful to Megan for her help. They had taken a day trip to Seville across the border into Spain and bought a beautiful wedding dress. It was ivory in colour, and at the top was a corset-like bodice that laced up as tightly or loosely as you needed. Ideal when she was growing by the day. She had chosen a lovely lilac bridesmaid dress for Megan, and a matching coloured dress for Tori. Tori's had the same corset like bodice; she would be a little bigger than Lara by then. Lara knew the sewing machine would probably come out the night before, but wasn't that half the fun of the preparations? Her mother may not think so!

Megan had organised a suit for her father, with a tie that matched the lilac of the bridesmaid dresses. Lara somehow had to make sure her father brought over a suit. She had a brainwave and phoned her mum and told her they would need posh clothes as Rob was taking them to a very salubrious restaurant, silver service, and the lot. She'd also asked her mother to tell Adam he'd need a suit too. Megan bought ties for both the men, in case they didn't bring one. Most places seem to allow suits with open-necked shirts, especially in the heat. But Megan wanted everything to be right for her dad and Lara. She was getting used to the idea of a new woman in her dad's life, but she still had moments when she was quite possessive of her father. She confided in Chloe one evening.

"I don't think you are possessive, Megan, I think you are being protective. They are two very different things. You don't exactly want Lara to disappear from your lives, do you? You just want to make sure your dad is always there for you, and he is happy and he doesn't get hurt." Megan wondered when Chloe had done her psychology degree.

"I suppose you are right. If I'm honest I think Lara has been very good for my dad. She seems to have brought his fun side out. I hadn't seen that for a long time. But when the baby comes I'll be away at school and they will be their own little family over here." Megan was feeling sorry for herself.

"There's an easy answer to that." Megan looked at Chloe wondering what gem she was about to come out with. "Why go to English boarding school? You could stay here with me and go into our sixth form. A Levels are the same, wherever you take them. Perhaps in two years' time we could go off to university in England together, by then you would probably love to get away from an annoying toddler." Megan jumped into the air and high-fived Chloe.

"You are brilliant. Dad didn't want me to go in the first place. I just thought it would be fun, but now I can have fun with a new brother or sister. It's quite exciting really." Chloe was grinning. "Why are you smiling like that, you are worrying me." Chloe hugged her friend.

"I would have missed you so much if you had gone to that school. My parents said they wanted me to stay here, no way would I have been allowed to board." Megan felt quite selfish. She loved Chloe but she hadn't thought of Chloe's feelings.

"Why didn't you tell me before? I didn't think you minded me going off." Chloe looked Megan in the eyes.

"You are my best friend, and you had your heart set on going. I didn't want you to stay because of me, or you may have regretted it and blamed me." Megan laughed.

"Chloe, Chloe. You will always be my best friend. That wouldn't change even if I become famous and started living in LA. Your house would be next door to mine and we'd share a private jet to bring us home to see our folks as often as we want." Chloe started laughing too. She'd have her best friend for a few more years anyway. She wasn't naïve enough to think it would last forever. Fame may get in the way, but more likely boys!

"Who are you going to tell first? Your dad will be happy, but you need to tell Mr McCarthy. Not sure how he'll react." Chloe sniggered. The headmaster of their school had breathed a sigh of relief when Megan told him she wasn't likely to stay into the sixth form. Although Megan was a good student, and was courteous and helpful, she did have annoying habits that got her into trouble with some of the teachers. One being her constant humming during lessons that she didn't realise she was doing. The other was falling asleep in lessons after a particularly late night singing. But if the truth be known, Mr McCarthy rather liked Megan's spirit and had actually told Rob on the golf course that he'd miss Megan. Rob hadn't told Megan, she'd have been unbearable for days.

"I'll tell Dad. He can ring Mr McCarthy, or Lara can. After all he'll be her boss after the holidays." Chloe hadn't thought of that; Lara would be teaching at their school. "I'll go and tell him now and let you know his reaction. After all the hard work with Lara helping change his mind in the first place, I'm not sure if he's for or against it now." Chloe actually felt sorry for Megan's dad. Megan left Chloe's feeling happy about her life-changing decision. Chloe was left feeling even happier.

Lara was getting nervous. Her family were due any moment and trying to hide her bulge was futile. It was too hot for long jumpers and so it was going to be obvious at first sight. Rob had borrowed a seven-seater car from a golf partner to pick them up from the airport. Megan was trying to calm Lara down.

"They'll be thrilled, you know they will." Megan hadn't known them long but she knew they were a very close family. "Just think you and Tori will be able to share babysitters." Trust Megan to see a positive note.

"I was hoping that would be you." Lara smiled up at

Megan. Megan smiled back. She hoped it would too. Both Lara and Rob were delighted to hear that Megan had decided to stay in Portugal for her A Levels. Lara had found it more and more difficult to bite her tongue when talking to Megan about the babies and her family. One would be her sibling the other her cousin, and her real grandma and granddad were on their way over. She knew it was the fact that she was pregnant again, bringing back feelings of guilt that made her want to tell Megan the truth, but having discussed it at length with Rob, then was not the time to drop the bombshell. For Megan's sake, they needed to be sure of the best time. Lara hoped it would be sometime soon.

"They're here." Megan heard the car pull up to Lara's house. "Come on, we'll face them together." She took Lara's hand.

Pete had opened the back and was helping Debbie and Tori out while Rob and Adam were unloading the suitcases. Rob hadn't mentioned Lara's condition, although tempted to get them used to the idea before they saw her, so as not to upset her, he felt it wasn't his place, and Lara had been quite strict on the subject. Tori was waddling up the path as quickly as her figure would let her, smiling at her sister.

"Lala, we're here at last!" Tori was stating the obvious as usual. She suddenly stopped in her tracks. She moved again, slowly, squinting. Had her sister put on weight? Was it a trick of the light? Megan shifted slightly to give Tori the full view of her sister. "Oh my God, Lala. You're preg..." Lara went forward and hugged her sister before she managed to blurt it out.

"I think I need to tell Mum first, don't you?" She and Tori smiled at each other. Tori whispered in her ear.

"Congratulations, you naughty girl." She unclasped her sister and made her way to Megan. She knew she'd hear all the gossip from her. Debbie caught sight of Lara, smiled, and then the familiar squint came onto her face too.

"Hello Mum. Good journey?" Lara was playing. "Dad, lovely to see you both." Pete had caught up to Deb with the suitcases. He put them down and went forward to hug his daughter. Why his wife had stopped halfway along the path, in the way, he didn't know. That was until he got nearer Lara.

"Oh my God, you're pregnant!" He smiled at Lara, turned to see Rob grinning and hugged Lara with all his might. "Congratulations, clever girl." He kissed her and turned to see what Debbie was going to say. "Look Debs, both our little girls are having babies. Isn't it wonderful?" Pete couldn't read Debbie's face. To Lara and Rob's relief, Debbie ran up to Lara, crying and hugging her.

"I'm so pleased for you Lara. I was beginning to think you'd never settle down to a normal family life." Lara wasn't sure if she should take that as a good thing or a bad thing, but she didn't care. Her parents were happy and her sister was thrilled. Rob came up behind them all.

"Champagne anyone?" Bless Rob, thought Lara. He rounded the strays up and got everyone inside. Megan had shown everyone where they were sleeping, and went into the kitchen to help Rob with the glasses and the champagne. After a few minutes, the whole family were in the kitchen.

"A toast. To my darling fiancée, and her family, welcome to Portugal." Rob held up his glass and then chinked it on Lara's and Megan's. "Cheers everyone." Lara looked around her kitchen and saw everyone she loved, together, smiling.

The silence was broken by Tori.

"Well, when is it due? Do you know the sex yet? Oh my God, I'm so excited. My baby will have a cousin the same age to play with. They'll be like twins." Adam put his arm around his wife.

"If you calm down for a moment, Lara will be able to answer your questions." Everyone laughed.

"It's due in January. We don't want to know the sex until it's born. We are very happy about giving Megan a sibling to play with." Megan smiled and hugged Lara. She could see what Lara was doing and appreciated it. Lara looked at Rob. They had decided to tell them about the wedding as soon as the dust settled from the news about the baby. Was that look Lara was giving him his sign? He wasn't sure. Megan sighed and looked at them both.

"And you are all cordially invited to the wedding between Lara and my father on Sunday at the All Saints Church, Almancil. We hope you haven't any other plans!" Tori screamed. She ran over to Lara and hugged her again. Lara was beginning to feel slightly bruised, but was enjoying every moment. Rob mouthed a 'thank you' to Megan. She smiled back, glad to be a child for a little longer; adult's lives seemed so complicated.

"Well it's a good job I've brought my best frock!" Debbie was laughing and thumped Pete. "You see it was something important. Thank goodness you listened to me and packed your suit." Pete rubbed his arm.

"Yes dear." Pete humoured her. He'd have the last laugh when she realised he'd packed smart trousers and a sporting blazer, thinking most important events happened at a golf course, in his world. Adam got a signal from Rob to join him outside with a beer. Pete had a bottle thrust into his hand by Megan and followed the men out into the garden. They knew baby and wedding talk would follow and it certainly was no place for any self-respecting man.

If the babies were on time, they'd be born four weeks apart. But given Tori was two weeks late and Lara was two weeks early, the date may be nearer, which meant they could be Christmas babies.

"Well Holly and Gabriel would be good names for a boy and girl." Megan was enjoying Tori's company. "Or Carol and Noel. Or Nicholas and Mary."

"Oh, I quite like the name Nicholas." Tori wasn't sure whether she wanted to be told the sex of her baby at the next scan. Adam's parents wanted to know if it was a boy so they could put his name down for a good school. Adam wanted what Tori wanted, and so they would probably wait until the birth.

"I rather like the names Rudolph or Gloria." Everyone looked at Lara, not sure if she was joking. Megan was the first to break as she knew what they had chosen already, and it was a secret. She burst out laughing.

"Your faces!" She picked up the bottle of champagne and poured a little more for Debbie and filled the sisters' glasses with orange juice. She winked at Lara. Debbie noticed the bond that had grown between Lara and Megan, but there was also something else there she couldn't quite put her finger on. Mannerisms? Even their colouring and stature were alike. Lara wouldn't have any problem passing Megan off as her own. They'd be a lovely family, thought Debbie. She was very pleased for her eldest daughter.

"Well, come on, let us know the plans for Sunday." Lara

was thrilled her mother hadn't taken offence at not being included in the planning stage.

"I've got a bridesmaid dress for you Tori. It's in my room at the back of the door." Megan took Tori's hand and led her to Lara's bedroom. "It may need altering Mum." She looked at her mum with a pleading expression. Her mum shook her head.

"Less than forty-eight hours until the wedding, you are cutting it fine, young lady. Oh Lara, I'm so happy for you. What a lovely surprise, a baby and a wedding all in the first few days of our holiday. Please tell me there are no more surprises so we can relax for the remainder." Lara giggled.

"No, not that I'm aware of. My old work friend Tina has organised all the paperwork for me to make the marriage legal. That was a weight of our minds. We have decided to have a honeymoon after the baby is born. We're getting to the busy season for Rob's work, and I really don't want to travel to exotic places and pick up an equally exotic disease until I'm sure the baby is safe."

"I quite agree. Anyway, we'll need you here to help with our salon move. Did you hear Josh and Kate and Hayley are all coming too?" Lara was so happy her family were actually moving to Portugal. Not just for babysitting purposes!

"I knew Josh and Hayley were coming out, there was a question mark over Kate." Debbie nodded.

"I had a cosy lunch with her mum, and told her she'd be safe over here. I've told them about all the footballers who come here regularly and the prospects are very good. It swayed her dad, and her mum was tempted by free holidays. Mercenary but human." Tori walked into the kitchen, the dress fitted almost perfectly. With a different bra and adjusting the laces at the back, it would be fine.

"Phew, that was pretty good judgement, although I say so myself." Lara was relieved. She didn't really want her mother to spend the next day on the sewing machine. "Did you show Tori the ties?" Megan nodded.

"And my dress. I didn't show her yours though. That's your prerogative." There was an interrupting chink of glass on the kitchen door. Megan noticed an empty beer bottle being waved at her. She went to the fridge and took out three more. She took them out for them.

"She's a poppet, Lara. She's ever so pleased for you and her Dad. I thought she'd be jealous." Lara smiled.

"We've had our moments, but she knows that she is the most important person in her dad's life at the moment, and the baby won't change that. I don't want to change that either." Megan came back in.

"Would you like me to help you out of the dress Tori? I've got to rehearse a song for the wedding, perhaps you could listen and tell me what you think." Tori said she'd loved to. They left Lara and Debbie talking about what the boys would be wearing and what the plans for the reception were.

"Your mum's getting quite excited. It's a little different to your wedding." Tori had to agree, it was. "I think Lara just wanted the baby to be born in wedlock. She's quite old fashioned, your sister. My friends think it's sweet." Tori had managed to step out of her dress. Megan put it on the hanger.

"It doesn't bother you, the wedding and a baby? It's all happened so quickly." Megan sat on the edge of the bed.

"It did at first. But Lara has made it very clear that I'm gaining a friend, not losing a dad. She's very clever. She makes my dad very happy too. In fact, when I'm famous and have to spend most of my time in LA, I'll know he won't be lonely." She fell back on the bed and laughed. Tori laughed with her. She did like Megan. She reminded her a little of her sister at that age. Both were full of life and ambition.

"So, when you are rich and famous, what will you be called?" Tori didn't think it wasn't going to happen. Megan would be famous. It was just a matter of time.

"Well, Adele and Leona used just their first names. Megan doesn't seem to have the same effect. My initials like JLS would be a no no. Then you have J-Lo. If I take some of my first name and surname I'd end up with Meg-Sim. Now I don't know about you but that sounds like something from a computer or a mobile phone." They were both laughing on the bed when Lara and Debbie walked in to see what they were laughing about.

"Megan's stage name is going to be Nokia!" Tori spluttered. They were both rolling about on the bed, laughing. Lara and Debbie couldn't see the joke. Debbie stood in shock.

"Oh, my goodness. Just seeing you two like that has given me déjà vu. It's just like the old days when you and Tori were giggling over a lad or something that had happened that day at school." She shook her head. Lara smiled. Her mother was going to work it out sooner rather than later. One thing her mother wasn't was stupid. Something had to be done, but what? She'd discuss it with Rob after the wedding.

Saturday was filled with decorating the garden at Rob and Megan's house for the reception. Luckily Rob had kept the floating lily candleholders and ribbons from Megan's sixteenth birthday party. When it was looking wonderful, Debbie, Tori and Lara went off to buy the food. Adam and Pete had been taken up to the driving range for an hour, which left Megan and Rob alone. They were sitting in the garden on a festooned bench.

"Are you ok poppet?" Rob was stroking Megan's hair. He hadn't done that for ages, she thought. Was he having second thoughts about the wedding? She'd heard it was normal.

"I'm fine, Dad. How about you? Are you nervous about tomorrow?" Rob realised his little girl had grown up.

"Not nervous, apprehensive. After all it will be Lara's first time. I'm an old hand at it." He laughed. Megan noticed the laugh was slightly forced.

"Dad, you know Mum would be happy for you, don't you? She would have wanted you to move on. Who better to marry than someone she loved herself?" Rob's face, usually so stoic, had completely crumbled. He nestled his head onto Megan's shoulder and let out his pain in front of her for the first time. Megan just stroked his head. Role reversal at its best. After a few minutes, Rob got up and turned to his daughter.

"I'm sorry Meggie Moo. I think my hormones got the better of me. This being pregnant lark isn't all it's cracked up to be for a chap." Megan laughed. She had her dad back. "I know you miss her too. That was selfish of me. But thank you for saying what you said. It means a lot to have your approval." Megan got up and cuddled her dad.

"I've had all my friends to talk to, and cry with. You wouldn't cry in front of me so it all got bottled up. I'm glad you were able to treat me as a friend as well as a daughter.

I may only be sixteen, but as Mason Morgan said, I've had to grow up quicker than most." She smiled up at him. "And he should know, he's amazing." Rob laughed. He had his teenage daughter back, but funnily he felt closer to her than he ever thought would be possible.

"Come on, let's go down to Vale Do Lobo and I'll treat you to a cocktail." Megan liked that idea.

"Not a Shirley Temple I hope." After all, she was a grown up now.

"No, you can have whatever one you like, just remember you will be walking your future mother down the aisle tomorrow, so we don't need you getting a fit of the hiccups like the last time you had cocktails." Megan smiled. That wasn't the only side-effect of the pretty coloured cocktail, but she wasn't going to mention that until after she'd got the drink from her father. Anyway, toilet humour seemed inappropriate after their heart to heart.

That evening they all went to Nelitos Restaurant for a wonderful 'last supper' as Rob called it, teasing Lara.

"Well, who'd have thought the last time we were here that we'd be sitting toasting your wedding the next day?" Tori was again stating the obvious. Megan was so pleased she would soon be able to call her Auntie Tori. She was so cool. Lara looked at Rob, they were thinking the same. Was it really only last year? Thank goodness she went off to find them both. Her life would have carried on in the same mode until she retired into lonely spinsterhood. With only her nieces and nephews for holidays, and perhaps a few cats living in. She had been functioning, not living.

"Lara? Hello, are you there." Lara suddenly realised she was the focus of attention.

"Oops, sorry. I was reminiscing." She smiled at Rob.

"Still too much thinking, I thought we'd got you out of that bad habit." He frowned at her, with a smile trying to break through. The owners, Linda and Manuel, had brought out a bottle of champagne and wanted to toast the happy couple. Linda and Manuel had met in London, where Manuel was a chef at the Savoy. They fell in love and married. With Manuel being Portuguese, they moved down to the Algarve where they opened their own successful restaurant. Lara arranged for Linda to go over for coffee the following week to help Debbie with the ins and outs of buying a business in the area. They'd see them at the wedding, but it was a day of celebration, not business.

"To the wedding of the year, tomorrow. *Nós desejamo-lo felicidade e luz do sol.*" With a few puzzled faces Manuel translated. "We wish you happiness and sunshine."

"Thank you, Manuel. Cheers." Rob saluted his host with his glass.

"*Saúde.*" Manuel and Linda chanted.

"*Saúde.*" The party chorused back. Manuel patted Rob on the back and kissed Lara on the cheeks and then disappeared back into the kitchen.

"If you want to have the specials, Manuel will have to cook them for you." Linda grinned. "But I'm in no hurry, now Debbie, I hear you want to open your own business." Debbie and Linda were in full flow when Megan suddenly tried to hold in a scream.

"Don't look now, but Jason and Melanie from *So You Want to Sing* have just walked in." Tori looked round. "I said don't look." Megan turned back to her table and as nonchalantly as possible, dunked her roll in the oil and balsamic vinegar. Linda looked at the door and realised she had to be the hostess.

"I'll be back later. Luis, Table Six is ready for that party." She was talking to the maître 'd, who was holding the door open for the celebrities, not realising who they were.

"She knew they were coming and didn't tell me." Rob looked at Megan, trying to act normal.

"I wonder why." Everyone laughed except Megan.

"But Dad, it's Jason Parker and MelanieCourtney. You know you love her. Oops, sorry Lara." Lara smiled. She was sure that Rob wouldn't be normal if he didn't love Melanie Courtney. As they passed their table they all smiled at them. Both Jason and Melanie had their partners with them.

"They've come for a nice quiet dinner out, I think we can respect their privacy." Debbie wasn't in the least bit moved by the arrival of celebrities.

"Mum, you know you love Jason and Russ in that jungle program. Who are you trying to kid?" Tori had seen through her mum's fake composure. Debbie looked up from her lap.

"She's busy texting all her friends." Pete could see exactly what his wife was doing. Everyone laughed again. What a wonderful evening, thought Lara. Rob had turned to make eye contact, and his face was saying the same as her thoughts.

The meal was to die for. Everyone tried to eat all their puddings, but were beaten. The Quinta Do Crasto, Rob's favourite wine from the Douro region of Portugal had flowed as beautifully as the conversation. Megan had managed to take her eyes off Table Six, but found it hard.

"Do you realise that in a few years holiday makers will

be sitting looking over at our table, wanting your autograph." Tori had said it in such a matter-of-fact way that everyone nodded.

"Phitt!" Was all Megan could say. She'd had her glass filled more often than anyone had realised, thanks to her ally Felix, the waiter. He'd managed to put equal amounts of soda water in while Megan's head was turned, on Linda's orders. She knew Megan was a bridesmaid the next day. A massive headache she didn't need.

As they were all talking, no one noticed Jason Parker walk over to Megan. He tapped her on the shoulder. Megan turned round and was so grateful she hadn't anything in her mouth, as it had dropped open on a reflex action, not attractively. Josh laughed.

"Sorry if I startled you. I just wanted to see you close up. I've seen your YouTube video and we caught sight of one of your performances in Vale Do Lobo a couple of nights ago. I was wondering if you were thinking of going on *So You Want to Sing*? You'd be the best they've seen this year." Megan was spellbound.

"Megan, close your mouth darling, not attractive." Rob was laughing. "Hello, I'm her father. She's auditioned for *Make Me A Star UK* on the other side, I'm afraid. She got through, but I've been a bit of a party pooper. We are going to get her through her A Levels first, then she can follow her own choice of career."

"Well, I hope it will be singing. Bye, Megan. Let me know when you are ready, here's my card. Perhaps I can help point you in the right direction. It's a cut-throat world, and someone as talented as you needs to be protected from the likes of Mason Morgan." He winked.

"He sent me a letter. He wants to produce me." She wasn't sure whether Jason was being serious. Mason Morgan was her idol.

"I was kidding. He is a great chap. We were only talking to him yesterday, and he mentioned you. He knew we were in Vale Do Lobo and he remembered that was where you were. You see, you are famous already! I won't take up any more of your time. Nice to have met you all, and I hear from Manuel that you have a big day tomorrow. Congratulations and good luck." He put out his hand for Megan to shake. "Bye Megan, I look forward to hearing you sing again, in the future." He shook hands with Rob and waved to everyone else and went back to his table. Megan's cheeks were bright red. She could see the other people at their tables looking over wondering who she was that a big celebrity had gone over to talk to her. She sat up straight and smiled. She could get used to fame.

"Here you are. As you seem to be so famous, you can pay the bill." Rob had put the saucer with the till receipt in front of his daughter. Everyone was laughing, Megan joined in. One day, she thought, she'd take them all to a wonderful restaurant in Miami, or LA or just there would be nice. Megan yawned. "Come on, let's get you home. We've a busy day tomorrow." They said goodbye to Linda and Manuel and left for home. Rob had kept the seven-seater for the duration of their stay, which was very helpful. He'd drop the Allen party off on the way round. Megan stayed in the car as the rest got out at Lara's house. Lara hung back until her family had gone into the house.

"Goodnight Miss Allen. I hope you sleep well. I'll send Megan over nice and early for her hair and make-up. You can send the men over to me, if you like. Otherwise I'll be all on my own." He had a pouting sulk on his face. Lara giggled.

"I thought your best man was coming over to be with you. He is in the country, isn't he?" Rob had kept his best man a secret from Lara. She knew he had to fly over from England, but who he was was a mystery. She had visions of a hippie or an ex-biker. She couldn't work out, if he was normal, why Rob had kept it a secret.

"All will be revealed tomorrow. Barring ash clouds, air traffic control strikes, and mechanical failure of the aircraft, he should be landing any moment now. I've sent a taxi down to pick him up. You can see him at the wedding. By the way, have I told you how much I love you?"

"Not recently, it was at least three hours ago." Lara gave as good as she got. She felt a yawn coming. "I must go in and get my beauty sleep. I've left it a bit late, but hopefully I'll get enough to make a pretty blushing bride." He leant down and kissed her.

"Will you two please wait until tomorrow? I know the 'virgin bride' bit is a little antiquated, but too much of that kissing business could be damaging for a child my age to observe." They could hear her giggling in the back of the car.

"I'll take her home and beat her for you." Rob was winking.

"Hey, I was only joking. Night Lara. See you in the morning." Megan decided to get into the front of the car. She went over and kissed Lara on the cheek. "I think I may be too excited to sleep, but I'll try." She got into the car and waited.

"Better go. Night night, my lovely Lara. Sweet dreams." Rob cuddled her one more time.

"Night night Rob, tomorrow is the first day of the rest of our lives, together. What a wonderful thought to sleep on." She pulled away from him, and gently pushed him towards the car. Poor Megan was wacked. She needed her bed almost as much as Lara did. They waved goodbye and Lara went into her house.

"Come on young lady, let's get you home. We should have a visitor by now." Rob winked at Megan. She knew who his best man was.

"Lara will see the funny side, I hope."

"So do I. Too late to get another best man." They drove off round the corner, both grinning. The taxi was just pulling away as they drove up. Megan got out to give him a massive welcome as Rob waited for the gates to open.

"Josh, how brilliant you made it on time. I've missed you. Come on in and have a drink." Megan was thrilled to see Josh.

"Well, after the journey from hell, seated in a smelly aeroplane for two and a half hours, then queuing to put my passport through that machine, only to get there and be told they were out of order. A drink? My dear, I need an intravenous drip filled with vodka, no less." They walked up the driveway hand in hand. Rob had unlocked the front door.

"Josh, glad you could make it." He shook his hand.

"I cannot believe you asked me to be your best man. What an honour." Josh was finding it difficult to control his inner emotions. He wanted to cry and laugh at the same time. He was just so excited. It made Megan and Rob smile.

"And then you tell me to keep it a secret. Do you not realise how difficult it is for gays to keep anything a secret?!" Rob laughed. He was glad he had chosen Josh. At least no one would be able to call it a boring wedding.

"I had to choose you, Josh. You were there at the beginning of our romance, it seemed only fitting you saw it through." Rob had poured Josh a vodka and cranberry juice, remembering it was one of his favourites.

"Oh, my goodness, you remembered what I drink." Josh was welling up.

"Perhaps you two should be getting married." Megan couldn't help comment. Josh loved the idea. Rob shook his head.

"I really don't think you could cope with the wrath of Debbie." Josh agreed. They'd leave the status quo, and he'd just be their best man. "Off to bed young lady. You can catch up with Josh in the morning." Megan shrugged. She'd have loved to have stayed and chatted, but even she realised that her eyes were going to need matchsticks if she stayed up any longer. She must have had more wine than she thought.

"It's a shame you couldn't come to the meal tonight Josh. Guess who was there?" Josh shrugged. "Well, it wasn't Russ." Josh opened his eyes wide.

"Not Jason?" Megan nodded. "Oh my God. Did you get his autograph?"

"I got one better than that. I got his business card, with his telephone number and email address on. He'd heard me sing the other night and wants me to contact him when I'm in London next, and Melanie Courtney was with him." Megan was walking towards her bedroom, trying not to make eye contact with her father, who was looking stern.

"Ooh, scandal." Megan opened her bedroom door.

"No, not together, they both had their partners. But Jason came over and talked to us, and Melanie waved." Rob coughed and pointed to her bed. "Must go to bed now. Will tell you all about it in the morning. Night Josh. Dad, will you come and tuck me in in a few minutes?" Rob nodded.

"She's so excited about tomorrow, but I think meeting celebrities tonight has taken her over the Richter scale of excitement. Well, that and the consumption of a little more wine than normal. Glad you could come Josh. Should stir things up a little tomorrow." Rob smiled. "I'll just go and tuck my little monster into bed and I'll be with you." Josh was happy just being part of the family. He stayed in the kitchen sipping vodka and picturing Tori's face the next day in church. Rob and Megan had made up a small bed in their box room. It was just the right size for Josh. It was only for one night. With Lara sleeping there the next evening, they'd be a free room at Lara's from tomorrow. Rob managed to get Josh and himself to bed within the hour. They had to be up early, and Josh had been at work all day. He'd managed to get a plane from Southampton, as there were no flights till Monday from Bournemouth. Had the rest of the family known, he could have come with them. But the secret was more fun. It also gave Megan something to organise for her father, without anyone else helping. He hoped it would make her feel important, which it had. Rob could only hope that Lara was getting more sleep than he was. The clock seemed to be going round very slowly. Each time he looked only another half an hour had gone. Luckily two o'clock seemed to be the last time he noticed.

Lara was luckier. Whether it was the baby, or just

tiredness, she shut her eyes and surrendered into the arms of Morpheus almost immediately.

CHAPTER 10

~~~

The wedding day was upon them. Rob could only imagine what Lara's house was like. His was serene. He'd made a pot of coffee, and was debating as to whether he should wake Megan and Josh. The calm and tranquillity would be gone. But he also wanted to share his excitement. He'd get Megan up first as she had to have her hair and make-up done by Tori. He'd taken her dress over the day before, so there was no need for him and Lara to see each other until the service.

"Poppet. Time to get up." Rob was rubbing Megan's forehead. She roused and saw her father and smiled. Suddenly she remembered what day it was.

"What time is it? Oh my word. Daddy, you're getting married in a few hours." Rob nodded, smiling.

"I know." He left her to run into the shower while he woke Josh with a coffee. By the time everyone was up, breakfast was on the table, warm croissants, French stick, cheese, hams, jam and fruit juice.

"How lovely. Continental, my fav." Josh sat down and tucked in. Megan thought he was phatt. What a shock Lara and Tori were going to have. It made Megan giggle.

"What's tickled your fancy?" Josh was giggling too; it was infectious.

"I was just picturing Lara and Tori's faces as they walk down the aisle and see you at the other end. I hope the photographer does a close up of their expressions." Rob hoped it didn't backfire. The last thing he needed was for them both to suffer a miscarriage through shock.

"I wonder whether you should go round and say hello. It will still be a nice surprise, but less of a shock for them." Rob was chickening out.

"Don't you dare. After all the planning and both of us keeping it a secret too. The strain was almost too much to bear." Josh nodded in agreement. "It'll be fine, Dad. It will be a pleasant shock, they won't give birth on the spot." Megan had worked out what Rob was worried about. Rob smiled. She was right. "Anyway, I've got to go in a mo. Josh, keep an eye on him. And make sure he gets to the church on time. It's your job remember. I'm trusting you with my father's life, don't let me down."

"No, don't say it like that. You've scared me." Josh was a baby. Rob and Megan laughed at him. He was trying to wipe strawberry jam off his mouth and making it worse. He was a bundle of nerves. Megan was using reverse psychology. Rob would be so busy calming Josh down, that he'd forget about his own nerves. So far so good. It was working. She left Rob putting some kitchen towel under the tap and passing it to Josh.

"See you later. Break a leg." She kissed her dad and decided to kiss Josh. "You'll be fine. Just remember the ring." Megan did it again. She knew Rob hadn't entrusted Josh with the ring.

"The ring. Did you give it to me? I don't remember you giving it to me Rob." Rob shook his finger at Megan.

"Go now, before you give him a nervous breakdown. And Megs?" Megan stopped at the door. "I love you, poppet. Always." He smiled.

"Love you too Dad. Enjoy today. You deserve it. See you at the church." She was gone.

"Oh, good grief Josh. You aren't crying, are you?" Rob went to fetch some dry kitchen roll. He couldn't help but laugh. He was actually pleased with Megan's idea of a best *man*, but could see the irony in the name with Josh.

Lara's house was relatively calm, not at all what Megan had anticipated.

"Hello Megan dear. Has the best man arrived?" Debbie had seen Megan through the kitchen window and had gone out to greet her. She gave her a motherly hug.

"Yep." Megan said, giving nothing away. Debbie was feeling great affection for Megan. She didn't know if it was just the wedding emotions or the fact that she reminded Debbie of Lara at the same age. She was confident, without arrogance, and bubbly, but with a little vulnerability that was endearing.

Lara noticed her mother bringing Megan in, and the facial expression that meant her mother was near to the penny dropping.

"Megan, how's your father? Oh, and has the best man

arrived yet?" Megan nodded.

"Yes, the best man is with Dad, and they are both fine." No need to panic Lara at this stage. But she wasn't sure whether the best man had had his breakdown yet. She smiled to herself. At least it was taking her Dad's mind off the jitters.

"Come on and let's see how you want your hair." Lara grabbed Megan from her mother's clutches. Her mother was smiling. Had she guessed? Lara had no time to worry. She took Megan into her bedroom that had been converted, temporarily, into a salon. Nails were being filed, hair was being piled and nerves were riled. That was just the men! Wait until Tori started on the girls, Megan thought. She was so enjoying this family life. She had loved her mum and dad but wondered what it would have been like to have a bigger family with aunts, uncles and cousins. She was getting a sample now, and was enthralled by it. She sidled over to Lara's iPod, Rob had bought her as a 'welcome to your new home and forced confinement in due course' present, plugged in the external speakers, and clicked it onto shuffle. Immediately the atmosphere relaxed. Megan hadn't realised she was singing along to the first track, which made everyone listen. Calm had been restored. Good old Olly Murs, thought Megan. If you need something light and cheerful, he was your man.

The men had had enough after a few more minutes, and decided to go and join Rob. They were itching to see who this infamous best man was. Megan wished she could have gone back with them, just to see their faces, but she had already been pulled into the warm, newly vacated chair and her hand was in Tori's, who was tutting.

"You're a nibbler. Tut tut. They won't look good on camera. Lara nibbles too. The pair of you need to manicure every week; that will stop it." Lara giggled at Megan. Tori was quite strict about beauty. Luckily Lara and Megan were laidback about it.

"My mother always said that beauty comes from within. If you are a good person and kind to others then people don't notice your faults." Megan was being a little mischievous. She knew Tori held beauty above all other attributes.

"That may be very true, but bitten nails and split ends would still make Mother Theresa not quite so saintly." Lara and Megan burst out laughing. They didn't mean to wind up Tori, she was a lovely person, it was just so easy. Debbie walked in with coffee and a squash for Megan.

"What's tickled those two?" She nodded towards the laughing hyenas in the corner.

"Me, apparently." Tori looked miffed, but her mum could see she was just keeping up the pretence for the sake of her sister and soon to be niece. "If we are to get you down the aisle on time, we will have to start taking this seriously, you two. I have my work cut out. Mum, perhaps you could start on Lala and I'll do Megan. Thankfully her hair is gorgeous, we'll ignore the nails for now. One out of two ain't bad."

"Ooh, that's a song from your day, isn't it? Meat Loaf I think." It was Tori's turn to laugh.

"Nearly, it's two out of three ain't bad." Megan looked round and everyone was laughing. She knew the real title, but the ploy worked. They were all in harmony again.

Lara hadn't even thought about her nerves since Megan came over. She had a laidback attitude to life that was calming and almost serene. She could see that Jill's last months on earth must have been easier with Megan by her side. Her love for her daughter was growing into such a deep affection that she would find it difficult not to tell her the truth soon.

"Ouch!" Debbie had gently hit Lara on the head with the hairbrush.

"I've been talking to you. I don't know where you go sometimes, Lara. Now, would you like it up or down?" Lara assumed she was talking about her hair as she had a clump of it in her hand.

"I don't mind. How are you having yours Tor?" Tori had already done hers. She looked at her sister with a frown and a face that was trying to stay straight. Unfortunately, Megan couldn't hold her giggle any longer and they all burst out laughing again. When they settled down Megan looked at Tori's hair, piled up with little flower buds, and decided they would all look lovely the same.

"I'd like my hair like yours, Tori, please." Megan smiled at Lara with her eyebrows up in a question. Lara took the hint.

"I'd like mine like yours too, Tor." She turned to Megan and in an aside that could be heard by all. "Creep!" Again, the girls were in fits of laughter. If they all got to the church on time it would be a miracle, but it was Lara's day, and she was enjoying every minute of it.

Rob had opened the electronic gates from his kitchen when Pete had buzzed. Josh went into his bedroom and kept quiet until the big reveal. He was so excited; he had gone to the loo at least twice since Megan had left.

"Morning groom. How are you feeling?" Pete shook his

hand, followed by Adam.

"I'm ok. It's my best man who's a bag of nerves." He led the men into the kitchen. "Beer or coffee?" It was a difficult decision. On the one hand beer would be good, on the other smelling of alcohol at the church would probably upset the girls. They all looked at each other, knowing they were thinking the same. Pete was the bravest.

"Beer, then a coffee." Rob and Adam thought that was a brilliant compromise. Rob took out three beers.

"Your best man not a drinker?" Adam was intrigued. He was under strict instructions to text Tori the minute he knew who it was. Rob had anticipated the news being leaked.

"My best man will be out in a moment, and he prefers a little wine. When you know who it is, I'm hoping you will keep it a surprise as the full impact at the church will be a joy to behold." Rob was smirking.

"You're evil." Pete loved it. Rob nodded and raised his bottle of beer.

"Cheers." They were tilting their bottles into their mouth at the moment Josh had decided to make an appearance.

"Mine's a spritzer please, Rob. Don't want to be tiddly down the aisle." They showered their beer simultaneously across the kitchen floor. Rob had managed to set his mobile on video. Megan was going to love it, he thought.

"Oh my God, Rob. It's brilliant. The girls are going to love it. What a stroke of genius." Adam was gobsmacked.

"Bloody hilarious, Rob. Well done mate." Pete was thinking about the impact on the girls on their walk down the aisle as they catch a glimpse of Josh.

"Let's keep it a secret then, agreed?" Adam and Pete

nodded. Adam wanted to see Tori's face. "It was Megan's idea. She thought it would make everyone very happy." He looked at Josh. He didn't want to offend him. Josh knew exactly what impact he would make, and was thrilled to be part of it.

"I could say at this juncture that I am not the entertainment. But I'd be lying... bring it on!" The one thing Josh loved above all else was being centre of attention, so the arrangement worked well for everyone. Rob passed him a very diluted white wine spritzer.

"Cheers, to the groom. As best man, I'd like to say a few words. 'A few words' ha ha. Oh, my goodness, I've just realised I've got to make a speech. Rob, what do you want me to say?" Rob laughed. He took out a piece of paper from his pocket and straightened it out.

"Megan has written it for you. She knew you would flap." Josh was so grateful to Megan at that point.

"I love that girl." He raised his glass. "To Megan, the best teenager in the world." At that moment, Rob had to agree. The atmosphere was getting deep.

"To Lara, the bride and soon to be my wife." They raised their bottles again, only to notice the bottles were nearly empty. "Just one more. We need to toast the bride."

"And the bridesmaids and the bride's mother." Adam wasn't worried about Tori's reaction to him drinking. She'd be far too busy as matron of honour. Pete, on the other hand did not want the wrath of Debbie.

"Better make this our last. I'll put some coffee on for later." Rob smiled at Adam. Poor Pete. Perhaps when they'd clocked up over thirty years of marriage, they could judge. Pete noticed their glances between each other.

"It's all to do with compromise." He may act like the downtrodden husband, but he'd not swap Debbie for all the tea in china.

The girls had organised sandwiches for them all to eat before the wedding. The Sunday family service ended at eleven o'clock, which gave Father Kevin time to go home and have a bite to eat, and back for the service at 12.00 pm. The idea being that everyone should be back at Rob's for a proper spread by 1.15 pm. Lara was worried about tummy rumblings, especially her and Tori, so decided that a few sandwiches would fill a gap, but not spoil the meal after.

Pete looked at his watch while eating a ham sandwich.

"Better get over to the girls' camp. You and Josh should be at the church in the next twenty minutes. Adam, you coming with me or going straight to the church?" Adam looked at Rob and then at Josh, who was trying to fix his tie with hands that were shaking more than James Bond's martini.

"I'll stay with Rob and Josh. I don't want to be interrogated by my wife. I may divulge the secret." He winked at Rob. Rob looked at Josh who was pacing up and down the kitchen looking at the notes Megan had written for him.

"Thanks." Rob said to Adam. It said it all.

"Ok, see you later. By the way, my lips are sealed. I'm looking forward to seeing the girls speechless for once. A moment to enjoy." He went off down the drive, laughing to himself.

"Right Josh. Let's adjust your tie so it looks more uniform." Rob wondered if Josh thought he was doing up his shoelaces. It was more like a bow than a knot.

"I can't remember the last time I wore a tie. It must have been at school. I'm a little out of practice." Rob smiled.

"So, who's the vicar? Is he a friend of yours?" Adam wanted to keep the conversation going so Josh could lose a few of his nerves.

"Father Kevin. He's a golfing partner of mine. Great chap. He lost his wife a few years ago, and moved over here when the position became available. He's loved it ever since. The dear lady expats swarmed round him like a honey pot. He's the exception; there are a lot of widows. A widower with all his own teeth was a Godsend, if you excuse the pun." Josh was giggling.

"I say, Kev the Rev. How jolly." Rob hadn't thought of that pseudonym, he'd have to use it the next time he beat him at golf.

"Right, if you two are ready, my car awaits." Megan and Lara had draped Rob's car in ribbons. It was to take them from the church to their reception. Adam said he'd drive them back. The girls had the seven-seater, all draped in ribbons, the bridesmaids and mother of the bride were going to the church first, driven by Martin who had volunteered as the chauffeur for the day and then he'd go back for the bride and her father.

Lara and Pete were waiting for Martin to return with the car. Pete looked at his daughter and noticed how happy she was.

"I was beginning to think that life would pass you by, but looking at you now, about to be a wife and mother." He was bursting with pride. "You have made me the happiest man alive today." He hugged her so tightly. "Rob is a fantastic chap. And that daughter of his is a credit to him and Jill.

You are going to make a wonderful family. I hope you have a lovely life together." Lara swore she heard a sniff.

"Dad! I'm getting married, not leaving you forever. Hopefully we will be living down the road from each other for many years to come. You will always be my dad. I may be getting a husband, but you will be my dad forever." She straightened his tie for him and brushed imaginary dust off his shoulders. "Now, let's get this show on the road. I'm starving and need food."

"You have to say 'I do' before you can eat anything." They both heard the car pull up. Diesels had a distinctive sound. It reminded Lara of the London taxis. It seemed like a world away, and it was.

The nerves started to kick in on the four-and-a-half-minute journey to the church. It didn't help that Pete had a fixed inane grin on his face. Lara didn't mind the fact that he knew who the best man was, but she did object to the hilarity that was going on between all the boys. A thought suddenly occurred to her. She prayed it wasn't Hugo. Both Megan and Rob had found the story of her date with him hysterically funny; it would have been their sense of humour to have him as a best man. 'Please God, don't let it be Hugo,' she whispered to herself.

"You ok darling?" Pete had noticed Lara's face contort and drain of colour. He thought perhaps she was exhausted. "Mum put some water in that cool bag, would you like some?" Lara looked at her father and shook her head.

"I'm finding it difficult to sit, Heaven knows how I'd fare if I needed the loo. I think I'll leave liquid refreshments until I'm back at home." He squeezed her hand and looked out of the window.

"Well, if you want to back out now is your chance." He had a smile on his face. They had just pulled up outside the church and Tori and Megan were waiting for her.

"No Dad. I've been ready for this day most of my life. I just had to wait for the right man." He and Martin helped her out.

"Well timed, two minutes late. How very civilised of you." Tori was teasing her sister. She remembered at that moment a few months ago; she was very nervous, and a bit of levity on Lara's part helped her, she was just repaying the kind gesture. Lara looked at Tori and then at Megan. Her two favourite girls in the world and they were sharing her big day. She could feel a tear welling up. "Don't you dare cry. That mascara isn't as waterproof as the manufacturers advertise." Bless Tori, thought Megan. She was the perfect sister. Perhaps Lara's little baby would one day be her perfect sister. Or would she be a half-sister? In fact, there'd be no blood tie what so ever. She had to snap out of her thoughts and concentrate on the job in hand. She helped Tori straighten Lara's veil and train. They were ready. Tori gave the organist the required 'thumbs up' and he started the 'Bridal Chorus'. Pete took hold of Lara's arm and started the procession, followed by Tori and Megan. Lara caught sight of Rob at the end of the aisle, he turned to see her and smiled. She felt totally at ease once he had made eye contact with her. Bring on Hugo or whoever, she didn't mind anymore. To her surprise and great delight, as she neared Rob the identity of his best man was revealed. Josh turned round to Lara and beamed. Lara grinned. All the wedding party were smiling with stupid Cheshire cat smirks on their faces as soon as they spotted Josh. If the vicar hadn't been party to the small deception about the best man, he would have thought he was part of a reality TV show. Lara was level with Rob and Pete stepped back. Tori took her posy of flowers and helped Megan pull her veil over to reveal her beautifully made-up face. Rob was the happiest man on the planet at that moment. He looked into Lara's eyes and spoke.

"Thank you." She tried not to cry again. It was getting more difficult. Bloody hormones, she thought. But she knew it wasn't the hormones. It was the fact she was standing with the love of her life, and he was making her feel special. It was almost as if they were on their own. She reached up and kissed his cheek and whispered in his ear.

"No, thank *you*." They both looked at each other and for some reason they then both looked up to heaven. They knew Jill was there, watching and approving. Father Kevin coughed, very subtly, but it brought the bride and groom back to the reason everyone was in the church.

"Dearly beloved..." Father Kevin's voice was melodic and soothing. His words were being said as if he was talking to Lara and Rob personally. Debbie had a few tears in her eyes. She was glad her daughter was marrying such a lovely man. Her worry was the 'baggage' the man brought to the marriage. She hoped their friendship was strong enough to get through the difficulties she envisaged. She was jolted out of her thoughts by Father Kevin asking Lara to take Rob as her husband.

"Do you Lara Megan Allen..." Of course, that must be where Jill and Rob had got Megan's name from. Deb had obviously known Lara's middle name, after all it was after her mother-in-law, but for some unknown reason she hadn't put that part of the jigsaw together. Megan was born around the time Lara was with them in Portugal. Her name was Lara's middle name. She had the longest legs and bluest eyes, more Allen traits. How could she ask her daughter about it? It was blatant that Megan knew nothing of her real parentage. She could do more damage by making accusations. She would have to hold her tongue until Lara mentioned it. She looked at Megan and the more she stared the more she saw of Lara. Was it psychological now she was curious? Was it like a new-born baby when both sides of the family see the characteristics they want to see, only to find they were looking at the wrong baby through the nursery window? She was jolted out of her daydream by Pete jabbing her. Everyone was standing for the next hymn except Debbie, so deep in thought. She snapped out of her reverie, where she hoped that Megan was her granddaughter, she was such a lovely girl, and started singing.

The service was beautiful. During the signing of the papers Megan sang 'Morning Has Broken' with the backing track from Cat Stevens. Jill had loved the song and the artist, and with permission from both Rob and Lara, Megan thought it would bring her Mum to the proceedings without making people feel uncomfortable. As usual, by the time she had sung the last note, she had the congregation captivated. They were jolted out of their absorption by the organist striking up the 'Wedding March' and Megan managed to join the procession as they walked back along the aisle to the doors and the sunshine outside.

The photographer, also a golfing friend of Rob's, was busy clicking as they appeared through the church doors. Lara was bursting with happiness and Rob with pride to have such a lovely woman on his arm. Megan was cross with herself. She loved Lara, but was starting to feel something that wasn't very positive. Her father was now married to the woman who had his blood child in her womb. Where did that leave Megan? She now had an adopted father and a stepmother and a sibling that was neither her blood nor family. Tori jabbed her playfully.

"Oy, smile for the camera!" Megan tried to smile but was feeling more and more dejected. Rob had spotted Megan's face. His heart went out to her. She would be missing her mum more than ever that day. While Lara had all her family around, he made a pact with himself to spend quality time with Megan. He realised he wouldn't have very much time once the season kicked in, and then shortly after that the baby would be arriving. He managed to catch her eye and smiled at her. Megan felt spiteful and looked away. Then she realised how childish she was being, the last thing she wanted to do was ruin his day. She looked back and smiled at her dad. Unfortunately, he had noticed the effort it had taken her to be civil. Perhaps it was time to tell her the truth. He didn't have any more time to think about it as at that moment the car had arrived at the front of the church and Lara was already getting into it. Debbie had been waiting on the pavement and had noticed the looks that had passed between father and daughter. She'd have a word with Megan at the reception to see if she could help. It must be so difficult for her to see the only parent she had left leave with his new wife. She hadn't had to share his love for a long time. She'd give her some step-grandma advice when she could get her alone.

The reception was in full swing with the food having been devoured almost as soon as they arrived back at the house. The speeches went without a hitch. Josh had used Megan's notes and had got a rousing applause.

"Thank you so much for the speech Megan. I would have gone to pieces if I hadn't had your notes." He hugged her. Megan had started to feel a bit better. Rob had cuddled her and Lara had thanked her for being a wonderful bridesmaid and for her Cat Stevens rendition in the church. Debbie had managed to talk to her and had asked her if she would do her the honour of calling her Grandma Allen. Megan was thrilled and felt like part of the family after all.

"Clever girl." Pete had overheard the conversation and was very proud of his wife. She looked up at him and smiled.

"I just hope it has helped. That is one very emotionally mixed-up kid at the moment. She's tried to act grown up, but she is still very young. Lara has her work cut out, but Rob seems to be able to cope. It will all come right in the end." She hoped.

Megan didn't like herself one little bit. She had withdrawn to her bedroom while the party went on in the garden. Chloe had noticed her absence and had gone looking for her.

"Why are you in here missing all the fun? You were going to sing again, weren't you?" Megan nodded. "I don't feel like singing."

Chloe gasped. That was the first time she had heard her friend say that.

"Megs, what's the matter?" Megan burst into tears. Chloe shut the door. She didn't want Lara and Rob's day ruined. She sat on the bed and put her arm around Megan. "Come on, tell me. Is it because your dad has a new wife?" Megan shook her head.

"I think I just miss my mum so much and today has made me realise that I now have to share my dad. It's so juvenile, Chloe, that I'm really cross with myself for thinking it. Maybe I'm just tired." Chloe felt sorry for her best friend. Megan was a good person. Having thoughts like that was probably making her feel guilty. Chloe wondered what she could say to help.

"I know Lara will never take the place of your mum Megs, but you like her, and your dad was probably lonely for female company before Lara came back into his life. You will be off on your career in a few years. The last thing you now have to worry about is your dad being alone." Megan sighed. Chloe was saying everything Megan had told herself, but she still felt anxious about the arrival of their baby.

"I have got used to Dad being with Lara, it's the baby that worries me. It'll be theirs. I will feel even more adopted with it around. How can I be so selfish on my dad and Lara's wedding day Chlo? I hate myself for feeling like this, today of all days." She shook herself and screamed. "Aahh. Pull yourself together Megan Grace Simpson. Right, I think I'm ready to sing. Point me in the direction of my public." Megan gave Chloe a big smile. Chloe relaxed. Tantrum over, Megan was ready to face the world again. "And Chloe, thanks for listening." Chloe opened Megan's bedroom door. She turned back to Megan.

"What is a friend for, if she can't listen to the mad ramblings of the future Brit Awards winner for the year 2020." Megan laughed.

"Excuse me, but I hope a little sooner than that." They both went out laughing and giggling as usual, to find Rob and get the sound system ready.

On their way back to the garden, they bumped into Josh and Tori having one of their numerous, good-humoured arguments.

"But I had to swear on my life, Tor. It was such a responsibility to keep a secret, and from you of all people. You don't understand the strain I was under. Look!" He pointed to his head. "There are fewer hairs there than a month ago. And look!" He pointed to his face. "Lines. Can you see them? Look, around my forehead and the bags under my eyes." Tori couldn't help but laugh. It was infectious. Megan and Chloe, who had been trying to be sympathetic, exploded. Josh was so funny when he was mock angry. He looked at the girls and realised he had an audience. "Well, thank you for caring... Not!" He succumbed and started giggling.

"When we get home, I'll work some magic on your face Josh." He felt better. Tori was the best beautician he knew. "Then I'll get some hair off the shop floor and spin it into a toupee for you." The girls creased up, with tears streaming down their cheeks. With mock indignation, Josh strutted off to find some sympathetic soul to listen to his self-pitying twittering.

"Come on Megan, give us a song. That'll get Josh out of his hissy-fit!" Tori put her arm round her 'new' niece.

"Good idea Auntie Tori." They looked at each other and smiled. That name sounded good to both of them. "Perhaps something from the musical *Hair* would be apt." Again the laughter came naturally. Tori loved her niece's sense of humour, it was uncanny how alike they were, she thought.

From the garden Rob and Lara had watched the contretemps between Tori and Josh. Realising the reason for their argument, they thought they should intervene, but as Megan and Chloe appeared they stayed put and watched from a safe distance. Rob was happy seeing Megan laugh. He'd noticed her on a couple of occasions that day looking glum. Lara could see a bond had already formed with Megan and her Aunt and Grandma. Perhaps it was time to tell her the truth. She'd have words with Rob at bedtime. Megan had organised to stay at Chloe's for a few days to give the newlyweds some privacy. Debbie had wanted her to stay with them, but hadn't reckoned on an extra guest in the only spare room, bless Josh.

As the light started to fail, the garden took on a more romantic hue. Locals were arriving to pay their compliments to the happy couple and the candles were lit to set the evening scene. Lara and Rob took to the makeshift dance floor, too near the pool for Debbie's comfort, but she had every faith in the guests to be careful. Megan stepped up to the mic and at her father's and Lara's request sung the song that had started the ball rolling, 'The Way You Look Tonight' for the traditional first dance. Halfway through, Chloe turned up the volume on the amplifiers, to try to drown out the wailing sound coming from Josh's mouth. He had a little too much sangria and was very 'in the moment'. She wasn't sure if he was crying or singing, but whatever he was doing, she wasn't going to let him caterwaul all the way through her best friend's tribute to Rob and Lara. Fortunately, Tori pecked Adam on the cheek and went to her niece's rescue. She took hold of Josh, and steered him onto the dancefloor for the traditional Maid of Honour/Best Man dance. Much to everyone's merriment Josh could waltz beautifully, but had always taken the female lead. Tori didn't mind playing the male role, she thought it would be safer. She swivelled Josh on a couple of occasions, away from the pool's edge. She caught sight of her father and husband in absolute hysterics. She had a sudden thought that their dance may be detracting from the bride and groom's first dance. But as she managed to manoeuvre Josh from crashing into the bar-b-que, she noticed Rob and Lara were holding each other, on the edge of the dancefloor area, giggling like a couple of schoolchildren having been caught kissing behind the bicycle shed. For the last verse Tori took Josh off, to a rousing applause, to get him another drink, and made way for her sister and her new husband to dance one more time on their own for the photographer and their finale kiss.

Megan had managed to sing the whole song without giggling or stopping. It had been her hardest audience to date. To carry on against such adversity, she realised she'd make a good solo artist.

"OMG Megan. How did you keep going without laughing?" Chloe was in awe of her friend.

"I was picturing myself in the Albert Hall, and tried to be professional. You don't know what may happen during a concert, but I thought if I could survive a family wedding, I could survive anything." She had been winding Chloe up. She had actually just kept her eyes closed and had concentrated on the music. They found themselves by the bar table. "I'm not singing anymore numbers tonight, so..." She poured Chloe and herself a glass of sangria. "Fame costs, and right here is where you start paying for it, in sweat and tears and sangria. Cheers, Chlo." They clinked their glasses and drank the ice-cold, alcoholic refreshment.

Rob could see Lara's energy was waning.

"Are you ok, Mrs Simpson?" Lara looked up at her husband and smiled. She did like that name. "I could tell everyone to go if you like." He continued in a low voice so only they could hear. "Excuse me everyone, bugger off now, my wife and I need some marital nooky." She laughed.

"Just to get into my pjs and clean my teeth will take all the remaining strength I have left. Sorry to be so unromantic." Rob sat down next to her on a sunbed and squeezed her gently in an embrace.

"I have been waiting for this evening for a long time. Just to have you next to me, feeling your body close to me, for the whole night, is all I want." She felt the same. It would be odd, she thought, sharing a bed forever, but she was looking forward to the novelty. Tori noticed her sister was looking like she felt.

"Adam, could we make tracks soon. I'm dying on my feet. If we start leaving, hopefully there will be a mass exodus and Lala and Rob can get to bed too. She looks tired." Tori motioned over to Lara.

"I'll have a word with Deb. She's the one for subtlety." Adam wandered over to where Debbie was talking to Christine.

"Please thank Martin again for all the expert driving. And thank you for letting us borrow your lovely house." Christine looked over to her husband.

"I don't know if you will be thanking me tomorrow. I've just overheard your husband and mine organising a game of golf at the crack of dawn." Deb shook her head.

"That's fine. The girls and I will be looking at properties tomorrow, he'd only get under our feet." Both women laughed.

"I'm the same. Martin tries to help with the paperwork on a Monday, but it takes me till Wednesday to sort out his helpfulness. I can finish by Monday lunchtime if he plays golf." Kindred spirits had united.

"Deb? Tori wondered if we could organise a mass exodus, surreptitiously. Lara and Tor are very tired." Debbie turned to find Pete. He was with Martin.

"So, I'll pick you up at 6.30 a.m. if that's ok? Any later and the back nine will be unbearable in the heat." Pete nodded. He bowed to superior knowledge until he'd played for a while in Portugal.

"I'll be ready. And thank you for letting us have the house for a bit longer. With the girls out looking for business premises, I think looking for a house will be last on the agenda." Pete shook Martin's hand.

"Pete. There you are." Debbie wondered what scheme she had interrupted. "Hello Martin."

"Hi Debbie. I've just been talking to Pete and I see no reason why you can't continue in the house until you find a more permanent home. Same rent as Lara was paying, the house next door won't be ready for at least another six months. So as long as you can put up with the noise?" Debbie smiled.

"Well I have to say that is a weight of our minds, Martin. Thank you very much. Now I need to drag my husband away, I have a job for him." Pete was steered through the throng, until Debbie had got him inside the kitchen. "Right,

I need you to make an announcement that the bride and groom are leaving." Pete looked puzzled.

"I thought they were staying here tonight." Debbie explained that Lara needed her bed and that the only way to get people to go will be to do the traditional wave off of the bride.

"They can be waved into the house and we can all leave around the side path. That way people hopefully will get the hint and the newlyweds will be left in peace and quiet for a good night's sleep." Pete understood. "Now to let Lara and Rob in on the plan." Debbie went back outside to talk to Lara.

"Ladies and gentlemen." Pete had turned on the mic, with Megan's help. "As the bride's father I would like to thank you all for coming. The bride and groom now wish to retire and so, without further ado, I'd like to wish them a long and happy marriage. Three cheers for Lara and Rob, hip hip." The guests joined in with the 'Hoorays' and, with all the cheering over, Lara and Rob made a dramatic exit into the house with waves, kisses and 'goodbyes'. Debbie went round to say goodbye to many of the guests, and the visitors all seemed to have taken the hint as they made their way through the garden and around the house to the open gates.

"Well executed, mother-in-law." Adam had come up behind Debbie and put his arm around her. "I knew I had chosen the right man for the job." Debbie laughed. She mock cuffed her son-in-law.

"Cheeky boy. Now let's get your wife home. I'm amazed she's lasted this long." With only a few stragglers left, Megan and Chloe decided it was time to call it a night.

Martin rounded them up and put them in the car. Christine said goodbye to Debbie and told her they'd be round in the morning to help with the clearing up while the men played golf. Both the girls in the back of the car pulled a face, then giggled.

"I've got a feeling there will be a few hangovers to compete with in the morning." Debbie knew the giggles were alcohol-based. Christine laughed.

"They'll be fine in the morning. I was watching them and the sangria they were drinking was mainly lemonade." She winked at Debbie. "The hard stuff stayed out of sight in the kitchen." Martin started revving the car.

"I've only got six hours to get some sleep, come on chatterbox." Christine tutted and shook her head.

"Men!" Christine kissed Debbie on the cheek and said goodbye. Debbie waved them off; she liked Christine.

Rob watched through the bedroom window as the guests left.

"Rob come away from the window. You look like you are checking to see no one has stolen the family silver." Rob turned from the window laughing. He moved over to the bed and jumped in it. He cuddled his wife.

"Hello gorgeous wife of mine. Happy?" Lara didn't think she could feel any happier.

"Very. Thank you for a wonderful day." She kissed him on the lips and he responded, gently. He knew they were both too tired to start something more amorous. They snuggled down in a loving embrace and both were asleep before Debbie and Pete had seen off the last of the guests.

They quietly put away as much of the food they could

save and Pete blew out all the candles. They locked up the back door and took one more cursory look of the garden, when Pete thought he'd heard something coming from a pile of sunbed cushions. He went over to investigate and beckoned Debbie over with a finger to his lips and a 'shush' sound coming from his mouth. Debbie stifled a giggle. There, lying between the cushions, draped in a towel, was Josh. Sound asleep and his thumb in his mouth.

"Should we wake him and take him home?" Pete was worried he'd wake-up disorientated and fall in the pool.

"He'll probably not move until I get back in the morning, but just in case we can put a barricade up with a few of those chairs." They placed a couple strategically and left the little sleeping beauty until the morning.

CHAPTER 11

~

Pete tried to get ready for golf as quietly as he could, but the room was strange to him and he bumped into many objects, with a few expletives being uttered a little louder than he realised. Debbie pretended to sleep through it, but as soon as Pete had gone, she got up and knowing she'd not be able to go back to sleep, made her way over to Rob and Lara's. Josh was still in the same position she'd left him in the night before. It would be a shame to wake him, but the job in hand was too much for one. She didn't want Rob and Lara to get up to the mess, so she unlocked the back door and made some coffee.

Within the hour she had roused Josh and put him to work. The pair of them had made good progress and Debbie decided to make Josh a little breakfast. She was warming up some croissants while he, in Marigolds and an apron, tried to clean the worst of the bar-b-que.

Tori had woken early. The baby was pressing on her

bladder and she needed the loo fast. She knew her dad would be at golf, so she popped her head round her mum's door to see if she was awake. She'd already gone. Tori went back to her room and had a shower. She made her way to Rob and Lara's leaving a sleeping Adam. As she walked up the side path, she heard Josh humming. She had worked with him for long enough to recognise his tuneless hum. She peeked round and saw him. She quickly got out of sight. She raised her phone and put it into camera mode and pointed it round the corner. She snapped the picture and pulled it back before Josh noticed. She had to stifle a laugh when she saw the vision on her phone, of Josh in a pinny with Marigolds and a metal brush. She clicked a few more points on her screen and tagged him in Facebook. Within seconds Josh's phone beeped. He took off a rubber glove and looked at his phone. He found a picture he was tagged in under the title 'scrubber!' on his Facebook profile.

"Bitch." He shouted, looking all around to see where Tori was. Tori couldn't keep quiet any longer. She came from the side of the house laughing so loudly that it brought Debbie out of the kitchen wondering what was happening.

"Shush you two, you'll wake Lara." Josh turned to her with a pout on his face and showed her the picture. She looked at Tori and frowned, but couldn't keep it up. She burst out laughing too. Josh looked at the photo again and had to admit, it was hilarious. He joined in the laughter. Well if that didn't wake Rob and Lara nothing would. Tori went into the kitchen to help her Mum and make herself a cup of tea. As she went to get the milk out of the fridge, she noticed a note magnetised on the door.

'We have gone to watch the sun rise and have a romantic

breakfast at Issabel's. See you all later, don't work too hard!'
How romantic, thought Tori.

"Who's Issabel?" Debbie hadn't had the full story. Josh was standing with a soppy look on his face. Tori decided to tell her mum.

"Issabel's is the restaurant that Rob and Jill used to own. It was called Jilly's Restaurant then." Debbie suddenly realised the significance of their visit to that restaurant.

"Of course, going back to where it had all started. That really is romantic." She pulled herself together. "Well this isn't getting the clearing done. Come on you two, there's still lots to be done. Let's see if we can finish before they get back." It wouldn't take so long now, they were safe to make as much noise as they wanted.

Josh was just tying up the last bin bag when Lara and Rob appeared.

"What immaculate timing. I surprise myself sometimes." Rob couldn't resist teasing Josh. 'You've missed a cup." He pointed to the table.

"That's my coffee." Rob patted Josh on the back.

"Only kidding. Thanks for all your help, and for yesterday. The best Best Man a chap could want." Josh wasn't sure if Rob was continuing in the frivolous mode or whether he meant it.

"He means it Josh. Thank you from me too." Lara gave him a peck on the cheek.

"What about us? We've been slaving away since early dawn." Tori was sitting with her feet up. "Well *I* haven't exactly, but Mum and Josh have. I'm a little incapacitated, I'm sure you understand." Lara laughed. Her sister was a bit bigger around the midriff than her; it had to be said. But then Tori was a few years younger than Lara. She should be able to cope better.

"Thank you Mum. What a lovely surprise." Debbie had heard them and had come out of the kitchen to say hello.

"It's all done now. Just relax and enjoy your post-wedding glow." Debbie hadn't seen Lara look so healthy. "Tori and I will take Josh to look at the properties you've printed out for us. We'll see them from the outside and then perhaps we could borrow you tomorrow to arrange with the agents to look internally at the ones we like." Lara was almost as excited as her mother. Tori got into the driver's seat of Lara's car, Josh and Debbie got in the back.

"I could come with you now if you like?" She turned to check Rob's reaction. He smiled and winked at her. He knew until Lara's family were settled and living close by the time the baby arrived, she wouldn't be entirely stress free.

"Go on if you want. I'll go and find Megan and give her some dad time." Lara thought that was a good idea. "See you back here at lunchtime, somehow we have to eat up all the left overs before the family go home, otherwise the food will be in my sandwiches for the next few months." Lara hugged him. She wondered what she had done to deserve such a wonderful husband.

"Thank you, Rob." She smiled at him.

"What for? I haven't done anything yet." He squeezed her tightly, and whispered in her ear. "I love you so much. Thank you for becoming Mrs Simpson." Lara was changing her mind about going with her family.

"Come on Lala. We don't know the way. Where's Quinta Do Lago again?" She shrugged. She was being pulled both ways. Rob made the decision.

"We have the rest of our lives to be together. They are only here for a few more days, go on." He gently pushed her towards her car. Tori got out and went over to the passenger seat. Lara got in and drove off, waving at her new husband. Rob had a few moments to himself so decided to phone his mother and tell her all about the wedding. He had missed her at the wedding, but had promised to visit her very soon with plenty of photographs.

Lara took them to four different properties. The first was in Quinta Do Lago, frequented by footballers and their wives and a great deal of other celebrities. The salon was in the Plaza with expensive restaurants and bars all around.

"This is a bit posh." Josh wasn't sure if it was what they wanted. He loved the thought of all the celebrities, but wondered if he'd be able to concentrate if he actually had to colour their hair.

"The downside here is the cost. As a going concern it is very expensive. You would be taking on their client list." Lara was almost quoting what the agent had said to her.

"That's if they stay. We could pay for them and they then could go off and find another salon." Tori was worried. It was a lot of money. Lara decided to show them property two. It was in Vale Do Lobo, attached to the golf course. Debbie wasn't sure about that one.

"It's all very well for golfers' wives, but what about passing trade?" Lara could see what she meant. It would have to be advertised for people to know it was there. She turned the car once more and headed for property three. That was a hairdressing salon in the heart of Almancil itself. Passing trade would be in abundance. There was one major problem.

"This salon is mainly for the locals, isn't it?" Josh asked. Lara nodded. "Well how will we be able to talk to them? You are the only one who can speak the language, and unless you can give us all an intensive course, we'll be stumped." Debbie knew Josh was right. She looked despondent. Lara could see her face in the rear-view mirror. It was time to put them all out of their misery.

"My pièce de résistance is on the road back to Vale Do Lobo. It's a few roads from our house, and therefore between Quinta Do Lago and Vale Do Lobo. The best of both I'd say." She stopped the car after a few minutes. Tori looked around. Was she being dense?

"I can't see a salon." Lara got out of the car and the others followed. Boarded up in front of them was a double fronted shop. Next door was a golf shop.

"That was Rob's first shop. It was all he could afford at the beginning. He was thinking, eventually, of expanding into this shop, but opened another golf shop in Vilamoura instead. It's quite large, and Rob owns it. He's happy for you to convert it into a hair and beauty salon, and has builders on standby to get it started." Debbie was crying. It was ideal. The location was amazing, and the size was just right.

"He's happy to let you have it rent free until you are showing a profit, or to buy the lease outright when you've sold everything in England." Debbie ran over to Lara and hugged her.

"Why didn't you show us it first?" She couldn't understand why they had looked at all the other properties.

"Because Rob said he didn't want you to take it so as not to offend him. He wanted you to see your options first and then decide." Tori and Josh were peering through the boards. Lara had one more surprise for them. She got out the keys and opened it up. Inside was an empty canvas. It had painted white walls and a new tiled floor. There were three rooms to the side of the main floor area.

"I can have two treatment rooms going." Tori was so excited.

"The third room could be a kitchen, I suppose." Debbie was picturing it.

"If you go through the back, there already is a kitchen and two toilets, and a staircase." They went through to the back. The staircase was outside, but in the Algarve weather that didn't matter.

"What's up there?" Josh was so nosey. Lara pointed up the stairs, and handed them another key.

"Go and have a look." Josh and Tori went up to look. Debbie stayed downstairs still envisaging what should go where. "There is a two bedroomed flat upstairs. Rob thought staff could live there." Debbie couldn't believe her eyes or ears. "They'll need doing up and furnishing, but the views are lovely and the room sizes are doubles."

"I cannot believe Rob kept this quiet from us. It's the answer to our dreams." Lara smiled at her mother.

"He was going to use it himself up until a few months ago, but another property came up in Vilamoura in exactly the position he wanted. This one was going on the market, but he held it back until you saw it." Debbie was worried.

"Has that left him short of cash? We could pay him for the lease just as soon as we have completed at home." Lara nodded.

"He knows that. It would be handy, but there's no rush. He has other plans for that money." She looked sheepish.

Debbie was intrigued.

"Are you going to tell me?" Lara smiled.

"He's going to pay for Megan to go to the Brit School in London." Debbie looked puzzled. "The London School for Performing Arts and Technology, to give it its proper name. It's a surprise he's organised with the help of Mason Morgan. She's going to stay with her Grandmother, who is thrilled. Please don't tell the others though, we need to find the right time to tell Megan first."

"She's going to love it. The only problem is, with the baby coming, she may feel like you are pushing her out." Debbie was very astute. Rob and Lara had thought of that.

"She has the option of doing her A Levels here if she wants, but it is her dream. She will be over every holiday, and with the cheap flights we could probably get her home most weekends, if she wants to come. I'm sure she will realise that she is just as important to us as the baby, once it arrives." Debbie hoped it would be that simple. "If she decides she wants to go she could start this October. We will leave it up to Megan to choose."

"Choose what?" Tori had come back down the stairs.

"What she wants for lunch. What did you think of the flat?" Lara changed the subject brilliantly, thought Debbie. All those years working for the government had paid off. She smiled to herself.

"Mum you should have a look. It's got two bedrooms and a bathroom and kitchen. There's also a small lounge, but it has a large balcony which Josh said would make a good sunbathing spot." Josh came running down the stairs.

"Debbie, tell her we'll take it. It's amazing. I've just phoned Hayley and Kate and sent them pictures of their bedroom. They love it. Can we have it, please?" He was like a little boy wanting an ice cream. "Please, please?"

"Alright Josh. Calm down. I'd already said we'd have it just by looking at the important part, the shop?" Josh laughed. Debbie was playing it cool, but Josh knew she was just as excited.

"Well let's get back to Rob and tell him the good news." Lara locked up and got everyone back into the car. "I think it will make a marvellous *Cabelo e Beleza* salon." They all looked at her. "Hair and Beauty salon. If you don't learn any other words, you ought to know those." They all tried to say it, but it wasn't going to happen. They'd leave the Portuguese to Lara.

Rob had taken Megan into Faro Old Town. Zara had a sale on. He never understood why women found clothes shopping so therapeutic. He would rather go to the dentist. By the time they got home, Lara had set out a feast. Tori had put knives and forks inside napkins and Debbie had made jugs of ice-cold squash. Adam was arranging chairs around tables in the garden and Pete was having a shower, after his game of golf, at their house and would be along as soon as he was ready. Tori noticed the bags Megan was carrying.

"Ooo, what have you bought?" Megan smiled and walked to her bedroom, beckoning Tori to follow. Lara went over to Rob.

"Clever boy." She kissed him on the cheek. "You certainly know the way to a woman's heart." He looked round the kitchen at all the food.

"And you seem to know the way to a man's." Debbie laughed with Lara. Men were so much easier to please. "I'll go and help Adam." He sidled over to the fridge, grabbed a couple of beer bottles and went outside to find Adam. Lara shook her head at her mother, they both smiled.

"It'll be lovely having all of us together. I'm so glad you all want to live here in Portugal." Lara knew it was a massive change for her parents.

"We didn't take a lot of persuading, did we? I'm just happy that the next generation of the family will be brought up together." She looked at Lara's tummy. "And we'll all be here to enjoy it." Megan came out of her room dressed in one of her new outfits.

"Oh Megan, that's gorgeous." It took Lara's breath away. She had on a very short pair of white shorts, with a pretty pink lacy top and a scarf around her neck. She looked at least two years older and her legs seemed so long. She actually was a beautiful girl.

"She's promised to take me out and help me choose some clothes. Don't you think she has amazing taste, Lala?" Lara had to agree with her sister. Debbie wasn't too sure about the shorts. They were very provocative, but perhaps she was being a little old-fashioned. She'd keep it to herself. Megan needed all the positive feedback she could get, at the moment.

"What do you think, Grandma?" Megan was looking straight at Debbie. Lara had a lump in her throat. It was the first time she'd heard Megan call her mother by that name.

"I think they are very pretty colours together." Debbie said diplomatically. Tori laughed.

"That means she thinks the shorts are too short and you probably have too much make-up on. But she likes the colours." Megan and Tori were laughing. "You'll get used to Mum's code. You just have to watch the wrinkles on her face to see what she's saying."

"I'm sorry I'm so predictable." Then she frowned. "What wrinkles?" They were all laughing and hadn't noticed Pete walk in. He walked straight out again to find the men. Women were scary at times. He was dying to tell somebody about his amazing two under par on the hole with the flamingos in the lake, he thought it was the fifteenth or maybe the sixteenth. Rob would know. Listening to the women in the kitchen and then seeing Adam and Rob sipping beer, in the sunshine, on a hammock, Pete wondered if life could get any better than that. Portugal was definitely the best decision they'd made, shame they hadn't made it sooner. Delivering post where, on average, there was only seventeen days of rainfall a year, would have been wonderful. Rob spotted Pete escaping from the kitchen.

"Pete, over here. I wouldn't go in there if I were you. The women are on a mission. Why they always have to make such a big production of meal times I don't know. Sit here and I'll get you a beer. Another for you Adam?" Adam nodded.

"Beer, sunshine and food. I think we've gone to heaven, Pete." Pete nodded.

"I was just thinking the same thing." He turned to Adam and sighed. "We are lucky buggers, aren't we?!"

The closer it got to the end of their holiday, the more unsettled Lara became.

"They'll be back for good soon. Then we can be one big happy family." Rob was on the sofa next to Lara. It was quite late, but Megan was still out singing at Vale Do Lobo. Tori and Adam had taken Josh to the airport, he had to get back for a birthday party, and then gone down to watch Megan. Debbie and Pete had just left Rob and Lara's for an early night. Debbie said she couldn't keep up the pace with the youngsters anymore. Pete agreed, but had a cheeky look in his eye when an early night had been mentioned. He and Rob had shared a look. Lara had ignored it. After all, they were her parents. They were too old for 'that sort of thing'.

"I know I'm going to miss them, but that's not what's worrying me." She faced Rob and held his hand. "We have to decide when to tell Megan. The longer we leave it the more difficult it will get. The baby has already unnerved her." Rob knew Lara was right, but he'd just managed to get Megan to brighten up after the wedding. He wasn't sure it would be a good thing yet.

"Perhaps we should wait until the baby is born, then we can buy her a t-shirt that says *'I'm the real big sister'*." He looked up from Lara's lap, where he had placed his head. She was smiling.

"You really are an idiot sometimes." She stroked his hair and tutted. "Can't help but love you though." He started to purr like a cat. "I don't think we are ever going to come to a decision about this." She looked down at Rob. In a way, he was right. It would be stupid rocking the boat so soon after Megan's anxiety at the wedding. Perhaps there would be an opportunity that presented itself in the near future. Until then Lara saw no point in worrying if Rob wasn't. He was a good influence on her. "Are you ready for bed?" Rob looked up and saw that same look he'd seen in Pete's eyes.

"I'm ready if you're willing." He grinned. "I reckon we've

got half-an-hour before Megan gets back."

"So long? We only need five minutes." He jumped up and grabbed her arm to pull her gently to her feet.

"I think we could kill the other twenty-five minutes, thinking of England." Lara burst out laughing. He certainly wasn't setting the appropriate mood, but she was so relaxed, anything could happen.

The day before they left, Tori and Lara had gone off shopping. Tori was finding it difficult to find summer clothes for her size, in England, that didn't resemble an adequate canvas home, sleeping room for two persons, from the Army and Navy Store. Adam and Pete had gone to golf with Rob and were due back by lunchtime. Debbie had invited Megan over to enjoy her company and get to know her a little better.

"So, Megan, apart from singing, what other subjects do you like at school?" Megan was munching on an apple. She felt so at ease with Debbie.

"Languages are my forte." Debbie coughed. She had just swallowed a sip of coffee.

"You must get on well with Lara then, she excelled at languages at school." Debbie had managed to cover up her surprise.

"We have fun teasing Dad. He can only speak basic Portuguese, Lara and I speak it fluently, so we often talk without Dad knowing what we are saying. He doesn't seem to mind. I love hockey too." She added as an aside.

"Lara loved lacrosse. I suppose that's like hockey. What do you not like?" Lara liked nearly all her subjects at school. She may not have been good at them, but she liked trying.

"I don't think there is anything I don't especially like. The subjects are ok, it's the teachers I had problems with. They are forever putting on my report card 'could try harder. Megan has a tendency to daydream'. Dad tells them I'm not daydreaming, I'm thinking. He says I've always been a big thinker." The child in front of Debbie could be Lara. How come no one else had noticed the similarity? Before she left she would have to talk to Lara. If Megan is hers, surely to goodness Megan has a right to know. "Do you mind awfully if I go home for a quick swim? I've got my costume on under my shorts. It's getting so hot." Unfortunately, Lara's pool was way too small for a swim, and it also hadn't been cleaned recently. The cover had a layer of builders dust on it. Lara had been using Rob's and thought it was an unnecessary expense for Christine and Martin after they had been so kind. Debbie thought that was a brilliant idea, and she may join her before the men got back. Megan liked the fact that Debbie wanted to be with her.

"Give me a tick to write a note for your Grandpa and Uncle Adam." Megan smiled at her. She was making her feel like part of the family already. Megan put her apple core in the bin and Debbie's empty coffee cup into the dishwasher while Debbie wrote a quick note. She went off to her room and came back with a grin on her face. She was carrying a small book.

"I thought you may like to look at some photos of Lara and Tori when they were young." Debbie had an idea brewing. It may work, or backfire dramatically. She hoped it would be the former. "We'll have a look at them when you've had your swim." She attached the note she had written to the fridge and walked back to Megan's house with her.

Debbie dangled her feet in the pool while Megan showed off in front of her Grandmother, diving and swimming lengths with different strokes. Debbie was impressed.

"The advantage of being brought up in Southern Europe means swimming is as popular as skiing in Northern Europe. My new brother or sister and cousin will have all the fun I had growing up here." She looked at Debbie. "With a big family around them." Debbie smiled.

"You have a rather big family now, Megan. It must be very strange for you." Megan dived under the water. Debbie thought she was ignoring her. But she came up almost immediately.

"Sorry about that. I was trying to get rid of a pesky fly. Yes, it is strange, but in a good way. Dad and I have had each other for a long time, but there were times that I felt he needed a mate. I had my friends at school, but he just had his golfing buddies during the day and his evenings were taken up looking after me. I was very pleased when Lara came back to Portugal." She disappeared back under the water for a few seconds again. "Damn fly. I have to admit at first it was strange, but Lara is very easy to like." Debbie nodded in agreement. "We seem to have loads in common." Debbie bit her tongue. It was hardly surprising, she thought, but let Megan go on. "And of course, she was my mother's best friend, so it was easier in a way to see Dad with a woman I know my mum loved." Debbie was beginning to realise why Lara and Rob had said nothing. It was heart-breaking to listen to Megan when she talked about her mother. Perhaps she'd forget about the photos. Rob and Lara knew best. She shouldn't get involved. It was their business and their responsibility. She hadn't noticed, but Megan had got out of the pool. "Shall we go in and look at those photos now? I'm dying to see what they were like as children." Too late; Debbie had to see it through.

"Hello you two. Had a nice swim?" Rob had just got back from golf. "Pete and Adam are having showers and then will be over for some lunch. I'll just pop in and have a quick shower myself. It has started to get too hot for golf in the morning. Think I'll leave it for evenings now Lara can keep an eye on you." He was looking at Megan. She laughed.

"I'm not a child, father. I no longer need a babysitter." She had dried herself. "I'm just going to pop on something dry and I'll be back to see your album." Debbie looked at Rob's face.

"Album?" He looked worried.

"It's photos of Lara and Tori as little girls. I thought it would be fun for Megan to see them. Is that ok?" Rob thought he saw something in Debbie's face. Had she guessed? He wasn't sure, but maybe that was the way forward. It couldn't be left for much longer. Debbie seemed like a very wise woman. Very like her daughter.

"What a lovely idea. Let me have my shower and I'll get some of Megan out for you to see. We could compare notes." He winked at her.

"As long as you are happy about it." Debbie hated being cryptic, but she had to be 100% sure and at that moment she was going on hunches and coincidences, which were enormous, but not proven. Rob went into the kitchen and got Debbie a large glass of white wine and went off to change. It left Debbie wondering why he thought she needed such a large glass of alcohol. She would be over the moon if her hunches were fact. She may have lost out on sixteen years of being a grandma, but she had plenty of time to make up for that. And time spent with Megan now was quality time. She was such a lovely young woman. She knew they'd be good friends, first and foremost.

"The sun is too bright out here. We'll get a better look at the photos inside." Megan had popped her head out of the kitchen door. Debbie agreed and carried her wine inside. She took the album out of her bag on the way through to the lounge, where Megan was already sitting on the floor cross-legged, just how Lara used to sit.

Megan took the album off Debbie and started at the beginning. There were photos of Lara in a cot. She was only a few months old.

"Aah, she looks so cute." Megan turned the page and found Lara with a little bonnet on her head, sitting on a lawn, looking very cheeky. "What had she done there?" Debbie leaned forward to see which one it was.

"Oh yes, she'd got up and ran off three times before we finally told her she could have a sweetie if she stayed still for a minute. That was the usual bribe and she had cottoned on to it from a very early age." Megan was laughing.

"Good job she'd grown out of it by the time the wedding photos were being taken. I can't imagine the look on the guests faces as they had to feed her sweets to make sure she kept still." Debbie and Megan were laughing so hard they didn't hear Rob come in. He looked over their shoulders and saw the picture of Lara. It was so like Megan it took his breath away. "Dad. Look at Lara, isn't she cute?" Rob nodded in agreement. Megan turned the page and Rob took another deep breath. Lara was about three years old, on the beach in Bournemouth, with a bucket and spade and just some knickers on. Rob looked over to the bookcase and took down a picture of Megan, on the beach at Vale Do Lobo, with a bucket and spade, wearing only bikini bottoms, around the age of three. He showed it to Debbie.

A mother sensed these things, and although sixteen years ago she had her suspicions over Christmas, she never voiced them. But in front of her now was the proof. Megan noticed the look her dad and Debbie had passed to each other. She took the album off Debbie and looked carefully at the photo. She took the picture frame from her dad and put them together. She looked up at her Dad.

"I don't understand. Or maybe I do?" Debbie pulled Megan up off the floor and sat her down on the sofa next to her. They both looked up at Rob for an explanation. Where was Lara when he needed her? He'd try to explain as best he could. Debbie could see how difficult it was for him.

"Would you like to wait for Lara?" Rob shook his head. "Take your time. Just tell us why the photos are so alike." Debbie was trying to make it easier for Rob, for which he was very grateful.

"When I met your mummy, we were childhood sweethearts. We were in the same class at school, and we lived a few doors from each other. We had decided to get married and have lots of children as soon as our parents let us. But fate stepped in and at the age of seventeen after a routine smear test found abnormal cells, Jilly had to have a hysterectomy to make sure they got all the cancer." Rob wanted to hold Megan, tears were streaming down her cheeks, but he needed to carry on. Debbie held Megan tightly. "After she'd recovered I had a battle on my hands. She wanted me to marry someone who could have my children. I told her I loved her and we could adopt if she wanted. I won and we got married just after her eighteenth birthday." Rob finally broke down. Megan wanted to go to him, but he took a deep breath and continued. "Unfortunately, we kept hitting a brick wall in England over adoption. Because of her medical condition she was classed as high risk, and the wait would have been forever, with no guarantee of a child at the end." He looked up at the ceiling, took another breath, and went on. "My father died shortly after we got married, I'm glad he was able to get to the wedding." He smiled at the memory. "And left me and my mum his pub. We sold it to a big chain of family pubs, and made a nice profit. I bought my mum a bungalow and kept enough in England to keep her happy and safe, and the rest Jill and I invested in a restaurant here. The weather improved Jilly's health and we were very happy. We just had one thing missing. We didn't feel like a family. Then Lara came into our lives like an angel from heaven." He smiled at Debbie. "She worked so hard that first summer. Then one night, for the first time, she went out and got tipsy. She hadn't had any alcohol for a long time. Lara was very trusting where people were concerned. She saw the good in everyone. She woke up in a strange house, and crept away. She didn't want to upset Jill or me so kept the whole episode from us. It was a few weeks later that she started fainting, and Jill took her to see the doctor. She was pregnant. She knew at that time," he looked Debbie in the eyes, "that you and Pete were so proud of her getting into university and she thought it would have been a bad example to set her little sister, so she knew she couldn't keep it. You." He corrected himself and looked at Megan. He couldn't work out her facial expression, but had to go on so she saw how difficult the decision had been. "Lara could never terminate the pregnancy, she said that babies were a gift from God, and wanted to give us that gift. She knew we would look after you and love you so much. So she stayed with us until you were born. She fed you so you got the best start. But it was getting harder and harder for her to see you and know she wasn't going to take you home. She knew Jill was in love with you and you were her only chance of ever having a daughter. The bond she had with you was getting stronger by the day, so she made the agonising decision to go home. She left you with us and didn't think it fair to herself or to us to keep in touch. It was her defence mechanism to cope with losing you. We named you Megan, Lara's middle name so you had something from your real mother, and Jilly said it was a reminder to all of them what a selfless thing she'd done. You know the rest. She came over for Tori's hen weekend and they went to Monty's. She heard you sing and her maternal instincts knew who you were." Megan got up and hugged her dad. Debbie tried to stop her tears, but they just kept on falling. "I'm sorry we didn't tell you sooner, poppet. But it was a very difficult story to tell." He was hugging her so tightly, but she didn't mind. He tried to look at her face, to see if she was ok, but Megan didn't want to let go of her dad.

Lara and Tori had arrived home, to find Adam and Pete hovering outside.

"Not sure what's going on in your lounge, but it sounded deep, so we thought we'd wait for the all clear." Pete was such a coward. Adam was just as bad. Tori looped her arm in Adam's and followed Lara into the house. Pete felt braver now he wasn't in the lead, and followed his daughters. As Lara opened the lounge door the other three pushed their way in. Rob was standing in the middle of the room with tears running down his cheeks. Megan was holding onto him like she'd never let him go, and Debbie was on the sofa pulling out tissues, wiping her eyes and discarding them as quickly. Lara wondered if anyone had died while they'd been shopping. She was too scared to ask. Suddenly Megan noticed her. She unclenched her father's arms and ran towards Lara.

"I love you so much, mummy."

THE END

If you enjoyed this book look out for 'Postman's Knock' by Elaine Ellis available in hard copy or in eBook from Amazon or to order from all good retailers or Romaunce Books.

The old proverb 'The grass is always greener' turned out to be an artist's impression, not real life at all.

When Charlotte Whitfield – known to everyone as Charlie – receives a letter from her best friend Libby, she has no idea that her life is about to change forever. Libby and James, Charlie's husband, have been having an affair, and James has decided to leave the marriage and move in with Libby.

But if Libby and James thought that Charlie was ready to be a victim, they had forgotten the tough resourceful woman they had both known and loved. Calling on all her strength, Charlie takes control of her own life, despite losing a baby as well as a husband.

When James, for whom the grass turned out not to be greener on the other side, starts to threaten Charlie his erratic behaviour turns quickly into dangerous obsession. Charlie is forced to re-evaluate everything, and find out, for the first time, what it is she truly wants. Beside her all the way is Libby's ex-husband Bruce, whose underappreciated grace and charm become a bedrock for Charlie. Are they too falling in love?

Elaine Ellis's *Postman's Knock* is a moving story of the way life continues to surprise, and how the actions of other people, for better or worse, make us look anew at ourselves.

ND - #0151 - 270225 - C0 - 203/127/16 - PB - 9781861518330 - Gloss Lamination